TOM B. NIGHT

Circadian Algorithms

First edition

This book was professionally typeset on Reedsy.
Find out more at reedsy.com

For CJ—Dream big, little guy

Chapter 0: Darwin

At four o'clock on Christmas morning, Darwin Johnston briefly forgot the imminent threat to his life and marveled at the rivers of red and white lights. Who were all these people? Where were they going at this hour on this day?

He could partially answer those questions about himself. He had been a neuroscientist, and a damn promising one at that. Recently he was a stay-at-home dad. And now...he wasn't so sure. A wanted man in more ways than one. He was going to San Francisco International Airport. The next logical question—why—made increasingly little sense.

Darwin's understanding of the relationship between cause and effect had undergone something of a paradigm shift.

He hated driving at night. The red and white starbursts, streakier than usual in the rain, reminded him he was no longer a young man at the age of thirty-six. More alarmingly, they highlighted that he hadn't slept in over five days. At least he thought it had been that long; the many harmful effects of extreme sleep deprivation included short-term memory loss. But they were still preferable to long-term memory loss, slipping further and further away.

While surveying the myriad points of light in front of him, he did his best to ignore those behind. Paranoia and hallucinations were expected given how long he'd been awake, but he was convinced the obnoxiously bright pair of headlights following him had been there since leaving his adopted safe-house. He did not think it a coincidence. He no longer believed in such things.

"Call Madeline Johnston," he instructed the dashboard.

"I'm sorry, I don't recognize that name," replied the car in a voice that had almost ascended out of the uncanny valley. Oh, right.

"Call Madeline Lockhart." The car understood this time, but her phone went straight to voicemail like it had for several days.

"Hey, this is Madeline." Her voice was bubbly like it used to be; she'd had the same greeting for years. The sound made his throat tight. He had a creeping suspicion this was the last time he would hear it. He still loved her despite the pain they'd caused each other and how much she had changed, an especially salient feeling under the circumstances. "Sorry I missed your call. Please leave a message, or, better yet, text me."

"Maddy, it's Dar again. I hope to god—yes, god—that you're alright. I ah...I think I really messed up this time. I'm on my way to Tokyo but...I'm not sure I'm going to make it. I'll find you if I do. Please tell the girls I love them, and not to believe everything they may hear or read about me. Merry Christmas."

For several minutes Darwin drove on through the pre-dawn in silence, the only sounds those of a car speeding in rain that would be snow if the temperature dropped a few degrees. The car in front of him put on its left blinker, which was odd given it was in the left lane going eighty-five. It followed its telegraphed intention and veered into the barrier separating the two directions of traffic, launching up into the air. Darwin's delayed reactions didn't even afford him time to brake, but when he glanced in his rearview mirror to survey the damage, he saw nothing out of the ordinary. He shook his head and blinked hard.

A plane appeared out of the clouds ahead and above, or at least that's what his eyes told him. It was logical given his location, so it was probably real. The plane's blinking red lights looked something like Rudolph leading Santa and his sleigh. Maybe Madeline was right, and he should have let the girls believe, but Mister Rational just couldn't let that stand. Strange how his mind wandered even at a moment like this.

A morbid mix of curiosity and fear propelled him to spare another glance in the rearview mirror. The intermittent windshield wiper cleared the glass, fortunately not leaving behind streaks of smeared blood. The offending headlights' height made it look like they belonged to an SUV—not a good sign given his present worries. On the bright side, he was too terrified to be tired.

"Shit shit shit," he whispered. He was ten minutes out from SFO, where hopefully the lights, crowds, and surveillance would discourage the worst kinds of violence. That meant they would likely make their move soon.

Honking shifted his attention back to the headlights ahead of him—one pair in particular. They were conspicuous amongst the flashing red taillights on the wrong side of the freeway and seemed authentic given his fellow drivers' reactions. Someone who'd had too much eggnog and driven up the offramp? No chance, though presumably that's what the media would report.

The car ahead of him began to brake and move to the left

shoulder. Darwin followed suit, and the oncoming vehicle changed trajectory so that it was now heading straight for him. Unsurprising. He braked further only to have the trailing vehicle rear-end him, propelling him forward and confirming his worst fears and that it was indeed a black SUV occupied by at least two serious-looking men.

His smartwatch alerted him that his heartrate had spiked to over two hundred beats per minute, more than four times its resting rate. He was having a heart attack.

Darwin briefly thought about swerving to the right but only had time for one decisive action, and his subconscious had already made up its mind and started to put his body in motion. With his right hand he reached onto the passenger seat for the Glock 17. An actual fucking gun riding shotgun. Who had he become? It was insane how fast everything could change, especially for the worse.

But Darwin had a more pressing concern: The weapon was not there. It must have been jolted onto the floor. He took his eyes off the road and both hands off the wheel, leaned down, and frantically felt around in the dark for the black, full-sized handgun.

There.

Darwin twisted as he sat back up, his right hand gripping the Glock and pointing towards the back window. It was reckless but hey, it was better than getting smashed to pulp on the 101. However, the trailing SUV must have slammed on its brakes and was now dozens of feet back. When he twisted to face forward again, he knew why. His heart had been attempting to pound, but the sight that awaited him made it stop and drop: The onrushing vehicle was much closer than anticipated, its high beams blinding.

The gun's lack of a traditional safety gave him enough time to get off a single, startlingly loud shot through the Volvo's windshield and into the approaching vehicle, and also to realize it would do no good; although there was someone behind the steering wheel, which wasn't a given in this day, age, and area, they were clearly not awake. The sleeping mask was a dead giveaway.

The gunshot had been quiet compared to the crash that came next. Shattered, blood-stained glass spilling onto the asphalt joined the cacophony of the downpour, which now sounded like thousands of tiny gemstones falling from the sky.

But Darwin, his heart now stopped, no longer saw the shining diamonds and rubies of head and taillights, only darkness.

Part 1: Somnolence

Six months earlier

Chapter 1: Madeline

The Dream Journal of Madeline Johnston

Tuesday, June 18th, 2019 — 6 hours of sleep (on a plane)

Sex. Again. And not with Darwin (again); it was my new assistant. How old is he, twenty-four? Remember to act normal next time you see him. I wonder if he's had similar dreams about me. Or the same one. That'd be a trip.

Why do these dreams make me feel guilty? It's not like I have control over them. I suppose I could try not sleeping on my stomach, which allegedly causes more erotic dreams because... friction. But a thirty-six-year habit is hard to break. Am I afraid these nighttime fantasies are what I really want, when Darwin says my overactive prefrontal cortex—my 'CEO brain'—in charge of executive functions like judgment, planning, and moderating behavior is offline?

Boy do I need to ensure he never reads this, for more reasons than one.

In red letters comprised entirely of right angles, the hotel clock on the nightstand informed Madeline it was five minutes after three a.m. She could still get almost four hours of sleep if she fell asleep right now and skipped breakfast. It was far from ideal but would at least get her through the coming day's presentation. There were various prescription pills she could take that would probably knock her out—her travel bag was full of the downers, uppers, lefters, and righters needed to get through modern life—but she couldn't afford any subsequent grogginess. She had to be perfect. The company was on the brink.

Madeline had awoken to an alarm seven days a week for the past fifteen years and carried a perpetual sleep deficit. She'd never had any trouble falling asleep for most of her life and could get seven hours by being in bed for seven hours and five minutes. Her sleep efficiency was close to one hundred percent. She often joked it was her superpower.

But now, jet-lagged after a flight across the Pacific, she was sharing in the ancient human experience of lying awake in the dark thinking strange thoughts. It was an experience she had become increasingly familiar with over the past few years, since taking the reins as CEO. The 'patented sleep-assist technology' embedded in the rooms of her preferred hotel chain was apparently just marketing. She could respect that. But sometimes her travel schedule made it feel as though she'd come unstuck in time, her circadian body clock and the ones on her iPhone and elsewhere having no relationship at all.

She took solace in the fact that things would radically change soon. She would have a real superpower.

She tried to clear her mind and meditate, but mere moments later forgot what she was supposed to be doing and was again lost in whatever images and words bubbled up out of the ether. After twenty more minutes of regrets about the past, anxieties about the future, and sanity-straining thoughts, she'd had enough. Why did everything seem so much worse, every problem so unsolvable, in the middle of the night? Better to make the most of the extra time than lie in bed with her eyes closed in a downward mental spiral.

For Madeline that meant work. Her job was an infinity pool into which she could dip anytime and for as long as she wished. There was always more to learn about a new technology, a competitor's product, a relevant historical anecdote. She could always be better.

Madeline dove in, running through the deck for the twentieth time. Good presentations were like a story, with an initial hook then building to a climax. But when she reached the crescendo (the live product demo), the application crashed. Madeline sighed. So much for 'fail elegantly.' Last week the DDoS attack, now this.

It was almost lunchtime yesterday in San Francisco, her 'home' time zone and city, if you could credibly call them that. One upside of an internationally distributed workforce was that there was always someone running with the baton, chasing the sun. The number of unread emails in her inbox was a constant reminder. She looked forward to being able to run with the baton for as long as she pleased.

"The whole team is working on it. We suspect it's a memory leak, which can be a particularly tricky kind of bug to fix," said her CTO Vipul over the video chat. He appeared nervous on the bright screen, his face illuminating her hotel room.

"What?" Madeline asked.

"A memory leak is when a program fails to discard memory after using it, resulting in less memory being available for other programs that *do* need it. It can cause degraded performance and ultimately system fail—"

"I have a degree in computer science," she interrupted. "I know what a memory leak is. I meant how is this happening now. The product has been stable for days. I can't sell vaporware up there."

"To be honest I'm not sure what caused it. Not yet, anyways. We're in code freeze. We haven't pushed any changes since Thursday. But don't worry—it'll be fixed by the time you wake up."

With her side of the video chat off, Madeline smiled to herself; you can't wake up if you never went to sleep in the first place. "Thanks, Vipul. I know you'll figure it out. Please keep me posted," she said as she closed the MacBook and sighed. There was nothing she could do to help; fixing a memory leak usually required editing a program's critical source code, and she hadn't written a line of code in years. The benefits of specialization had been drilled into her in business school. It was best to let the full-time engineers figure it out.

With the laptop closed, the only light in the room came in through the fiftieth-floor window from Tokyo's twinkling late-night cityscape. She felt like she was in the movie *Lost in Translation,* except she was fluent in Japanese. The view reminded her of another infinity pool she fancied taking a dip in. It was surely closed this time of night but was worth a shot, if only to get out of this damn room.

A few minutes later she wore a plush, white robe over her red, one-piece swimsuit and watched the elevator count its way up to sixty-five. She felt free with her phone back in the room; it was hard to truly relax with it nearby.

The elevator doors slid open, and she was pleasantly surprised to see that the one to the rooftop pool was itself ajar, though on further inspection it looked broken, possibly forced.

Strange. It should have been fixed right away with what she paid per night to stay here—the property was part of the Stasis Hotels *Suspended Animation Collection*, after all—but for the same reason, she also felt entitled to use the facilities whenever she pleased, even if they were technically closed. There were probably cameras; they were everywhere in the panopticon of modern society. But so what if in ten minutes the graveyard shift security guard came up to politely tell her she couldn't be here? She had plausible deniability.

Madeline walked through the broken door and out onto the vast, empty terrace. It was a still, comfortable summer night, the only sounds the sparse traffic far below and soft splashing of water. Most of the light came from inside of the large rectangular pool. It contrasted starkly with the rest of the roof and looked like it ran right off the side of the building and into the night. Recently opened, she'd read it was the world's highest, surpassing the Marina Bay Sands in Singapore, except here the view wasn't marred by oil tankers for as far as the eye could see.

She untied her robe and let it fall on top of her slippers. She noted the marked depth, then disregarded the 'no diving' sign and plunged head-first into the cerulean water. The temperature was perfect. She swam to the far side and rested her arms on top of the glass wall as she took in the bright night comprised of other skyscrapers in the Shinjuku district and beyond. How many pictures had she seen of others in this exact same pose?

Almost *forty million people*, the most populous metropolitan area in the history of the world, she thought. Why do we live on top of each other like this? Even in a relatively small country like Japan, slightly smaller than California, every individual

11

person could in theory live on their own thirty-thousand-square-foot plot of land, three-quarters of an acre. Globally there was enough biologically productive land for each human alive to live on that much. She'd done the math. And yet, rural towns in Japan, like in much of the world, were dying. She knew the reasons why, of course—economics and opportunity—and that those in wealthier countries consume several acres worth of resources every year. But she couldn't help wondering if perhaps on some level we craved the paradoxical sense of loneliness and anonymity found in an overcrowded metropolis.

Madeline sure did.

"Quite a view, is it not?" The sound of a male voice with a slight Japanese accent startled her. Security must have arrived faster than anticipated. But when she turned her back on the nine-hundred-foot drop, ready to play dumb and apologize, the man standing at the edge of the pool did not appear how she expected.

He was about her age and wore a fitted black suit, but that was where any semblance of being put together ended. Everything was wrinkled, his white shirt untucked and stained with what she hoped was red wine but looked distressingly like blood. The bags under his sunken eyes were visible from fifty feet away as the floodlights in the pool shined through the gently rippling water and danced on his disheveled face. His left hand tousled his long black hair, and his right held a half-empty bottle of Yamazaki whiskey he must have raided from the rooftop bar.

Well, that explained it, Madeline thought, a little relieved. A salaryman who'd had too much to drink trying to impress his boss, then perhaps got his hands on a little coke. But what was he doing at one of the most expensive hotels in the city? Come to think of it, she thought she recognized him, but his unkempt appearance made it hard to place him.

"Ou peut-être en français—tout à fait une vue, non? O en español—toda una vista, ¿sí? O italiano—abbastanza una vista, sì?" he asked in French, Spanish, then Italian.

"I understood you the first time. Nihongo o tsukau koto mo dekitadeshou," she replied in English, then Japanese. "Yes, the view is lovely."

"Ah, American." He continued in English, "Some people are afraid to look down from such heights, but there is no difference between five stories and fifty. Either way, if you fall you're dead, which is preferable to surviving such trauma."

"Can I ask what you're doing up here at this hour?"

"I could ask you the same thing. You showed no hesitation walking through the door I broke open. You're welcome, by the way."

"I can't sleep."

The man burst into laughter. He dropped the bottle of whiskey, shattering it, but did not seem to notice. So much for 'no glass allowed in pool area.' He sat down on the edge of the pool and dipped his feet into the water, still wearing tattered designer dress shoes like a goddamn psychopath, and sighed. "Can't sleep. Ain't that the truth."

Madeline became hyperaware of just how alone the two of them were on the roof. This stranger wasn't a big guy; he couldn't have been any taller than her five feet eight inches. And she had years of kickboxing and Krav Maga classes under her belt. But the prospect of fighting in water was distressing and not a scenario for which she'd trained. If only security would in fact arrive about now. She was no longer a spring chicken and didn't receive the kind of male attention she had in her twenties, but the look in this man's eyes was unlike any she had seen before.

"I fancy your swimsuit. It reminds me of..." he looked down at the red stain on his shirt, then back up at her and said, "...that old American show Baywatch."

"It brings out my eyes."

Hysterical laughter again, this time ending in a yawn. Then he seemed to notice her looking past him towards the elevator, no doubt telegraphing her concern, and said, "Security already came. They won't be bothering me again tonight."

What did he mean by that?

"But there is no need to worry, Miss American Pie. The only person currently in physical danger is me. Do you know what is the longest anyone has intentionally gone without sleep?" He glanced at his expensive-looking watch and continued without waiting for her to answer. "Twenty-two days and just about six hours." He started laughing and shaking uncontrollably, then abruptly stopped. "Those who stay awake for half this long end up dead as a result."

"Are you ok? Do you need help?" This wasn't the behavior of someone who was simply drunk. More importantly, Madeline took shit from no one.

"I do need help, but not the kind you can provide." He yawned again, then shook his head violently as if trying to shake off drowsiness. "Even the strongest of stimulants no longer work. I'm just...so...tired..." he said quietly as his eyes closed. Then he slumped forward and splashed into the pool. A moment later his head surfaced, coughing up water, bloodshot eyes looking around wildly.

For a terrifying second it appeared he was going to swim towards her. Instead he slowly and painfully pulled himself back up out of the pool, leaving behind red whisps in the water.

His soaked suit dripped all over the terrace when he got back to his feet, and his white dress shirt clung to his torso, revealing a heavily tattooed chest. He swept the wet hair off his face with a hand missing most of its little finger to stare at something beyond her, blinking intently every few seconds. His head was steady, but his eyes still darted around.

"Tell me...do you believe in dragons?" he asked in an awed voice as he began walking along the length of the pool, his shoes squishing and the glass shards crunching underfoot. His gaze was still fixed somewhere behind her, off the roof. He picked up his pace as he rounded the pool's corner and was at a full sprint by the time he approached the edge.

"Stop!" yelled Madeline, but it was too late. In a surprisingly athletic maneuver, he bounded with his left foot off the last chaise lounge chair and over a bed of stargazer lilies, then planted his right on the top of the railing and launched himself out into space. From her position on the glass wall, she saw him clear the ledge that caught the infinity pool's overflowing water and plunge silently to the street below.

He didn't move at all on the way down, almost as if he fell asleep as soon as he leapt.

Chapter 2: Darwin

Darwin watched the shadowy phantasm creep towards him out of the corner of his eye. Like starlight, the creature was easier to see by looking at it obliquely; it disappeared if observed directly, though it was still coming for him.

And deciding whether or not to look was the only option available to Darwin—his eyes were the sole part of his body over which he had any control.

The specter continued towards him, drastically out of place in the sunny living room covered in multicolored dog hair. When it reached the couch where he lay, it climbed onto his chest, making it difficult to breathe, and screamed a deafening hiss in his face.

But Darwin was not afraid, and not because he was particularly brave. He'd been terrified the first time it happened, many years ago, but he now knew exactly what was going on down to the level of neurophysiology: sleep paralysis. He was stuck in a partial dreamscape, somewhere between sleep and wakefulness. His body was still paralyzed like it is during rapid eye movement (REM) sleep, so you don't act out your dreams, and part of his mind was still hallucinating. Many accounts of aliens and the paranormal were attributable to just this phenomenon. He merely needed to remain calm and wait to fully wake up.

The buzzing phone on his chest was just the catalyst he needed. The sinister apparition vanished as he regained control over his body. His device was perpetually in Do Not Disturb mode, with only a handful of people exempt. Thus he was unsurprised—and glad—to see that it was his wife; her name on his screen still brought a smile to his face.

He *was* surprised, and pleasantly so, to notice that he had an erection. An average healthy man had three to five per night, every night, and often while napping. Good to know it still worked. Madeline's libido hadn't exactly been through the roof lately given all the stress and sleep deprivation from work.

Darwin answered the video call and said, "Wow am I happy you called when you did. I was in the middle of—"

Madeline interrupted and recounted the events from the Tokyo Stasis Hotel's roof without letting him get in a word. Darwin fiddled with his wedding ring throughout, something he'd spent hours doing every day for the past eight years.

"Oh my god...that's terrible," he said after she finished. "I'm so sorry you had to witness that. And you haven't slept at all? You look awful."

"Thanks, dear."

"You know what I mean. You have to cancel the presentation. Surely they'll understand."

"No, no, I can't. It's too important. We've been preparing for months, and people have flown in from all over the world. I'll take an Adderall and a beta-blocker and catch up on sleep later. Anyways, I wanted to tell you and see if by chance the girls were home yet. After seeing something like that, all I want to do is talk to them."

"On Tuesdays they have soccer practice right after school." No extended summer breaks at this private school, even in the first and second grades. Maybe that explained the eye-watering cost.

"That's right. I've lost track of what day it is. I'd better get back to preparing. I have a week of follow-up meetings scheduled but will see you next weekend."

"Good luck."

"Thanks," she said as she flashed a forced smile and hung up.

Darwin looked at the time on his phone: almost three p.m. He must have inadvertently dozed off. The instructor in the ninety-minute hot yoga sculpt class had kicked his ass that morning, and the afternoon sun had been a welcome break from the May Gray, June Gloom, No-Sky July, and Fogust that characterized a San Francisco summer. At least in Seattle they'd had a few months where it was predictably nice.

His phone also showed a voicemail from someone who was definitely not exempt from Do Not Disturb: Balthazar Abadi. It was a name that most people alive would be ecstatic to see in their list of missed calls, much less voicemails; the man was worth tens of billions of dollars, after all. But not Darwin. All it caused was a tinge of annoyance. Still, he pressed play.

"Chuckieeee," Balthazar said, using a nickname no one had called Darwin since college, "it's the tzar. I get the feeling you're avoiding my calls, texts, and emails. I'm going to hire a skywriter next. Seriously, I had someone look into it. When are you going to visit me on the *Arianna*? She's almost as beautiful as some of the women on board. I've literally been asking you for years. I'm making some big moves out here and want to loop you in. Just give me a date, time, and airport. I'll send the PJ. Your birthday is coming up. That seems perfect. Come alone if you want. I know you have shit else to do. Or bring the family. There's plenty of space. Though, given the laws out here—or lack thereof—I should warn you that some areas of the ship probably aren't appropriate for children. Or wives. Let me know!"

Darwin shook his head and deleted the voicemail, hoping his jealously would abate with it. He'd had much better grades, higher test scores, and more work ethic—more ethics, generally. And yet their two lives had turned out the opposite of how a naïve person who believed past performance was an indicator of future success would have thought. A naïve person like Darwin. A few fortunate, reckless bets and Balthazar was on the cover of half the magazines at the airport, while one stroke of bad luck and Darwin was—

No. He would not follow the line of thought any further. He would not give in to quiet desperation. Raising children and shaping the lives of your progeny was a far more fulfilling and consequential way to spend your scarce, precious time than the majority of meaningless jobs people trudged through, frittering their lives away just to make a living. Maybe not as consequential as pushing the boundaries of our understanding of the brain...but still. He loved his life and family. That was enough.

Having kids was like crossing a singularity's event horizon: It was impossible to foresee the subsequent changes, and impossible to go back.

He opened the laptop sitting on a stack of *Neuron, Journal of Neuroscience,* and *Consciousness and Cognition* on the coffee table, determined to take advantage of what was left of the heightened creativity found when transitioning between dreaming and being fully awake. Many renowned creators including Beethoven and Edison were known to have done the same. The state contributed to both the melting clocks of Dali and the absolute (if ultimately incorrect) clocks of Newtonian physics. Some would nap holding a heavy object so that it would drop and wake them up as soon as they drifted off, their grip relaxed, and their subconscious came online. Darwin could have worn a more sophisticated device to monitor his biomarkers and rouse him when sleep started setting in, but he'd trained himself to make the most of these literal daydreams naturally.

What Darwin believed would be his break-out science fiction novel—*The Stardust Chronicles, Episode IX*—was already open, the cursor mid-sentence, right where he'd left it before taking a break to think and apparently falling asleep.

Darwin wrote, '...distant, technologically primitive civilizations believed them to be massive, collapsed stars, orbiting another dense object like a black hole or fellow neutron star. They gave them names like 'pulsars' and compared them to the lighthouses that existed on their own planets to help ships navigate and warn them of perilous shores. They were both more incorrect and correct than they knew. Light Station 739 rotated just beyond the event horizon of an unremarkable black hole at the center of an unremarkable galaxy. The artificial intelligence who kept the electromagnetic radiation beaming out into the cosmos was itself unremarkable except in one critical sense...'

He was thinking of the best way to word what came next when their rescued mutt Mofongo ran into the room, jumped onto the couch, and stared out the window with her tail wagging. Darwin rubbed what he liked to think of as his characteristic light stubble. It *was* Tuesday, right?

He glanced out the window to confirm who Mofongo was telegraphing must be there, then got up and opened the front door to greet his children. Christina and Evelyn ran the rest of the way when they saw him.

"You're home earlier than I expected," he said as he knelt and hugged both at once.

"Now we can spend more time with daddy," said Evelyn. They'd inevitably grow out of the phase where he was their hero, at least for a while during adolescence, but he was committed to cherishing it while it lasted.

"That's right!" he replied. Mofongo was impatiently waiting behind him, and the girls moved on to greet the dog. Darwin stood up, stepped out onto the porch, and waved to his neighbor, who was about to pull into the garage. She had driving duty today. Her daughter was the same age as Christina and played on the same team. Evelyn was a year younger, but the same retired hedge fund manager coached both grades.

She rolled down the Lexus window and said, "Coach had to cancel practice last minute. Didn't say why. I'm not surprised, though—I've felt some strange energy coming from him recently." Darwin wondered if she meant energy in the real, scientific sense, as in the capacity to do work. "A few of the other parents volunteered to hang out and let them scrimmage, but I'd prefer to avoid driving at rush hour later and figured you'd be around if I brought them home early."

"Yeah, no problem. I'll just need to find a way to burn off their extra energy. Have a good evening."

"Can we play fetch?" Evelyn asked when he walked back in the door. Their small backyard was just large enough for a viable game.

"We sure can. Let me just put my computer back to sleep." He'd have to write another time.

"Do computers dream when they sleep?" asked Christina.

Darwin's first instinct was to tell her that no, it's more like the computer is temporarily dead or in suspended animation than asleep, then reconsidered and said, "Yes, they dream of electric sheep. Do you want to play fetch too?"

"I wanna watch TV."

"Ok, but only for an hour. With the half-hour you watched this morning, you'll be at your TV limit for the day. And first you have to tell me the three most interesting things you learned in school today."

"Um...I learned that if you add two even numbers you get a even number, if you add two odd numbers you get a even number, and if you add a even number and a odd number you get a odd number."

"That *is* interesting, but I'm only going to count that as one. What are two more?"

"What's a odd number?" asked Evelyn. At age six she was still at peak curiosity. Darwin hoped it lasted forever.

"It's a number that can't be divided exactly by two. You'll learn all about them next year," he said.

"Hooray!"

"Um...," continued Christina, "I learned that all the planets are big round balls and go around the sun, which is a way bigger round ball."

"That's amazing! Some adults don't even know that," said Darwin. It was literally elementary school science.

"I wanna throw the ball for Mofongo," said Evelyn, patting the dog's head.

"Just one second," said Darwin.

"But she didn't say why they are all round. Why are they all round?" asked Christina.

"Because of something called 'gravity,'" he replied, "which means that everything pulls everything else towards itself, and the bigger something is, the harder it pulls!"

"Why does everything do gravity?" asked Christina.

Darwin paused; it was a more profound question than she knew. In science it often made more sense to ask 'how' than 'why.' He said, "They just do, sweetie. Gravity is one of the fundamental forces of the universe." She was probably too young to learn about electromagnetism or the strong and weak nuclear forces, which he wasn't even sure he fully understood himself. "Ok, what's the third interesting thing you learned?"

"Oh, I learned that your brain controls everything you do and talks to your body through the nervous system. My teacher said you *are* your brain."

"Now *that* is interesting. It sounds like you had quite the day. Did you know your dad used to be a scientist who studied the brain?" Darwin resisted the urge to add to or modify what Christina's teacher had told her, although he highly doubted you'd be *you* without your body. Madeline would be proud.

"Yes we know that, dad," interjected Evelyn. "You told us like a million times. Let's play fetch!"

"Ok ok. Go find the ball and I'll meet you at the back door. And I also want to hear about what you learned today."

Evelyn ran off with Mofongo hot on her heels. Christina jumped up on the couch. Darwin turned on the TV but paused before changing the channel to the one with his daughter's favorite after-school cartoons. The news was on.

"...successful and controversial Japanese entrepreneur Takayoshi Yamamoto killed a security guard then committed

23

suicide by jumping from the roof of the new Tokyo Stasis Hotel. Friends and colleagues say he hadn't seemed like himself for some time and was acting especially strange and erratic over the past few weeks, suffering from extreme insomnia. It had also been long-rumored that he had ties to Japan's notorious Yakuza organized crime syndicates. Authorities plan to conduct an autopsy, but the catastrophic damage from the impact may limit what can be concluded..."

What a coincidence.

Chapter 3: Madeline

Thursday, June 20th, 2019 — 6 hours of sleep

Work. The unglamorous kind (triaging a cash flow issue with accounting and delivering an underwhelming performance review, though I don't remember to who). It was like a normal Wednesday back at the office, which is surprising given how atypical the real yesterday was and how much press we're getting after the product announcement. At this point it feels like I've been on the grind nonstop for over twenty-four consecutive hours, including while asleep.

At least now I finally get a few days off.

The inside of the facility was calm and quiet, a welcome change from the frenetic energy and constant honking in the streets of Bangkok. Madeline preferred the controlled chaos of Tokyo; this was just chaos. The taxi ride from her hotel had only been fifteen minutes, but they must have been passed by hundreds of scooters and tuk-tuks zipping by, some with entire families crowded onto them.

But what relieved her more than the facility's tranquility was its upscale interior, especially compared to its bare exterior, which was considerably less impressive than many others in this part of the city. She could have been in a new medical office building back in San Francisco. She supposed they wanted to keep a low profile. Understandable. Long before it became one of the world's most popular medical tourism destinations, Thailand was a place many people came to do things that were illegal in their home country.

That was why she was here, after all.

The doctor, also an American, entered the room. That was why he was here too. She wondered if he also engaged in other kinds of tourism.

"Missus Johnston, good to see you again," he said, shaking her hand. She'd forgotten how tall he was. She hadn't seen him since her consultation in Palo Alto months ago. "How are you feeling?"

"Good to see you again too, Doctor Magnusson. I'm starving." She hadn't eaten all day. Madeline was more of a foodie than many of her friends, some of whom saw eating as a chore and did it purely for sustenance in the form of disgusting shakes. But sometimes having to consume so many calories multiple times every day was irritating. Perhaps one day science would solve that problem too, like it had with another biological need.

"Standard pre-surgery protocol. Have you been keeping a dream journal like I asked?"

"Yes, as best I can. It's amazing how fast you forget your dreams. Sometimes it feels like I only have seconds after waking up to write them down."

"Fascinating, isn't it? And you only remember the dreams you have immediately before waking, if you remember them at all. You could dream about all kinds of things without realizing it. The brain is just as active during sleep as while awake—*more so*, even—but in different ways. However,

26

REM sleep interrupts the neuron activity and neurochemical conditions associated with memory formation."

"Like being blackout drunk," said Madeline. She may have been an honor student but had still enjoyed college and remembered (or didn't remember) such experiences. She'd also had no problem pulling all-nighters back then.

The doctor forced a joyless smile but did not laugh. "Something like that. But we believe there's an evolutionary explanation for why we mostly don't remember our dreams. If you *were* able to, especially the mundane ones, it might be difficult to distinguish them from memories of reality. Some unfortunate people *do* experience this, often to great detriment. It's also thought that much of the phenomenon of déjà vu, things you don't remember you remember until you confront them, is caused by encountering what you previously dreamed."

"If we don't remember them, why do we dream at all?" asked Madeline.

"We don't definitively know, though there are many theories. It may be that we just don't *consciously* remember them. Some believe dreams serve a primary purpose, like helping your subconscious work through and make sense of recent experiences and feelings or prepare for potential scenarios you may encounter in the future. A way to derive value from otherwise lost time. Others believe they're simply a side effect of other important processes that occur during sleep. There are also more outlandish theories, but of course those aren't supported by science. Even fetuses experience REM sleep and dreams in the womb. I hope that one day we'll be able to discern what they dream about.

"It should, *however*, become easier to remember your

dreams from here on out. They will likely become more vivid, but also more fantastical, like fever dreams. You may also experience a higher prevalence of lucid dreams. It's important to keep a record in the unlikely event of adverse side effects, and so that if you *do* find yourself confused whether something happened in a dream or not, you have a reference."

Madeline said, "It already reads like the diary of an insane person."

Another joyless smile. "How have you been sleeping?" asked the doctor.

Should she mention the strange events of the other night on the roof? No, better to stay focused. "Not great. I've spent half of the past few months on the road."

"Jet lag aside, there's an evolutionary explanation for that, too. Your brain remains partially awake the first few nights sleeping in a new environment. It's believed this is because it doesn't know if it's safe, and thus remains more alert to potential danger."

Under different circumstances Madeline would have been annoyed at how much Doctor Magnusson sounded like Darwin—like a know-it-all—but right now she appreciated his confidence and intensity. He was yet to break eye contact during their conversation. It was reassuring given her reason for being here. "Can you please humor me and explain how this works one more time? Forgive me, but I'm a bit nervous before undergoing brain surgery."

"It's perfectly normal to feel nervous," he said. "But while endonasal endoscopy *is* technically neurosurgery, it's minimally invasive. I'll go in through your nose, not your skull. You'll be discharged in as little as two days and can return to your normal life, though there are some activities we

28

recommend you avoid for the next month. It's all covered in your discharge paperwork, and you can of course reach out if you ever have any questions or concerns."

"And there's no scar, no way at all to tell it was done?" She knew this already, naturally. It was a critical feature given the nature of the modified Huxley procedure and stigma that still existed in many places. The rich getting richer. Thus most recipients tried to keep it a secret.

"No scar, but *you'll* certainly be able to tell it was done. Every patient is different, but for the next week or so you'll likely experience some nasal congestion, along with blood or cerebrospinal fluid leaking from your nose. You may also have a headache—not from pain in the brain itself, of course, which contains no nerves—but from the tissue surrounding it."

"That sounds manageable, all things considered," said Madeline.

"However, it's in several weeks that you'll *really* notice something has changed. Sleep is critically important and must bestow a tremendous survival advantage to have evolved at all given how vulnerable it makes you to predators for extended periods. Think of the selective pressure to eliminate sleep and the boon it would be for a species. Or an individual.

"But we don't fully understand all the benefits of and reasons why we sleep. We *do* know that deep, or slow-wave sleep, is vital for converting short-term to long-term memory. And long-term memories comprise much of who you are. So, although the procedure will reduce the amount of *time* you feel you need to sleep to four hours or less, it will not reduce the *effect* of that sleep. An average sleep cycle takes about ninety minutes to move through the light, deep, and REM phases. Over time yours will compress down to about forty-five, but your brain activity will approximately double, giving you the benefits of a full night's sleep in half the time."

That, more specifically, was why she was here. Madeline wished she was one of the extremely lucky and extremely few with the genes that allowed them to get by with only four hours of sleep. For a while she'd deluded herself into thinking she was, but in reality had just been one of the many people kidding themselves, masking the problem with stimulants while doing significant harm to their health and depriving their bodies and minds of the closest thing in existence to a miracle drug. "And it's safe?"

"As far as we know, yes, but you should still avoid things you would be wise to avoid anyways, like prolonged exposure to ionizing radiation. Now, I would be a *fool* to tell you there's no risk. We only have longitudinal data on humans going back seven years to when it was first performed in China. As you know, the modified procedure is still not approved in many Western countries, which is why you and I are here."

That last point didn't bother Madeline. Like many, she thought the FDA was dragging its feet for overtly political reasons. "Sorry to ask all the same questions as last time. To confirm—it's irreversible?"

"For the foreseeable future, yes. We can take out what we put in, but the procedure also removes small sections of parts of the brain involved in sleep and regulating circadian rhythms—the thalamus, hypothalamus, and pineal gland. We can't simply put them back. There's a saying in neurosurgery—'you're never the same when the air hits your brain.'"

Madeline knew it was a 'type one' decision. She'd deemed it a calculated risk worth taking, despite Darwin's rants on the topic. She 'had it all' but found it lacking, and the prospect of several hours of extra time every day to spend with her daughters, on her career, and on herself was just too tantalizing. Perhaps she could get back the body she had at twenty-five or finally catch up on all those mystery and thriller novels.

She had been an early recipient of LASIK eye surgery and performed a similar rationalization—if it turns out there are adverse side effects decades down the road, hopefully the relevant science will have advanced to treat them. And even if not, the positive impact would still have made it worth it. A few people in her circles had had it done and said the results were astounding, which was how she'd been introduced to Doctor Magnusson. He was supposedly the best in the world and only took referrals. Plus, he'd actually had the procedure done himself, unlike her LASIK surgeon who'd worn glasses.

"Now," the doctor continued, "it looks like you're yet to list an emergency contact. We hope it's just a formality, *of course*, but can I assume there's a Mister Johnston who should be listed here?" He nodded to her ring.

Madeline hesitated, but only for a second, then said, "Let's put my brother, Preston. My husband doesn't know I'm having the procedure done."

Part 2: Hypnagogia

Three months later

Chapter 4: Darwin

Per the late inventor and industrialist Alfred Nobel's will, most Nobel Prizes are awarded in Sweden. Darwin had no idea how he ended up at the Stockholm Concert Hall, much less in a front-row seat, but that wasn't top-of-mind. No, Darwin's chief concern was the man wearing a medal and accepting a diploma with his left hand while shaking His Majesty the King of Sweden's hand with his right.

The orchestra played while the crowd stood on their feet and applauded. Some even whooped and cheered, which seemed wildly inappropriate given the ceremony's unbearable pomp and formality.

Finally, everyone took their seats. The grand auditorium fell silent. Doctor Gregory Huxley, Darwin's PhD supervisor at the University of Washington, took the podium. He looked exactly like he did the last time Darwin saw him a decade ago—like a wolf in sheep's clothing, but in this case the sheep was an old, bald man.

"Your Majesty, Your Royal Highness, Mister President, Excellencies, Ladies and Gentlemen," Doctor Huxley began. So, he even stole the start of his acceptance speech, this time from MLK, fumed Darwin. Did no one else notice? He felt insane. "I am so grateful for this tremendous honor. It is the culmination of a thirty-five-year career and truly feels like a dream. But what brings me even greater joy is the prospect this research has for improving the lives of so many who have suffered from acute and chronic neurological disorders. I—"

"It's my research!" roared Darwin, standing up. Doctor Huxley stopped and stared at him, as did everyone else in the concert hall. Looking down from the stage and at himself for the first time, Darwin realized there was likely more than one reason for the widespread gasps and whispers: Not only was he not wearing a tuxedo like all the other men—he wasn't wearing anything at all.

But that didn't bother him. He may have only seen a few minutes of playing time before the heart condition sidelined him, and even before that he'd been more focused on his biochemistry studies than athletics. But he'd still played linebacker on a D1 college football team and kept up a daily workout habit in the years since. He was not embarrassed by any part of his body. Quite the contrary.

All he felt was rage.

Darwin vaulted onto the stage and strode towards the professor. He didn't actually have a plan for when he reached him, but it was liberating to act only out of raw emotion for once. It appeared as if everyone else in the auditorium was frozen, Doctor Huxley with a look of abject terror on his face. But when Darwin got within a few steps of the podium, a sharp pain arose in his lower back. He looked down to see the tip of a ceremonial sword, dripping with blood, protruding from his stomach.

That seemed a bit drastic; they could have just tackled or tased him. I bet that's the first time that sword has ever been used, he thought as everything faded to black.

Darwin gasped as he sat up in bed, sweating. It was just a night terror, and one he'd had multiple times before. Doctor Huxley had not won the Nobel Prize in Physiology or Medicine, though many said he should have. Hell, the person who pioneered the lobotomy won one. Darwin had never even been to Scandinavia. And although the stabbing had felt real, there had always been reports of people experiencing pain during dreams, for whom pinching themselves wasn't a reliable marker of being awake or asleep.

There were many more such reports due to the proliferation of the modified Huxley procedure.

He turned to Madeline's side of the bed to apologize for waking her up. She wasn't there. Darwin was a deep sleeper and rarely woke up during the night. Maybe she'd got up to pee, which she'd told him was common. The perils of having a small bladder. But the bathroom off the master bedroom was dark and quiet. The curtains were open, revealing it was still hours before dawn. The blinking red light atop the near tower of the Golden Gate Bridge was barely visible in the distance.

Darwin turned to his nightstand and tapped his phone's screen. Four-thirty a.m. The sole notification was a text message from Balthazar. He'd thought his old friend had given up but should have known better; the man was nothing if not tenacious. Famously so. Darwin deleted the message without reading it.

If it had been a weekday, it would have been that awkward time when it's close enough to his alarm that he can't get in another full sleep cycle, and it might make sense to just get up. Sacrificing a little bit of shuteye was often preferable to risking your alarm going off in the middle of slow-wave sleep, which all but ensured waking up on the wrong side of the bed. But it was Saturday, so he could sleep in (as much as that was possible with two young kids). However, he felt dehydrated from the bottle of cab he and Maddy had drunk last night and figured he'd have another glass of water to head off any lingering effects given the busy day ahead of him.

He was also curious what his wife was up to.

Darwin hopped out of bed and used the light from his phone's wallpaper—a picture of his family at the beach—to navigate to the bedroom door. Mofongo was still asleep and snoring at the foot of the bed. Worst guard dog ever. No lights were on upstairs, and he tiptoed past the closed doors to his daughters' rooms, careful not to wake them. But he almost cried out when he stepped on an object so sharp it could only be one thing: LEGO. What had he told them about putting away their toys?

He cursed under his breath and walked downstairs to find the entire first floor also dark. He glanced out the front window and was annoyed to see the same old car parked under a streetlight in front of the house. Technically you were only allowed to park in the same place for seventy-two hours. He was going to complain to the city if the car wasn't gone by morning.

Wait, was something moving under the vehicle? His pulse increased slightly as he stared without blinking, trying to find a pattern in the darkness. Then something darted from beneath the car and into the streetlight. Then another. Then two more. A whole family of raccoons scurried across the street and disappeared into the shadows, probably to raid the trashcans of anyone who didn't take protective measures. Darwin smiled; he was glad some nonhuman animals thrived in the middle of the environment people had created.

He filled a glass of water in the kitchen, neglecting to turn on the light, then disarmed the alarm and walked out into the backyard. Silence. What a strange time of night, when the only places still open were the few after-hours clubs and all-night diners left in the city. All but the highest Friday night partiers were asleep, while only the most committed early risers were up.

And he was married to one of the latter. His wife got more done before nine in the morning than most people did their entire day, including on weekends.

Darwin went back inside and down the hall towards Madeline's home office. A faint light came from under the closed door. Figured. She worked more than ever now that her face was popping up on some of the same magazines as 'the tzar,' which was saying something. Darwin had never been on the cover of anything. He approached the office but paused before knocking. A soft humming sound came from within, and above it Madeline said heatedly, "...fuck me."

Interesting.

But in the silence that followed, Darwin recognized the humming sound as coming from her new treadmill desk. No surprise she was using it despite the early hour; she'd recently been on quite a fitness kick. Then Madeline laughed and continued speaking, "Yes, you're right. I'm sorry. They're going to fuck all of us, not just me, because that's what lawyers do. We'll have to make some major shifts if we don't clear the regulatory hurdles and get the green light from legal by Monday. I'll put together a contingency plan on the flight. Let me know if you hear anything over the weekend. See you Tuesday. Bye."

It was just business talk. What else had he expected to find, eavesdropping on his wife like some jealous, paranoid loser?

He knocked gently on the door.

"Come in," she said. He opened the door and entered. Madeline was indeed using the treadmill desk, wearing one of her standard work-from-home uniforms: a long-sleeve blouse and no pants. She looked incredible. Despite her increasingly hectic schedule, their sex life had taken a marked turn for the better lately. He wasn't sure why but also wasn't complaining. He would have made a move if not for his headache.

Madeline paused the treadmill, removed her AirPods, turned around, smiled.

"You're up early," he said. "I'm impressed given we finished that bottle."

"I could say the same to you. And you had more than I did, plus a nightcap."

"That's true. I'd forgotten about the whiskey, but it's precisely why I'm up." He raised the glass of water, neglecting to mention the nightmare. "What's your excuse?"

"I want to try and get a full night's sleep on the flight so I hit the ground running when I land in Japan. Hopefully this ensures I'll be good and tired later."

"I wish I was able to sleep on planes like you. You're such a road warrior. But I still think it's silly to spend most of your weekend traveling. You're the boss—can't you make a better schedule for yourself?"

"I try to set a good example at the top. Plus it's already almost Sunday in Tokyo."

"You could certainly set a better example of work-life balance, but I understand things are busy now with all the talk of taking the company public. Can I get you anything while I'm up?"

"I'm good, thanks."

"More importantly, are you still making breakfast tomorrow, or, I guess, today?"

"You're not the only one in this house who can cook, you know."

"What's that you always say about specialization and the division of labor?"

Madeline smiled. "There will be organic French toast and a fresh pot of coffee ready as soon as you and the girls wake up."

"Organic, as in carbon-based?"

"Don't be a smartass or there won't be any for you."

"Just kidding. I can't wait. Perfect fuel for the girls' soccer games." They had a new coach. The old one had inexplicably disappeared. "Goodnight, or good morning."

"You too."

Darwin went back upstairs, tiptoed past the girls' rooms again, then navigated his way through the dark to the California king-sized bed. Mofongo was still snoring. She twitched and paddled in her sleep. What did she dream about? He was up to date on the relevant literature and knew that whatever dreamland she currently frolicked through was just as rich as the one to which he was heading. Some aspects of dreams' content could be reasonably inferred by comparing MRI and fMRI when dogs (or humans) were awake versus sleeping.

It took Darwin longer than usual to fall asleep. As he lay still with his eyes closed, he couldn't shake the feeling that something about Madeline seemed off. If he didn't know better, he'd think...nah. No way.

Chapter 5: Madeline

Monday, September 16th, 2019 — 3 hours of sleep (the fewest yet!)
A double-decker A380 roared by overhead, so close that the wind it created almost knocked me off the edge of the cliff where I stood, overlooking a vast, lush valley. Behind the plane trailed an enormous red ribbon, perhaps fifty feet wide and many thousands long. I don't think I ever saw the end of it. The Airbus was followed by a 747, the Spruce Goose, a stealth bomber, and a B-29 Superfortress, all painted in psychedelic patterns. Each trailed a similar ribbon in orange, yellow, green, and blue.

They initially began flying in spirals around another ribbon, this one violet and being lifted slowly by a zeppelin that looked to actually be made of lead. The planes then began to swoop in perfectly choreographed patterns around the growing purple tower as it ascended towards the sun, miraculously avoiding each other and their attached ribbons while weaving some type of complex rainbow knot. It's like they were creating a rope for a giant, or a necklace for god. The rumble created by the engines and aerial maneuvers was deafening. And incredible. And—I realized at the time—not real.

It was another lucid dream.
I swan dove off the cliff. After falling for a few hundred feet, I swooped upwards and began what I imagine is most people's

go-to activity when they realize they're dreaming and in control: flying. There was now a ribbon trailing behind me, too. It was indigo, definitely the lamest color in the rainbow, but the only one left. I soared towards the kaleidoscopic spiral, and when I was about to make my first contribution, I woke up. Very disappointing. Reality was a bit of a letdown in comparison, but I knew there was no hope of falling back asleep to rejoin the show.

Madeline hadn't technically lied to Darwin—she *was* going to Tokyo; she'd just selectively excluded the simple fact that she was stopping in Bangkok for a night first. The truth, but not the whole truth, so help her god. He'd find out eventually, but often it was better to ask for forgiveness than permission. He would have been unbearably overbearing and cynical about the whole thing given his background.

Her follow-up appointment with Doctor Magnusson had gone well. Unless anything unforeseen happened she would only see him once more, nine months from now. Boy that guy was intense. There was something a little disconcerting about his persona, something that made her slightly uncomfortable. Perhaps it was that he almost seemed *too* put together, too professional. Perhaps it was that, combined with an office staffed exclusively by beautiful young Thai girls. Regardless, she had to admit he did great work. He'd earned his reputation, and she would definitely make referrals.

If only this procedure had been an option before she had the girls! How much easier it would have made being a new parent. Or when she was taking the redeye to New York in economy class every other week. There's nothing like snagging half the sleep you need while sitting at an acute angle, then changing in an airport bathroom stall while someone shits

41

next to you before taxiing straight into Manhattan for a full day of meetings. Oh well, no use regretting what couldn't have been. It was done now, and there was no going back.

In a sense she'd always looked forward to sleep, like most people, but up until recently it had been because of exhaustion. Now, after undergoing the modified Huxley procedure, it was because of the fantastic dreamscapes she visited each night. She'd close her eyes and drift off, wondering where she was heading and who would be joining her. It was like she was living many lives in parallel. She used to only get that feeling by reading novels, but now she was the protagonist.

After a short, harrowing drive from the doctor's office in rush hour traffic, her car pulled up to the Bangkok Stasis Hotel behind a red Ferrari, a silver Aston Martin, and a black SUV. Pretty standard lineup for one of the fanciest hotels in the city. The sun was starting to set, the hot and sticky day finally beginning to cool off. She deserved a drink at the rooftop bar before preparing for what awaited her the rest of the week. But when she stopped by her room to drop off her phone first so she could truly relax, the door's lock blinked red no matter how many times and ways she tried her key card. Madeline sighed. Sometimes the little annoyances got the deepest under your skin.

It took a few minutes to take the elevator from her high-floor room to reception. There was a line of people waiting to check in—bad form for a *Suspended Animation Collection* property. Fortunately she was able to use the VIP desk. At least *that* worked as it should.

This time her key worked. After dropping off her stuff and heading to the roof, she gazed out from a chaise lounge on the fortieth floor at the Bangkok skyline, sparkling in the encroaching dusk. The city had less than half the population of Tokyo, but it was a respectable metropolis nonetheless. Sexy in its own unique way (from up here, where the traffic and honking weren't your concern).

She started to think back to the strange night on the roof of another Stasis Hotel when a smartly dressed cocktail waiter approached her and said, "Excuse me ma'am, the gentleman over there would like to buy you whatever drink you like. I'm also happy to tell him that you're not interested."

Madeline glanced at where the waiter signaled. A man around forty subtly nodded and ever-so-slightly raised what looked like an old fashioned at her. Old fashioned indeed. She had to admit he was handsome. It wasn't fair men could be so attractive at that age, while most women peaked at nineteen in the eyes of the opposite sex, statistically speaking. His all-black outfit was overly debonair—did he think he was a fucking James Bond villain? But that was par for the course at these places. Perhaps he was just European.

"I'll have a glass of your most expensive champagne. Feel free to choose something that's not on the menu," she said.

"As you wish," the cocktail waiter said with a knowing smile before turning and walking away. The man must have been able to see her engagement ring from where he sat. Darwin hadn't exactly been flush with cash when he proposed back in grad school, but she'd upgraded a few years ago when the money started coming. So, either the man was a brash suitor—or worse—he recognized her and wanted to pitch something. She'd give him five minutes. That was worth fifty dollars before tax and tip given this leg of the trip wasn't going on the company card.

The man walked over and took a seat on the chaise lounge

43

across from her, said, "Such a beautiful evening in such a beautiful city. It'd be a shame for such a beautiful woman to spend it all alone." His voice was sonorous, befitting of his look. Madeline couldn't quite place the accent, which was unusual given the extent of her travels.

"Some people don't get the opportunity to spend much time alone. I assume a married man can empathize." He seemed to genuinely enjoy her response and held up his left hand to display the simple gold wedding band. Sometimes Madeline found them disarming. Right now she wondered if it was a prop. "Does your wife mind you buying expensive drinks for strangers?"

"Marcellino, my husband, does not mind." That explained a few things, if true. But for some reason, perhaps against her better judgment, she believed him. "And you are no stranger to me, Missus Johnston. I have followed your company for some time." That explained more. She hadn't thought so many people gave a shit about enterprise software and was starting to miss the anonymity she once had. Oh well—it came with the territory. Remaining in obscurity meant failure.

"Please call me Madeline. What should I call you?"

"Elias." He shifted his now-empty drink from right hand to left, leaned forward, and they shook. His dress shirt's top two buttons were undone, revealing the pendants on the several gold necklaces he wore. It looked like one of those 'Coexist' bumper stickers. What would Darwin the militant atheist have to say? To him, any answers to questions like 'where are we from?' or 'why are we here?' that originated before *On the Origin of Species* were null and void.

"And where are you from, Elias? It's unfair that you know so much about me."

44

"I am one of the lucky few born and raised in Malta, the heart of the Mediterranean."

"I've never been."

"Not many have, especially Americans. Most just think of it as a tax haven."

"Do you still live there?"

"On paper, yes, but I've lived mostly in hotels like this for the past decade." He motioned to the rooftop around them. "Though I am not complaining. I assume you are here on business?"

"Something like that."

"Lucky you. Of all the capital cities of Asia, Bangkok is among my favorites."

"I'm more of a Singapore girl myself."

Elias shook his head. "Too clean, too safe, too orderly, too *boring*. Now, Kuala Lumpur, Jakar—" He was interrupted by the cocktail waiter returning with Madeline's flute of champagne, then asked, "Can we please have a bottle of that?"

Madeline let out a single sharp laugh. "You're out of your mind if you think I'm finishing a bottle with you. Also, I have to admit it's not cheap."

"Go ahead," Elias said to the waiter, who walked off. "I'll finish whatever you don't drink. And don't worry about the cost—my firm owns a majority stake in Stasis Hotels."

"What firm is that?"

"Circadian Capital Partners. CCP."

"Don't take this the wrong way, but I've never heard of it."

"No offense taken. We normally act as a silent partner, and most of our investments are in Europe and Asia."

"I don't suppose the reason we're having this conversation is that you're looking to enter the US, perhaps by taking a stake

45

in a high-profile company on its way to a successful IPO?"

Elias smiled. "Like I said, it'd be a shame to spend such a beautiful evening alone. I'd actually prefer not to discuss work, if that's alright with you. I'm sure we both do enough of that."

Madeline glanced at her watch. His five minutes were up. What were another five?

Two hours and two bottles of champagne later, Elias said, "Dubai. The irony! It's almost as if the buildings are reaching to get as far as possible from the scorched earth that generated the wealth to fund their construction."

"That sounds like something my husband would say."

"Ah, Mister Johnston. Lucky man. Tell me—what is Darwin like?"

Had she mentioned his name? Probably. She was more than tipsy. "Hmm...let me put it this way—there's the kind of person who takes pleasure in pointing out that tomatoes are technically a fruit. Then there are those who feel the need to go one step further and explain that *actually* tomatoes are both a fruit *and* vegetable."

Elias smiled. "Say no more. Your turn. What's your favorite skyline?"

Madeline looked out at the now-dark Bangkok cityscape and contemplated. "Hong Kong."

"Come on! The city with the most skyscrapers in the world? It's admittedly something to behold, nestled around Victoria Harbour, but that's a cop-out."

"That or Tokyo," she said. "Which reminds me—I'm flying there early tomorrow and believe it's time for me to retire to my room for the night."

Elias had been true to his word and discussed only the

tangential aspects of their professional lives up until now. This was usually when the pitch came, in one form or another.

"What are you doing for dinner?" he asked. "There's a great night market nearby I'd love to show you."

"I plan on ordering room service. It was going to be a salad, but now I'm thinking pasta."

"Ok, well take my number for if you change your mind."

"I left my phone in the room."

"How enlightened of you. In that case here's my card." He handed her a matte black business card with silver lettering.

"Elias Sultana. Vice President. Fancy."

"Everyone in finance is a VP. Haven't you seen *American Psycho?* Title inflation helps us get meetings. And strokes our egos. Though it's not quite as fancy a title as CEO."

"'Your money never sleeps, and neither do we,'" Madeline read from the card, then laughed. "It's a bit cheesy, don't you think?"

"I'm not in charge of marketing. And it certainly hasn't hurt fundraising."

"I'm glad to hear that. Well, it was nice to meet you, Mister Sultana. Thanks for the pleasant company and champagne." She stood up for the first time since arriving on the rooftop and almost stumbled before regaining her composure. She hadn't drunk *that* much.

The waiter arrived and dropped off the bill. Elias glanced at it, raised his eyebrows, smiled. "Even if this were in dollars instead of baht, it would have been worth it. So nice to meet you too, Missus Johnston." He extended his hand to shake again. His sleeves were rolled up now, revealing tan, muscular forearms and a tattoo on his right wrist of what looked like a dreamcatcher...with people caught in it? "Don't hesitate to call if you change your mind. And if you don't, sweet dreams."

Madeline took the elevator the few stories down to her floor. She half expected her key card not to work but was relieved when the lock flashed green. She let the door close behind her, neglecting to lock the deadbolt.

What a strange, charming man, she thought as she fell backward onto the bed. She grabbed her phone from where it was charging on the nightstand. Twenty-five new emails, eight unread texts, and three voicemails. None from her friends or family. Fuck it—work could wait, as could turning off the light or brushing her teeth. It was only eight-thirty, but she felt more tired than she had since the procedure.

Stakeholders and fiduciary duties be damned, Madeline closed her eyes and fell instantly asleep.

Chapter 6: Darwin

Darwin briefly took his left hand off the bike's handlebars to glance at his smartwatch. He had heartrate to spare. No way he was losing. Not to this guy.

Preston was about twenty feet in front of him, standing up out of his ten-thousand-dollar road bike's seat and dressed like Lance fucking Armstrong. Darwin could hear his labored breath from here. There were only about a hundred yards left of winding climbing to the scenic overlook at the top of the Marin Headlands, the endpoint of a three-hour ride. And the song was getting to the best part. Game over.

He checked there was no car coming up the hill behind him, then turned up the volume in his headphones, downshifted, and increased his pace. When he got within a few feet, Preston did the same, but it was too late. Darwin had momentum on his side now.

He passed Preston and gave him a smile that was begrudgingly returned as Don Henley sang the last few lines of The Eagles' 'Hotel California' and Joe Walsh launched into the guitar solo. If only he could see the look in Preston's eyes behind the sunset-tinted, aerodynamic sunglasses. Darwin sustained the heightened pace into the almost empty parking lot; it was nice to avoid the weekend crowds.

He'd already removed his helmet and had a long drink of Gatorade by the time Preston pulled in and dismounted. The latter removed his helmet and sunglasses, revealing strawberry blond hair and bright blue eyes that were both precisely the same color as Madeline's.

They fist-bumped then took in the sweeping views of the sun-soaked San Francisco Bay—one of the best damn views in the world—without speaking for a few minutes as they caught their breath. They'd barely spoken since meeting up for the ride.

"Perfect day," said Darwin.

"Gotta love that Indian summer," said Preston.

"I wonder if that term is considered politically incorrect these days."

"Don't know, don't care."

Darwin glanced at his watch. "Two hours fifty-five minutes. Not bad."

"It seems the Peloton is working," said Preston. "I'd have won if I was your age. Thanks for the invite. I think that was the longest I've been out of the house this quarter. I don't know how you do it, man. Including Mofongo you're outnumbered by women four to one."

"I don't mind. Growing up it was zero to two. This is definitely preferable."

"I can't wait to start going back to the office and traveling."

"How long you been on paternity leave now?" asked Darwin.

"Almost two months."

"I didn't realize partners at venture capital firms have that kind of luxury."

"We're progressive like that. Though in reality I'm still working almost full-time, just from home. Thank god for the modified Huxley procedure. It's nice to be both a night owl and an early bird."

"Which god, the mighty Odin? I think you mean 'thank science.'" Darwin resisted the urge to add 'and me.'

"Yeah, whatever. I know that name is like 'Voldemort' to you. But your work is alleviating a lot of suffering, even if you don't get credit for it. Anyways, how's my little sister? She's barely seen her niece since she was born."

"She's in Tokyo for work, per usual. Things have been crazy now that they're on the road to going public."

"We're a family of overachievers, what can I say."

"I bet your firm stands to make a lot off an IPO."

"Not as much as you and Maddy. Have you seen the cap table?" asked Preston.

"That's not exactly my forte."

"Well, it might be time to upgrade the house. Maybe get a new zip code, down closer to us."

"I'm perfectly happy with our current place." It cost two million dollars, after all, even if it was only twenty-two hundred square feet.

"One day you'll learn to appreciate the finer things in life, Darwin. And you should really consider a safer neighborhood. Scary shit has been happening lately. I'm considering selling our townhouse in the city. You take my advice and pull the trigger on buying a gun?"

"No. You aren't even allowed to buy one in the city."

"But you *can* own one," said Preston. "In the land of the blind, the one-eyed man is king. And you can use it if you need to. California has surprisingly friendly self-defense laws for such a liberal state. Castle doctrine. Stand your ground. You gotta protect the family. Don't wanna become a victim."

"I don't know. I don't want to become a statistic, either. You're more likely to shoot yourself or a family member than an intruder."

"Darwin, you're a scientist. Or used to be, anyways. Broad stats about a general population don't apply to individuals. One in four Americans die from heart disease, but that doesn't mean *you* have a one in four chance. It depends on your individual genes and lifestyle."

Preston just had to use that example, didn't he?

"Think of all the idiots included in those gun numbers," Preston continued. "The statistics aren't relevant for responsible, well-educated people."

"Are you including us in that category?"

Preston grinned. "Most of the time."

"I'll consider it."

A colossal container ship approached the Golden Gate Bridge. The thousands of different colored boxes stacked on its deck resembled an abstract mosaic. Preston watched it approach and said, "Look at that beast. Probably came from China. I bet it's been on the open ocean for weeks. What a life. Speaking of which—you heard about what your boy Balthazar is up to? You gotta take me out there, man. Or at least make an intro. The guy is a legend. He makes everyone else in this industry look like an amateur."

"I wouldn't exactly call him 'my boy' these days. And no, I haven't heard, and I'm trying to keep it that way despite everyone I know requesting an intro."

"Suit yourself, but I think you should make an exception for your older brother-in-law. Hey, we got some police action." Preston pointed down at the suspension bridge. A police car's lights flashed from the near tower's base. Two other cruisers raced across the expanse from the San Francisco side. "Oh shit, we got a climber!"

Preston was right. Darwin could just make out a tiny figure standing atop the immense red tower. He said, "Let's hope he's not also a jumper. I thought they were supposed to put up suicide nets under the bridge by now." Dozens of people jumped every year.

"I don't think they'd do him much good from that height. How the hell did he get up there? Oh, that reminds me—I had a dream I jumped off a bridge last night, but it turned out I could fly. I have the craziest dreams, man. What do you think Freud would say about that?"

"Freud was a quack," said Darwin. "His ideas about dream interpretation were nonsense."

"But he *was* a certified doctor." Darwin saw Preston look at him and smirk in his peripheral vision but continued to gaze down at the bridge. Preston had urged Darwin to finish his PhD, despite the extraordinary circumstances. He'd insisted he would regret dropping out for the rest of his life. And he was right, which made the fact that he never let Darwin forget it that much more intolerable.

Preston turned back to look at the bridge and continued, "I think coincidences are just further proof we're living in a simulation. It's gotta be computationally expensive to model all this madness, so the program optimizes memory by reusing resources where it calculates it can get away with it."

"You Silicon Valley guys crack me up," said Darwin. "I agree that on some level your reality is already a simulation created by your brain from its sensory input—everything is filtered and manipulated into whatever was historically the most beneficial for natural and sexual selection. But we still don't have the slightest idea how consciousness arises. It's not a given it can be modeled on a computer."

"We only don't know how it arises because that's not part of the simulation," said Preston. "And it *does* explain other phenomena, like the measurement problem in quantum mechanics. It's just the program optimizing resources—something doesn't *need* to exist unless there's an observer. When a tree falls in the forest and no one is around, it makes a sound if the algorithm determines it's relevant to the simulation."

Darwin sighed. "You can use that reasoning to explain anything. It's like invoking an omnipotent god who works in mysterious ways, a devil who plants dinosaur bones to lead people astray, or an underground society that secretly pulls the strings and runs the world. It's just the technocratic creation myth. Intelligent design for those who rightfully ridicule intelligent design. Religion for people who think they're critical thinkers."

"Better than that many-worlds, multiverse nonsense. There *are* an almost infinite number of universes, but they're just other simulations."

"Multiverse, simulations, it's all the same. A theory is nothing but pseudoscience if it can't be empirically tested. Next you're going to point out there's approximately the same number of stars in an average galaxy as neurons in the human brain."

"Awfully suspicious, isn't it?" Preston asked. "On the subject of exploring consciousness—you still able to attend the men's ceremony next week?"

"Assuming Madeline gets home on schedule so she can watch the kids, I'll be there."

"She's cool with it? You told her the truth?"

"She encouraged it, actually. And yeah, we don't hide things from each other."

"Must be nice." Preston gave a strange smile. "You're gonna love it, man, especially with your background. It's a solid group of guys, and the facilitator is really good. He studied under a shaman in Guyana for a year."

There were now four police cars and a firetruck on the bridge. A few first responders had started the five-hundred-foot climb. Traffic was stopped in both directions. Preston said, "I hope this doesn't delay getting home. I've got baby duty starting at three."

"We may have to head back down to Sausalito and take the ferry."

"They should fine people who cause accidents or otherwise hold up traffic like this. Think about the economic impact of causing thousands of people to lose an hour of their lives."

"I'm not sure fining a suicidal person tens or hundreds of thousands of dollars is a good idea," said Darwin.

"Five hundred bucks says he jumps."

"You're an asshole."

Preston's watch buzzed with a notification. "Oh my god—that's Rick Larson."

"Rick Larson texted you?"

"No, *that's* Rick Larson." Preston pointed to the scene below.

"The guy who just illegally climbed up one of the Golden Gate Bridge towers is the CEO of a publicly traded company?"

"Apparently. It doesn't make any sense. The guy is as strait-laced as they get. I told you, some scary shit is happening. I'm gonna call him."

"Wait, you know him?" Darwin asked.

"We invested in their series D. We haven't talked in a few

months and aren't exactly best buds, but I have his number."

"That's a terrible idea. Let the professionals handle it," said Darwin, but it was too late; Preston was already holding the iPhone up to his ear, his mouth open in a look of disbelief. "What's up?"

"It went straight to voicemail."

"That's not surprising, all things considered."

Preston put the phone on speaker and held it out between them. "...got to keep the loonies on the path..." It was playing Pink Floyd's 'Brain Damage,' but with another voice—presumably Rick—singing along and crying. Darwin didn't think he'd ever heard someone do the two simultaneously.

Darwin looked from the phone to Preston and then back at the distant figure standing atop the immense red pillar. The first responders were making good progress on their ascent, and a police boat had arrived in the water beneath the bridge. The song built to the crescendo at the end of the first chorus, and Rick bellowed, "I'll see you on the dark siiide of the moon!"

Rick Larson jumped

Three hours later Darwin walked his bike into the garage and leaned it against the wall next to the highest-rated compact SUV in its class. They'd ended up cutting their losses and taking the ferry instead of waiting for the bridge to reopen. Rick hadn't jumped into the water, but the middle of the span below. He made a mess.

Darwin was physically and mentally drained. Just as he sat down on the couch to relax, Mofongo came bounding into the room to look out the window, tail wagging. No rest for the weary. He stood up and put on a smile, determined not to let the ruination of his day ruin that of his daughters. He wouldn't always be able to protect them from everything, but he could protect them from this, for now.

After greeting them at the door, Darwin asked, "What do you want for dinner?"

"French toast!" replied Christina.

"Breakfast for dinner!" echoed Evelyn.

"Are you sure? We just had that on Saturday." He'd hoped they'd say something he could order, like pizza. It was usually a safe bet.

"I like yours better," said Christina.

"Yeah," agreed Evelyn.

Well, he couldn't blame them for preferring Darwin's famous banana vanilla French toast. "Ok, but you have to promise not to tell your mom."

"Deal," they said in unison.

"Can we use fake maple syrup?" Christina asked. "Mom says it tastes like chemicals but I like it more."

"Yes we can," he said. They were probably too young to understand that technically everything is made of chemicals and tastes accordingly, even real maple syrup. "But first daddy's going to relax and watch some TV. Dinner will be ready at six."

The girls ran off upstairs. The stack of dishes in the sink from this morning that he was yet to do weighed on him. It sure took a lot of time and effort just to keep your family fed. Then he reminded himself that searching for food is how many non-human animals spend their *entire lives*. They would literally kill for French toast. He shouldn't complain, and instead summoned gratitude for the countless generations who went through the hardship of raising children and building the modern world so he could be here now.

Darwin turned on the TV. The local news was on, and they were unsurprisingly talking about the disruptions to traffic caused by the tragic and unexpected suicide of respected technology entrepreneur Rick Larson. Maybe Preston was right; maybe there was some scary shit going on. He changed the channel to one more focused on international news.

"...of African Trypanosomiasis, better known as 'sleeping sickness.' It's the largest outbreak of the disease since the Ugandan epidemic a century ago that killed over a quarter of a million people..."

He changed it to another.

"...an explosion that brought down a cell tower used in the rollout of the 5G network. Those who claimed responsibility for the attack say the technology is used for government mind control..."

And another.

"...when special forces tried to intervene, the pirates set the captured oil tanker ablaze, killing all aboard..."

He turned off the TV and shook his head. On second thought, Preston was wrong; anyone who knew anything about history knew there was always scary shit going on. It was now just being blasted at you around the clock by perversely incented people and companies paid to do so, recycling whatever stories generate the most fear and outrage every hour and destroying civilization in the process. Something Madeline often said came to mind: 'You'll never make the news if you waste all your time watching it.'

He got up and headed to the kitchen to start cleaning but stopped when he passed Madeline's office. No, don't even think about it. Then in a rare burst of impulse, he ducked inside and quietly closed the door behind him.

A wave of shame hit him as he surveyed the neat and tidy room. What was he doing? What did he expect to find? His wife was a private person. On one hand it annoyed him there always seemed to be things she kept from him—she still had a separate credit card—while on the other he had to admit it kept a certain spark alive in their marriage. Madeline was forever an enigma. A sexy enigma.

Darwin's curiosity overcame his guilt. He would keep going. Just a little further.

It was a modern office, so there wasn't a piece of paper in sight; anything of any interest would be stored on the computer. He turned it on, sat down in front of the monitor on the mahogany desk next to the treadmill, and stared at the blinking cursor in the password input box, his heart beating faster and faster.

'password.' Wrong. Of course that didn't work. Who did he think he was married to?

'password1.' Wrong again. Duh.

'Darwin.' He submitted it with a smug smile and tinge of hope. Wrong. Some hacker he'd make. The computer alerted him he had seven more attempts before it erased all its data. Best not to get too close to the limit in case Maddy incorrectly typed her password a few times when she next logged in. Time to stop messing around.

Darwin racked his brain, trying to think of people, places, and dates that were important to her. Mofongo, Christina, and Evelyn were contenders, as were the University of Michigan, where she did her undergrad, and UW, where she got her MBA (and met him). She was born on May 16th, like the Lagwagon song, in 1983. Their wedding anniversary was…August 14th, 2011. It had rained, which was supposed to be good luck. They'd stayed up all night listening to Fleetwood Mac's 'Dreams' while doing other things.

What were some of her other passwords? Did he really not know *any* of them? What did that say about their relationship? Looking around her sparse desk for a clue, his gaze fell upon a picture from their wedding day. They were soaking wet, smiling. He'd told her she looked *dazzling*.

Stop.

Darwin turned off the computer and the light. He shut the door and went to do the dishes and make his daughters his famous French toast.

Chapter 7: Madeline

Madeline awoke to sunlight streaming in through the window and onto her face. She'd stopped closing curtains now that she was always up before the sun. She'd also stopped setting alarms now that she no longer needed—

Shit! What time was it? She sat up and looked around frantically for her phone. It was in her right hand. Six-thirty a.m., and far too many notifications to deal with right now. She was supposed to be at the airport thirty minutes ago. Fortunately she hadn't even had the chance to unpack and was already dressed.

She sat up and walked straight out the door, grabbing her luggage in stride. She slapped the wall out of habit to turn off the light, but it was already off.

It wasn't until Madeline was in the taxi that she had time to reflect on how this had happened. She didn't recall going to bed. Not remembering the last few minutes before falling asleep was normal, but the end of the night was missing, and the whole evening was somewhat blurry. Her partying days were long behind her, but she wasn't a total lightweight. And she was sure she wouldn't have let herself have more than she was comfortable with, certainly nowhere near enough to black out.

A disturbing thought came to her: Had she been drugged? She was convinced someone had slipped something in her drink once in college and tried to remember how she'd felt the next day. Had her head hurt as bad as it did now? The idea of someone trying to date rape a thirty-six-year-old at one of the nicest spots in the city seemed unlikely. And she thought, though admittedly was not sure, that her drink had been in her hand the entire night. At least for the part she remembered, anyway. Well, luckily, like last time, she'd woken up alone and clothed in her room. She was confident nothing had happened.

Then something else occurred to her: She may not have had that much to drink, but it *was* the most she'd had since the procedure. She'd been honest when filling out the pre-liminary paperwork to see if she was a candidate, including the questions about alcohol and drug use (unlike when she was younger). Doctor Magnusson hadn't mentioned anything about drinking, and she hadn't asked. There must be others with far worse habits than her who've had it done. Should she call the doctor? No—the thought of his clinical disapproval on top of the light shame she already felt was too much in her current condition. She wouldn't be surprised if the man had remained dead sober his entire life.

Madeline contemplated calling Darwin too, but he still didn't know she'd had the procedure done. Or that she was even in Bangkok. And he'd probably judge her even more harshly than Doctor Magnusson would for drinking irresponsibly with a stranger...which reminded her. She checked her pockets and found the black CCP business card. Surely if you were going to drug someone you wouldn't give them your fucking card, right? She called her executive assistant.

"Hi Madeline, how was the flight to Tokyo?"

"The flight was ok, thanks. Sorry, I'm a bit short on time and have to be brief. Please do some research on an investment firm called Circadian Capital Partners and a VP there named Elias Sultana? Just the standard stuff."

"Of course. By when do you want it?"

"End of the week is fine. I won't have time to look at it until then. Gotta run. Bye." Madeline hung up. She'd do her own research on Mister Sultana and his firm later; just reading the business card in the backseat of this cab had made her feel sick. And she could peruse her assistant's report on the flight home to San Francisco.

Luckily it was early enough that traffic was light, though the drive still dragged on for ages. The flight was also slightly delayed due to storm clouds in the area. Hadn't she woken up to sunshine a half hour ago? She was happy to see the plane was a Dreamliner, then settled into her business class window seat and noticed the Wi-Fi symbol. It used to be that flights, especially international ones, were among the last remaining places you could be reliably unreachable. A perfect, guilt-free opportunity to relax and read or just space out. Not anymore—it was now a perfect opportunity to work.

But Madeline was exhausted. She must have slept for something like ten hours, which was unheard of, but felt like taking a nap for the first time in as long as she could remember; perhaps it was still possible to oversleep. The flight was six hours. She'd still have time to play some catchup on email after a brief rest.

Madeline closed her eyes, but right when she began to drift away, she was jolted back in her seat as the plane accelerated and took off. It felt like a rocket ship. Madeline stared at the back of her eyelids again, but the turbulence made it too bumpy

63

to sleep. It was of no concern to a seasoned flyer like her, but some of the other passengers were clearly disturbed. It sounded like the person in front of her was using the airsick bag.

"Hi folks, this is your captain speaking. Apologies for the rough ride so far. We encountered some unexpected turbulence on our way up to cruising altitude. It's nothing to be worried about, but please ensure you stay seated with your seatbelt fastened." He spoke in the calm, reassuring tone pilots were trained to use, but Madeline had the odd sense she recognized the voice. She didn't know any pilots, at least not professional ones. Oh well. Probably just her brain overly eager to pattern match.

The flight smoothed out a bit when they reached cruising altitude. Madeline stared out the window and was struck by how much one of the passing cumulonimbus clouds resembled a dragon. She was reminded, as she often was, of the strange conversation on the roof of the Tokyo Stasis Hotel with the man she now knew had been Takayoshi Yamamoto. Looking down from thirty-five thousand feet was even less scary than looking down from five hundred. It was all the same once you reached terminal velocity.

But Madeline wasn't looking down from thirty-five thousand feet.

From up here she could see the curvature of the Earth, a brilliant blue and white marble against the black backdrop of space, half-illuminated by the painfully bright sun floating above the horizon. It was like the videos she'd seen from the International Space Station. She had to be more than a million feet up, but—no longer inside the plane—her altitude was decreasing. In a kind of abstract sense, anyway.

She was still above southeast Asia, just much farther above, for now. But this did not feel like the skydiving on her honeymoon. It felt more like the vivid dreams she'd had while taking antimalarials. Madeline had the distinct sensation of being pulled into the Earth. She supposed this was technically what all falling was, but it gave her a new perspective on the mechanics of gravity. She could feel herself rolling down the curvature in spacetime created by the planet's mass. It was the kind of stuff Darwin always droned on about. It was also a revelation of sorts.

She fell in complete silence but could still breathe, which didn't make sense. Nothing made any sense. What was happening? She descended through the upper layers of the atmosphere, past a few satellites that whipped by at impossible speeds, and what was either a rocket or an intercontinental ballistic missile. She didn't care.

For a while her view was obstructed by the fireball all around her as she went through reentry. It only burned a little. Then her view of the ground became more familiar, like what she was used to from a plane. She was somewhere over the South China Sea and going to make quite a splash given how fast she plummeted.

There was something visible beneath the surface of approximately where she was going to land. A discoloration and disturbance in the water, far too big to be her shadow. And she was still tens of thousands of feet up. Even a blue whale, the largest creature in the history of the world, would have been difficult to spot from this altitude. Was it a submarine? Whatever it was, it was massive.

A giant maelstrom formed as the water continued to rush towards her. Perhaps it would break her fall. Moments before

65

impact the mouth of an enormous, dinosaur-like creature—a dragon with fins instead of wings—emerged from the swirling, bubbling water.

Madeline plunged right into it, and everything went black.

Chapter 8: Darwin

"I think this is just about where Rick landed," said Preston.

They were crossing the Golden Gate Bridge, heading north in the late afternoon sun. Riding shotgun, Darwin was looking east, admiring the view of the bay and trying to shake the lingering malaise from a nightmare he couldn't quite remember. "Thanks for the reminder. I'm trying to focus on happy thoughts, like you said. And you seem a bit cavalier about the death of someone you knew."

"I assume many simulations have afterlives in one form or another. It would be efficient to recycle his mind in some sense, almost like the idea of rebirth in Buddhism. It could also solve some ethical problems for Big Simulation."

"Do they have these afterlives for chimps? What about dogs? Flies? Amoebas? Where's the cutoff?"

"It probably varies," Preston said casually, "but the computing power required to keep an amoeba's soul happy has gotta be trivial."

"How much of this kind of crap am I going to have to listen to over the next twelve hours? We haven't even got to the drugs yet."

"You may very well become a believer, my friend. I'm bullish on the day. I can't believe you've never taken ayahuasca

67

before."

Darwin said, "I experimented a few times with acid and mushrooms in grad school but never DMT, the psychoactive ingredient."

"I smoked it straight up once. It was like a bomb went off in my mind, like I was strapped to a rocket and blasted off to an alien planet. I actually met the interdimensional beings that many people claim to meet."

"That's only because you've heard the stories. It influenced your trip, or at least how you remember it."

"What a classic Darwin response," said Preston. "What do you think of the speculation that DMT is responsible for dreams?"

"Unlike other tryptamines, it *is* produced naturally by the brain. And it's a cute theory, but I haven't seen any convincing data or studies to back it up."

"You're no fun. Well, no need to worry—ingesting it via ayahuasca is a bit more mellow, but it also lasts much longer."

"That's actually what I'm worried about," said Darwin. "I stopped experimenting after an eight-hour bad trip in Amsterdam that I still count among the bottom five experiences of my life."

"And *that's* only because you took too much in the wrong place with the wrong mindset. It's all about set and setting, man. And this isn't recreational—it's medicinal."

"It's not just an excuse for grown men to trip balls?"

"Hey, I never said it wasn't fun."

"What are we listening to, by the way?" asked Darwin. "I like it."

"*WHEN WE ALL FALL ASLEEP, WHERE DO WE GO?* Billie Eilish. It's what all the kids are into these days."

"Not mine. I think they're a bit too young given the subject matter. I've been trying to get them into Dream Theater without luck. I actually stopped taking *anything* once Christina was born. Getting high didn't really seem conducive to being a good dad."

"Don't be a hypocrite—you still drink, which is worse than most substances. I know hundreds of the highest-functioning people on Earth, and most of them regularly use 'drugs.' Shit, I micro-dosed LSD three days this week."

Darwin chuckled. "I mean, it's true that hallucinogens appear not to be neurotoxic, as far as we know. And they have serious clinical potential that has been stifled for decades because of government pushback to the hippies. It's kind of ironic because the psychedelic counterculture unwittingly emerged from earlier CIA-funded research into using LSD as a mind control weapon. Does Missus Lockhart know you micro-dose?"

"What Karen doesn't know won't hurt her. She *is* cool with the men's group, as long as I limit my mind benders to once a quarter. Madeline have any second thoughts?"

"No, but she's been acting a bit strange since she got home last night. I think it's just jet lag."

"Right. The facilitator also does couples' ceremonies, by the way. Maybe you two should consider it."

"She wanted to do one in Cusco after we hiked Machu Picchu. There are signs advertising them everywhere."

"You gotta be more adventurous, man."

"They looked pretty damn shady," said Darwin.

"Yeah, you're right. You gotta be careful down there. You don't want to end up dosed with devil's breath and happily withdrawing all your money from an ATM for a kind stranger."

69

"That's just an urban legend. An old internet myth."

"I swear it happened to my friend in Colombia," Preston said.

"In high doses scopolamine can cause delirium, unconsciousness, and amnesia, especially when mixed with alcohol, but it doesn't turn you into a zombie slave just by touching a business card that's been dipped in it. It's mostly used to treat motion sickness, and in some countries as a date rape drug. It's out of your system and untraceable within hours."

"You seem to know a little *too* much about this." Preston glanced at him and smiled.

"Fuck you. I was almost a doctor, remember?"

Ten minutes later they pulled up to an enormous wooden house in Larkspur, surrounded by trees. Darwin was grateful for how private it felt. Preston added one more Tesla to the half-dozen already parked in the driveway and on the street.

Darwin said, "Quite a place. Far cry from a hut in the Amazon."

"It's a safe space. And yeah, it's crazy how much further your money goes once you get out of the city. It looks like most of the guys are already here."

They got out of the car. "Smells good," said Darwin.

"Arlo must have already started smudging."

"Smudging?"

"Burning sage. It cleanses the space of negative energy. And promotes healing and wisdom."

"Does it, now?" asked Darwin. "I wonder what the mechanism of action is."

"I know it sounds like some woo woo shit, but it's an ancient spiritual ritual that developed independently in different cultures. Sometimes you have to accept things that aren't neatly

70

explained by science. Plus, it smells nice."

"Are you sure that isn't just what Big Sage wants you to think? I hope you do more rigorous analysis before making investments."

"I mostly handle deal flow," said Preston. "I'm basically in sales, but I sell money."

"Well, dad explicitly raised me to be a man of science and not a salesman like him."

"Yes, I recall Madeline's story about his coffin being slowly lowered for an excruciating seventeen minutes to the entirety of Pink Floyd's 'Dogs,' a song about not wasting your life chasing money in business. Except in the song he died of cancer, not a heart attack. I bet the guys in that band appreciated smudging."

"Do you know what they call naturopathic medicine with data that proves it works?" asked Darwin.

"No, but I'm sure you'll tell me."

"Medicine."

"Come on, man," said Preston.

"I guess the placebo effect *is* among the most reliable in all of medicine. And sage *is* in the same family as salvia divinorum. Smoking that was another bottom five experience, even if it technically only lasted five minutes."

"What are the other three experiences that round out the bottom five?" asked Preston.

"I'll tell you another time. Happy thoughts, right?"

"That's the spirit. Have an open mind. Remember—set and setting."

They went inside and Darwin was introduced to the group. There were a dozen men, at or approaching middle age, including a few he'd met through Preston once or twice. He worried about remembering all the new names except for two: Michael, whose house they were in and whose books he'd read (Preston hadn't given him a heads up, and Darwin was sure he came off as an idiot); and Arlo, the facilitator.

Arlo looked and dressed normal, like the rest. Darwin had half-expected him to be wearing a robe. He didn't even have long hair. But there was something different about the way he carried himself, the reassuring look in his eyes, and the way he gave you his full attention when you spoke to him. It calmed some of the butterflies in Darwin's empty stomach.

They settled into a large, beautiful living room covered with colorful blankets and cushions. This was where they'd spend most of the next eighteen hours. Or their bodies would, anyway.

Arlo spoke at a slow, measured pace while sitting cross-legged on the floor. "Thank you all for coming to September's men's ceremony. I am glad everyone arrived safely. And thank you, Michael, for once again welcoming us into your home." Michael smiled and nodded. Arlo continued, "We have been blessed with an especially beautiful day, amid a beautiful time of year. It may not feel like it around here, but it is indeed autumn, which is one of my four favorite seasons."

It was a cheesy joke, but Darwin found himself smiling anyway. Arlo said, "The season of harvest. The long shadows and changing leaves remind us that everything in this world is transitory, including all of us and our trials and achievements. And, like the seasons, we too are part of an endless cycle of life, death, and rebirth."

Darwin couldn't help thinking that wasn't technically true; everything was transitory on a long enough timeline, from the cycle of life on Earth to that of star death and formation.

Stardust to dust. Stop. Keep an open mind.

Arlo continued, "However, the time we have is also infinitely precious. We blink in and out of existence, but our actions reverberate for eternity and serve a much greater purpose. The medicine helps us appreciate and connect with that time on a deeper and more fundamental level. I understand that we have someone who will be joining us on this journey for the first time. Darwin, it is customary for us to go around and discuss what each of us is presently struggling with, that which we hope the medicine can help us see in a new light. Our society does not often afford men the opportunity to open up and be emotionally vulnerable with each other. But all human beings are physically and mentally fragile, despite how we may pretend otherwise. Let us begin with you."

The feeling of calm initially created by Arlo's words shattered as all eyes turned to Darwin. The lone noob. "Uh...hi everyone. Thanks for letting me join the group. I guess what I'm struggling with the most right now is...the sense of unrealized potential. I'm only thirty-five but have started letting go of many of the dreams I had growing up and in my twenties. I understand that I'm one of the most fortunate sentient creatures to have ever existed, and my current life would be a dream for most people alive today, much less throughout human history. But sometimes it's hard to keep that in perspective."

Arlo said, "Thank you for sharing, Darwin. It is important to recognize that our dreams change throughout our lives, and there is nothing wrong with that. One man's dream can be another's nightmare, and vice versa. This may even be true between different versions of ourselves. I am sure there are many here who can provide you with valuable insight

73

throughout the evening. Preston, how about you?"

"Hey guys, glad to be back. The most significant challenge in my life right now is recently becoming a first-time dad at the age of forty."

They went around the entire room like this. Someone was going through a divorce. Another had retired young after achieving all his initial goals and no longer found meaning in life. One was having trouble connecting with his kids now that they were adolescents. Another had recently sold a company and was looking for inspiration for his next. Someone had just lost both parents. One felt like he'd been dragging his feet his whole life and was now in a career and relationship from which he derived no joy. Michael was trying to decide on which creative project to focus.

Next Arlo led everyone in a twenty-minute meditation. The research on its benefits was promising, and Darwin had tried on several occasions to develop a practice over the years, but it never stuck. The fact that it had now entered the cultural zeitgeist hadn't changed anything for him. He found it intensely boring.

Afterward they took turns following Arlo to the attached kitchen, where he served them a bowl from the large pot on the stove. Despite its strange, earthy aroma, Darwin was looking forward to the soup. It would be the first sustenance he'd had other than water all day. Apparently the idea was to have minimum ammo for throwing up, shitting your pants, or both, if it came to that later. He shuddered and hoped his strong stomach would spare him. Fasting was also a proven method for increasing dreams' vividness.

Arlo ladled the soup into his bowl. Darwin gave him something between a head nod and slight bow, unsure of the proper etiquette. Arlo just smiled, relieving him of any awkwardness.

A nearby howling sound startled Darwin and almost caused him to drop his bowl. Other cries joined in, like a large wolfpack was dying in the next room. Had the scent of the soup alone caused hallucinations? Arlo was unperturbed.

"Unselfconscious, animalistic behavior can help dissolve the ego and connect us with nature," said the facilitator. What had Darwin gotten himself into?

The first sip of ayahuasca was all it took to dispel any illusions he had about enjoying the taste. It was thick, bitter, and salty with a hint of paprika, but he'd had worse.

When he reentered the living room, a couple small group conversations were happening. A few guys sat alone wearing blindfolds. Preston was talking to one of his golfing buddies and wildly gesticulating with his arms. Darwin sat down alone on a cushion adorned with a psychedelic elephant. Music played through the house's excellent speaker system, the kind of song you'd hear at an expensive spa. It prominently featured drums and what sounded like a didgeridoo. Interesting mashup of aboriginal cultures. Darwin assumed it was supposed to be profound.

Michael broke off from the guys he was talking to and took a seat on the ground next to Darwin with a soft groan. He said, "It's not as easy to get down here once you get into your fifties. I've been thinking about what you said earlier, Darwin. I may not have Arlo's clarity of thought, but I'm pretty sure I'm the oldest person here, which has to count for something. Perhaps I can impart some wisdom."

"I feel like you already have. If it wasn't clear earlier, I've read everything you've written."

"I assure you that you've only read everything I've published,

75

not written. And if that's the case, then you may know that I didn't publish my first book until I was around your age. I didn't even start writing until my late twenties."

"I was not aware of that."

"Believe it or not I was in accounting."

Darwin laughed. "I would not have guessed that."

"You'd be surprised. It's a more creative profession than you think. Perhaps too creative in a few infamous cases. But something I know for certain is that it's never too late to change your dreams, or to create entirely new ones. Arlo spent the first fifteen years of his career as a mechanical engineer."

Their conversation continued, with a few other guys dropping in and out over the next thirty or sixty or ninety minutes; he'd lost track. Eventually Michael moved on, and Darwin found himself alone again. He was still sitting on a psychedelic elephant, but it was now the size of a planet. And not just any planet—a gas giant—which he knew because he could see the blue and green marble of Earth far below. Relatively it *was* the size of a marble, tiny and fragile, liable to be trampled underfoot.

After contemplating this circumstance for several lifetimes, he looked up and discovered that the animal he rode was only one in a herd, a solar system of gigantic creatures. Darwin then realized he was no longer alone—the elephant-like animals had riders, cartoon versions of shamans and machine elves who beat the drums and breathed into the other instruments that created the sounds permeating every fiber of his being.

It was the most profound music he'd ever heard.

And the riders were made of stone. And they were made of metal. And they were made of wood. And they were made of flesh and blood. And they were made of trillions and trillions of combinations of electrons and protons and neutrons, which were made of quarks and gluons, which were both particles and waves and either so elementary to be nothing but expressions in fields at the rock bottom of reality, or made of something so small and fundamental to be not yet understood by 'great' apes who learned to build rockets and launched themselves into the sun, which through the process of thermonuclear fusion combined the quarks and the electrons and the protons and the neutrons into all manner of matter and scattered it to the ends of the known universe via supernovas so spectacular and yet so unsurprising, an inevitable endpoint of following a set of equations that could be written on a single page. And they were made of stardust. And they were made of nothing at all.

Sometime later he was more lucid, could remember what it was he was even doing and why. But then, literally before he knew it, reality would melt away, and he was gone again. Darwin rode this wave for an indeterminate amount of time that could have been six hours or six thousand. At the troughs he would confer with the other men in the room or write in his notebook. His emotions were more pronounced, easier to isolate and make sense of. At the peaks he lacked the words to describe the experience, even as a wannabe writer, and all he could do was try his best to hold on. On a few occasions Arlo, the only sober one, must have recognized the battle raging in his mind because he'd show up with a calming, friendly presence and gently guide him back from the edge.

Before finally falling asleep Darwin was positive of one thing: It was as if he'd spent his entire life looking through a window with rain streaking down it, but he could now see clearly out and into a gorgeous, sunny day.

Darwin awoke to the smell of fresh coffee and bagels. About half the group was still asleep, including Preston, but the others were having breakfast and talking quietly. Gradually the memories from the prior evening (year? millennium?) came back, though he was surely missing some of them. It wasn't quite like forgetting a dream, more that so much had transpired his mind didn't have enough memory to save everything.

Then he remembered the notebook. He found it beneath where he'd slept, wedged between two couch cushions. A few of the pages were crinkled, but he could still read his handwriting, even if few others could. It was almost like it was encrypted. He'd written more words the prior evening than the past month. It included no shortage of interesting ideas for *The Stardust Chronicles,* randomly interspersed with the ramblings of a mad man's mad lib, ridiculous cartoons from which he could discern no meaning at all, and surprisingly cogent insights into his life.

He also used his watch to review his vital signs for the prior evening. Yikes.

When everyone was awake and caffeinated, they went through what Arlo called 'integration,' taking turns discussing what they'd learned. Darwin was grateful he hadn't gotten sick like a few of the others. Preston had thrown up on his Patagonia vest. At least he had several more. Three guys had even met the interdimensional entities, about which Arlo had many questions. Had Darwin met them too? He opted not to mention it. Even in his newly enlightened state, he would have felt silly discussing such a thing.

"Thanks for inviting me," Darwin said to Preston after saying some touchy goodbyes and getting into the car. "You were right. It's a good group. I enjoyed it much more than I thought I would."

"No problem, man. I was sure you'd love it, even if you're the kinda guy who refuses to say 'namaste' at the end of yoga."

"You do yoga?"

"Hot yoga is the closest a happily married man can get to sex with other women."

Darwin smiled. "I guess no amount of medicine-induced insight can change everything about someone."

"You gonna come back next quarter?"

Darwin laughed and was surprised at its heartiness. It was the freest, least self-conscious laugh he could recall. "We'll see about that. I need some time to process everything."

It was a foggy morning, and though Darwin lacked the absolute clarity he'd briefly glimpsed in the eye of the prior night's hurricane, he'd arrived at a new, higher baseline. He didn't count himself among the many who converted from atheism after such experiences, but the green of the trees was greener, the gray of the sky grayer, and there was a deep sense of connectedness with everything he saw. As they drove home he felt rejuvenated, ready to be a better person for himself, his friends, and his family.

Chapter 9: Madeline

Sunday, September 22nd, 2019 — 3 hours of sleep

I was a piece in a game of Tetris. The worst kind, the one that almost resembles the letter 'Z.' No matter where it lands, something always remains. Evelyn and Christina were pieces too—the best ones—a two by two and a three by one. I was proud. But they were several pieces ahead of me. I tried to look ahead of them to see what was being built up below and how best to position us, but it was too far and my vision was obstructed. As we got closer the music played faster and louder until it was maddening.

Dun, dun-dun-dun, dun-dun-dun, dun-dun-dun, dun-dun-dun, dun dun dun dun, dun, dun.

Christina was up first and landed flat, the long way. It created a perfect two by two hole for Evelyn to fill, which she did. I was so happy as she fell perfectly into place. Then they both disappeared along with the top two lines of the stack. After a few poorly placed pieces, it was my turn, but I realized with terror that I no longer had control over my movement. I was in a game being played by someone, somewhere, and the speed was too much for them now.

Dun, dun DUN dun-dun-dun, dun dun, dun-dun, dun, dun dun dun dun, dun, dun.

I landed the long way, fully exposed, and the pieces piled up around me with as many gaps as blocks. I didn't know what would happen when they reached the top of the screen, and more importantly where my girls had gone, but I knew that I'd never see them again.

Madeline woke up soaked in sweat and with the taste of blood in her mouth. She moved her tongue around and confirmed that she'd bitten into it hard. Weren't you paralyzed while dreaming?

It was sometime in the small hours, her usual wakeup time. But while it was dark outside the window, there was a light—and sound—coming from the foot of the bed. Christina was playing Tetris on her iPad. *Dun, dun-dun-dun...*

In the dim light were the still-sleeping figures of Evelyn and Mofongo, the latter snoring away as usual, though thankfully she wasn't joined by Darwin adding a discordant harmony. A wave of relief washed over Madeline; her daughters were safe and hadn't disappeared off to some unknown place after completing a row in the game. The nightmare had felt so real despite its ridiculousness. World-consuming, as if it were all there was.

Although no longer anxious, Madeline was confused at the full bed until she remembered that she'd let the girls sleep with her, as she often did on the rare occasions Darwin was gone. It was only three hours ago when she became too tired to keep reading, admired her small, slumbering family, and dozed off herself.

She sat up and touched Christina's shoulder, whispered, "Hey sweetie, are you having trouble sleeping?"

Christina turned around and smiled. She put down the tablet and crawled into her mother's arms. "You kept making noises and I got scared. I tried to wake you up but I couldn't wake you

81

up."

"Aw, I'm sorry. Mommy's going to get up now so you can go to sleep. Do you want me to get you anything?"

"That's ok. I'm just glad you're ok."

"I'm fine, sweetie. There's nothing to worry about. Go back to sleep."

Madeline wasn't fine. She knew that now. She'd been awake for almost eight hours and was yet to pull out of the funk. She'd had dream hangovers before but never like this.

Come to think of it, things hadn't been the same since that bizarre night at the Bangkok Stasis. But she'd read the reports on Circadian Capital Partners and the lack thereof on Elias Sultana, who hadn't returned her call or email. She had trouble recalling the specifics—it was almost like remembering a dream. But she knew that nothing had jumped out at her. Nothing shadier than how most of these funds and their operators operated. She'd even talked to the hotel, and although she probably sounded like a paranoid psycho, asked them to review the relevant video footage. The manager had said that normally they only do that if there's an official investigation, but they'd obliged given her VIP status. Nothing suspicious came up.

It was time to reach out to Doctor Magnusson, perhaps even to tell Darwin. She was starting to regret having had the procedure done at all. Should she have let Preston talk her into it? What a turn of events. And on top of everything, Gwenivere Adams, one of her favorite actresses, had died. An overdose, likely intentional. How sad and surreal it was to get older and watch your childhood heroes die one by one. Gwenivere had seemed invincible. It reminded you that no one is that special.

She was about to schedule a call with the doctor when Mofongo glanced up at her with big brown eyes, then got up from on top of her feet and bolted out of the open office door. It startled her more than it should have, another sign she was losing it. Apparently the boys were back from wherever the hell they imagined they'd gone.

Madeline walked out the front door after Mofongo to find her husband and brother hugging in the driveway.

"So, is this what you guys do at men's group?" she asked.

Preston, who was facing her, said, "On some level, yes." Then he walked over and hugged her too.

"Are you able to stick around for lunch? There's something I want to talk to you about," she said, trying to use shared sibling experience to subtly convey the seriousness of the request without alerting Darwin.

"Sorry Maddy, I've gotta get home to Karen and your baby niece. Why don't you come down and see her this evening? I'm afraid you're not developing enough affection for her such that we can pawn her off on you later. Hey!" said Preston, looking over her shoulder.

Christina and Evelyn ran out the open front door, closely followed by Mofongo, who stopped quickly to pee. Madeline did a quick double-take—wasn't the dog already outside? The three girls rushed to greet their uncle Preston; for some inexplicable reason they had far more affection for him than he deserved. She turned her attention to Darwin. "So, how was it?"

"It was great. I'll give you the rundown when the girls aren't around. You hold down the fort here?"

"As best I could, though I didn't get much sleep. I think I'm coming down with something. Also, Gwenivere Adams died."

"Did she? Well, she had a good run. Life goes on."

"That's all? You seem a bit sanguine about it."

"No, it's just not what I was expecting, and I'm in a good mood from the ceremony. And, I mean, it's all transitory, like the seasons. Everyone and everything will die at some point. I don't see the point in wasting too much time worrying about precisely when and how."

"Who are you now, the fucking Buddha? Is that what you're going to say when I die? Or Mofongo? Or—god forbid—the girls?" Madeline didn't realize how much she'd raised her voice; the others were now looking at them. She found the entire concept of profanity ridiculous but still rarely used it around the girls at this age.

However, their looks caused no embarrassment or shame, only rage.

"I think that's my cue to leave," Preston said. "I love everybody. Enjoy the beautiful day." He got into his car and drove off into the fog. Awkward silence filled the driveway, except for...

Dun, dun DUN dun-dun-dun...

"Christina are you playing Tetris again?" asked Madeline more sharply than she intended. Her family just looked at her confused. Christina had both her arms wrapped around Darwin's leg. The iPad was inside. Why couldn't Madeline get this damn song out of her head? It was like an earworm burrowing deep into her brain.

With infuriating, Buddha-like calmness, Darwin said, "You seem like you're not feeling well. Let me know if there's anything I can do to help. I'm going to take a shower. I'll tell you all about last night afterward, if you're interested." He went inside with the girls.

84

Madeline stood alone in the driveway for several minutes, her left leg twitching. She tried to ignore the music looping in her head as she stared through the fog in her mind and into that of the late morning. The boundary was undefined. The song was getting faster, the multicolored blocks stacking up ahead of her and forming a jagged surface with nowhere safe to land.

What was going on? Who had she married? Was she going to lose her girls, like she'd lost them last night?

Chapter 10: Darwin

The UW Medicine Sleep Center, subject of endless sleepless in Seattle jokes, and somewhere Darwin had spent an uncounted number of hours. He didn't remember exactly how he'd gotten there, but it was the middle of the night shift, which he worked often. Such was the life of a grad student. Doctor Huxley rarely worked after five.

The polysomnogram displayed the inpatients' brainwaves, vitals, and muscle activity on hopelessly outdated computer monitors. All the telltale signs of narcolepsy. By now Darwin knew these people personally and felt terrible for them. He understood how frustrating it was for them to feel perpetually and overwhelmingly drowsy and be accused of laziness, how debilitating it was to unpredictably and uncontrollably fall asleep throughout the day.

It was how his mom had died.

Darwin had only been three years old and didn't have a single memory of her, at least one he was confident he hadn't manufactured later. She'd spent almost twenty-four hours flying home from a research trip to Cape Town, then fell asleep at the wheel and died in a head-on collision on the ten-minute drive home from the airport. And he was determined to help these people like he'd been unable to help her.

The cause and cure for narcolepsy were unknown—*were unknown*—until the insight that ultimately led to what was now called the Huxley procedure and should instead be the Johnston procedure, or at a minimum the Johnston-Huxley procedure. Darwin had had the initial insight sitting right here, at precisely three o'clock in the morning after his fifth cup of coffee while staring at pixelated screens from the pre-iPhone era with bloodshot eyes. But although the computer's clock read three a.m., this was not that night.

Darwin wasn't sure what night it was until he heard the distant shattering of glass.

Could it be the sleepwalkers? They were also studied on this floor. Some of them could turn violent, like zombies. However, for just this reason they were closely monitored in a room where they weren't a danger to themselves or anyone else. Maybe one of the other grad students had simply dropped something. Or maybe someone was breaking in. He should go check it out.

But there was no one in the hallway. Or the office next door. As he continued down the hall in the direction where the sound came from, past an empty reception desk, he developed the uncanny feeling he was the only person awake on this floor. When he reached the last office, he discovered he was wrong.

A junkie ravaged through the medicine cabinets, making a mess. No doubt in search of whatever drugs he or she imagined were kept here. The long unkempt hair made it difficult to discern sex from behind. But how had they got through security? Where was everyone? Darwin was trying to think of something to say when the person stopped, as if detecting his presence. Then they wheeled around to face him.

Darwin now understood how this person had gotten through

87

security.

He stared at the barrel of an old six-shooter, held in the erratically shaky hand of...Madeline? Darwin tried to hold up his hands, but they wouldn't move. He tried to speak, but no sound came out. He tried to convey the message 'don't shoot' with his eyes, the only option left to him, but it clearly didn't get through.

Madeline fired.

Darwin woke up to a loud bang somewhere outside. Was that a gunshot or a car backfiring? Was that even something that happened anymore? It was also possible the noise wasn't real and instead an incident of exploding head syndrome, a poorly understood but hilariously named phenomenon. But he could not confirm if the sound was authentic or not—there was no one else in the room to ask.

Darwin was unsurprised to be alone in bed; Madeline had barely talked to him all day and insisted on sleeping on the couch in a strange reversal of the usual cliché, even if she *had* recently taken to spending part of her nights downstairs and taking Mofongo with her. He used to love watching his wife sleep, safe and sound. He couldn't remember the last time he'd done so.

He went to the window and surveyed the empty street. Everything was still, until what at first looked like a dog came trotting down the middle of the road. On further inspection it was a coyote. It wasn't uncommon to see them this close to the Presidio. One had killed their neighbor's chihuahua last year.

Darwin was about to go back to bed when he noticed the time: precisely three a.m. It was either a crazy coincidence, or his eyes had been partially open and the information had made its way into his subconscious and influenced the dream, like the bang presumably had. Any other explanation was nonsense. One thing that *was* special about the time, however, was that it meant he could go back to sleep for several more hours. There were few better feelings than waking up to such a realization, and few worse than the opposite.

But a suspicion had crept into Darwin's mind. The bang had likely woken up Madeline...but what if she had already been awake? It was an outlandish idea, one that couldn't possibly be true, but he wouldn't be able to fall back asleep until he put it to bed.

The girls were hopefully drifting off again—they slept almost twelve hours a night, which was normal for their age—so Darwin tiptoed past their rooms and down the stairs. As expected, the living room was dark, but neither his wife nor dog were on the couch. There wasn't even a proper pillow or blanket. It was as if no one had slept there at all.

Unsurprisingly Madeline's office door was shut, a thin strip of light at the bottom. Darwin continued tiptoeing, his heart beginning to race, until he was close enough to hear the conversation happening inside.

"...you have three more hours of appointments after this? Wow. I figured it was the end of your workday in Bangkok. Quite a busy man. Ok I'll see you on Thursday and will take your advice until then. Thanks again Doctor Magnusson. Bye."

Bangkok. Doctor Magnusson. James Magnusson. Darwin knew the name and what it meant. Just like that, everything changed. Some kinds of knowledge were like one-way doors; despite humans' immense capacity for cognitive dissonance, some things were impossible to unlearn, even with recent advancements in neuroscience. The conversation was almost more devastating to overhear than if she'd been talking to a lover.

How could she do such a thing without consulting him, especially after the role he'd played in the procedure's discovery? She knew his thoughts on its use outside of helping those with debilitating conditions. It was potentially unstable. The risks were too great. Even if Darwin had ostensibly come downstairs to assuage himself of such a suspicion, he hadn't *really* expected to find anything, like a rational adult checking under the bed before going to sleep, just in case.

And now he stared into the face of a monster.

He heard the sounds of a chair sliding back and Madeline standing up, walking towards the door. Darwin couldn't think of anything to do; he just stood there in the dark with his mouth agape. Whatever clarity he imagined he'd found over the weekend was already gone, the window into a sunny day now coated in something thicker than blood.

Madeline opened the door and jumped when the light from within revealed Darwin standing outside.

They fought until dawn.

Chapter 11: Madeline

Thursday, September 26th, 2019 — 2 hours of sleep

First time intentionally sleeping since Sunday. It's better when I don't sleep, don't dream. Easier to pay attention, to differentiate between hallucinations and reality, remember who I am. But the flight was so long, and my eyes were going to bleed if I didn't let them rest. Now I'm not entirely sure what was real, what happened on the airplane vs. an interdimensional plane. Presumably the dragon keeping pace outside the window with wings like lungs freshly ripped from the back of a human giant, dripping blood and inflating and deflating as they flapped, was illusory. I'm not so sure about the rest. I should probably look through my sent email.

I'm fucked.

It was after midnight when Madeline entered the grand lobby of the Bangkok Stasis Hotel. She felt some trepidation given what had happened the last time she was here and had almost opted to stay elsewhere, but those damn rewards points make it so tempting. Madeline would have preferred not to stay in a hotel at all, to land and go straight to see the doctor, but had only had one flight option on such short notice. At least she no longer had to hide the trip from Darwin. Informing him was the last time they'd spoken, days ago. They hadn't gone that long without speaking since the moment they met.

Her appointment was first thing the next morning, which meant the next eight hours would be tough. She'd hoped to pass them working given the company planned to file its registration statement and formally announce its intention to go public in a few weeks. But now she didn't entirely trust herself. It was hard to be confident in your work when the numbers literally danced on the screen, the sixes and nines flipping back and forth.

Madeline checked in then began walking across the empty lobby towards the elevators, contemplating which combination of pharmaceuticals would best get her through the night. Looking blankly ahead, at first she didn't take any notice of the dark figure who emerged from an elevator and walked her direction. At second glance she stopped dead in her tracks in the center of the foyer.

Elias Sultana was ambling straight for her.

What should she say? The timing of the change in her was too coincidental, the night too bizarre. Damn what her assistant and the hotel staff had said, he had to have played a role in whatever happened. But when he got within several feet, he looked at her and gave nothing but a small, polite smile and nod, as one would to a stranger. He seemed ready to continue past her without stopping or speaking, so she sidestepped into his path.

"Apologies," he said in the unique Maltese accent she suddenly recalled as he went to step around her.

Madeline again moved to block his path and said, "Don't you remember me, Elias?"

His face showed either genuine confusion or great acting. "I think you have me mistaken for someone else, ma'am. If you'll excuse me, there's a car waiting for me outside," he said as he moved to walk around her again.

Was this a joke? He even wore the same outfit as the last time she saw him, just last week. It had to be him. Then she recalled something else and grabbed his right wrist with one hand while attempting to pull up his long sleeve with the other. The dress shirt was tailored and buttoned at the wrist, so she didn't make much progress before he ripped his hand away, but she thought she saw the beginnings of the macabre dreamcatcher tattoo.

"Security!" he called out, his voice echoing in the atrium. Someone strode towards them from behind the front desk.

Madeline was about to give him a piece of her mind when she noticed that he'd left bloody footprints all across the white marble floor, as if he'd come out of the elevator from *The Shining*. She looked back into the dark, startled eyes of the man she thought was Elias Sultana. Were they the same?

"Missus Johnston, Marcellino, is there a problem here?" asked the front desk clerk.

"No...I'm sorry...I uh, I'm just tired and mistook him for someone else," she said.

The man—apparently named Marcellino (where had she heard that name before?)—smiled as he fixed his shirt sleeve. "That's alright. After all, it's quite late. Sometimes our minds do strange things when they believe they should be asleep. Sweet dreams, Missus Johnston."

He walked across the lobby and out the huge glass doors, then got into a waiting black SUV. The clerk went back to behind the front desk. Madeline remained standing in the middle of the atrium for a few seconds, then finished making her way across the sparklingly clean, white marble floor to the elevators.

It was going to be a long night.

"Based on your brain activity and the reports of your experience, it seems as though your mind is drifting in and out of dreaming while otherwise remaining awake," said Doctor Magnusson. "It is utterly bizarre. The events that occur during these episodes may be difficult to recall, especially compared to the more vivid dreams you have when fully asleep."

"So...like I'm sleepwalking all the time or something?" asked Madeline.

"Your condition shares characteristics with sleepwalking and REM sleep behavior disorder, even night terrors, though honestly it is unlike any *specific* parasomnia of which I'm currently aware. This may be concerning for you to hear, but it seems to be without precedent."

"It hasn't happened to anyone else who's undergone the modified Huxley procedure?" Madeline had asked around while trying to downplay the severity of her symptoms. She'd also gone down some deep rabbit holes online. No luck, just speculation at best and wild conspiracy theories at worst.

"As far as I know it is without precedent in both my clinical experience and the medical literature. *However*, I plan to extend my knowledge as far as necessary to help you."

"Is it possible some of the recent high-profile suicides stemmed from something similar? The behavior of Takayoshi Yamamoto, Gwenivere Adams, Rick Larson, and others could be interpreted—"

"Rick Larson is dead?" Doctor Magnusson interrupted, looking...scared?

"He jumped off one of the Golden Gate Bridge towers last week."

"I'm sorry to hear that," said the doctor, regaining his composure. "I hope you understand that I'm unable to disclose the identity of my patients due to privacy concerns. I'm *also* not comfortable speculating on who may or may not have undergone various procedures. But rest assured, Madeline, I will do what I can to find an effective solution. Fortunately, the regulatory environment is shifting in the United States, so I may be moving the entire practice to Palo Alto sooner than anticipated, saving you the long flight."

She also wanted to ask him about something else. It was, she hoped, entirely unrelated—Doctor Magnusson looked like he'd been recently beaten up. One eye was black with a cut above it, and his lip was swollen. It was obscenely out of character. She'd almost brought it up when she first arrived but wasn't sure it was real, especially after the dark night of the soul she'd just wrestled through. Now, after hours of tests and neither of them acknowledging his condition, it was simply too late and awkward to mention it.

Better to keep her questions focused on the subject at hand. She asked, "Is there anything you can do to help me today?" The last thing she needed right now was anyone, from a Wall Street analyst to a family court judge, questioning her competency as a chief executive or mother. The stigma around mental health was too strong.

The doctor looked pensive. "I don't usually recommend unconventional or experimental treatments, but this is a unique situation. Are you familiar with dream hacking?"

"Like the movie *Inception?*"

"Perhaps dream engineering or incubation is a more appropriate term. Dreams are commonly affected by external sensory input. For example, it is possible to deliberately influence their content by introducing sounds and scents that trigger certain subconscious responses. This much is uncontroversial. However, it is also *ostensibly* possible to detect when someone begins to have these hypnagogic microdreams and arouse them such that they enter a state of lucid dreaming."

"They feel more like macrodreams to me." Come to think of it, she knew some people who were into just such activities. Self-proclaimed 'dreamwalkers' who took oneirogens like galantamine. They'd always seemed a bit crazy, but now that she was a lot crazy, she was open to anything.

The doctor continued, "Most of the data is self-reported and subjective, as well as susceptible to the placebo effect, but there are supplements and devices that purport to aid with lucid dreaming and recall. They may help you manage these scenarios when you unknowingly start hallucinating, to effectively turn them into lucid daydreams you can control."

"What kinds of devices? Please don't tell me I need to wear a headset like the one I had on all morning." She couldn't run a company like that.

"I'd like to propose trying two different experimental devices we have on site. They're modified versions of prototypes developed by some old colleagues at the MIT Media Lab. The first you'd wear when intentionally sleeping. It's transcranial and does resemble a pair of headphones that sit over your ears and temples. It monitors mentation and transmits electrical currents and sound for neurostimulation. It also includes an optional mask to track rapid eye movement with a neural interface on the back of the head over the visual cortex. It may take some time to get used to sleeping in.

"The second device you'd wear in your daily life and resembles a sort of futuristic glove and bracelet combination. It monitors and modulates your heartrate, dermal and muscular electrical activity, blood oxygen, and other biosignatures. You could conceivably wear a more normal-looking glove over the top to conceal its presence."

"And I'd wear it all the time?" asked Madeline. 'The gloved one.' Great. Still, better than jumping off a bridge.

"Admittedly, the data I have right now is limited, but given what you've told me, I recommend you wear it *as much as possible*, especially in situations where these microdreams could be dangerous. Again, we're in unprecedented territory. I hope to find a more permanent solution, but it will likely take some time. The devices aren't waterproof, so you may remove them to shower or when somewhere safe with someone you trust to monitor your actions. Is Mister Johnston still unaware that you've undergone the modified Huxley procedure?"

"No, he's aware...but..." Madeline paused for several seconds, "he's not going to be my husband for much longer. We're getting divorced."

Part 3: Light Sleep

Three months later

Chapter 12: Darwin

'Time moved relatively slow on Light Station 739, positioned as it was near the bottom of a black hole's deep gravity well. Nascent technological species like *Homo sapiens* had gotten many details of these celestial phenomena wrong, but they'd been (mostly) right about the effects of gravity. While the program who thought of itself as Lightkeeper 739 understood time dilation on an intellectual level, from its perspective time moved along at precisely the pace it was supposed to. Only on the rare occasions when it received a transmission from a passing starship, thanking it for the warning, was it reminded of just how warped its position in spacetime was compared to most other sentient beings. But although Lightkeeper 739 had been created specifically to perform this job—and knew how important of a job it was—on these infrequent occasions it also felt something difficult for it to describe: loneliness.'

Darwin's first time writing in months was not going well. He shouldn't have used third-person omniscient narration, but it was too late to change now; he was eight and a half books into the series. He was too old to finish his PhD or rejoin the rat race, not to mention he hadn't worked since Christina was born. Had he had kids too young? No, stop. But making a career out of writing was his best option. And it would let him spend time in fictional places more exciting and less dumb, political, and random than reality.

At least he would only need minimal income going forward, he thought as he looked at the tan line where his wedding ring used to be. The last thing he wanted to become was a single dad working late nights at the office, like his dad.

Darwin had been the one to first bring up divorce. He'd been enraged and not entirely serious. But Madeline had executed the process with the same ruthless efficiency she did everything. It was something he'd always admired about her, but not fun to be on the wrong side of, especially now that it was combined with the brazenness and impulsivity of someone who seemed to have lost many of their inhibitions. The business press called her a maverick. Darwin was convinced something else was going on. Who breaks their wrist kick-boxing so severely they need a plaster cast for twelve weeks? How much longer would she hide that she'd undergone the modified Huxley procedure now that the FDA had approved it? That the government had approved something so dangerous was almost as insane as it made Darwin feel. What kind of world would his daughters grow up in?

Technically they were still married; California had a six-month waiting period after filing the initial paperwork, for which Darwin was thankful. But Madeline had made it painfully clear it was over, and they'd both said things they couldn't take back. He'd even changed her last name in his phone to see if he could get used to it. She had no interest in couple's therapy, much less one of Arlo's couples' ceremonies. If Darwin were in a better mood, he would have laughed out loud at the thought of the awakening he felt he'd had at the men's ceremony, only to come home and immediately plunge into this nightmare. So much for the afterglow. He kept wishing he'd wake up and it would all turn out to be an extended bad dream or trip.

Admittedly he missed Preston, who he hadn't talked to since learning he was the one who referred Madeline to Doctor Magnusson. He *had* finally taken Preston's advice and bought a gun.

He was glad that came with a mandatory waiting period too.

Darwin closed the laptop and awoke his phone. It was almost two in the morning. He'd recently developed something like insomnia but guessed that was what happened when every day you slept until noon after hitting the snooze button a dozen times. Apparently using Queen's 'Don't Stop Me Now' as the alarm didn't have the desired effect.

The screen also informed him there were two missed calls. The first was from an unknown number with a 206-area code. Seattle. They left no voicemail and had only called once, which meant it must not have been that important. Probably just a telemarketer using his old home area code to increase the chance he'd answer. The second call was from Balthazar, which of course came with a voicemail. He was about to delete it out of habit but instead caught himself, reconsidered, and pressed play.

"Chuck, it's the tzar. An *actual* fucking tzar. I heard you're getting divorced. Bummer. I could never get married. I'd never survive for the same reason there are no great white sharks in captivity—you can't cage a true apex predator. Hmm, maybe using the word 'predator' in the context of sexuality is questionable. And we know almost nothing about the sex lives of great white sharks. Oh well. But fret not, my oldest and lamest friend—a single day in New Libertatia will make you wonder why you ever tied the knot in the first place. The offer still stands. Just give me a date and an airport. I don't care if you're on the run from the law—we have no extradition treaties. Don't forget your passport. Hope to see you soon."

How the hell did Balthazar know he was getting divorced? He and Madeline had agreed to keep it quiet until after her company went public. Darwin didn't plan to make any crazy alimony demands, but California was a community property state. The rational thing to do was help her maximize their assets' value while they were still theirs. Well, Balthazar was technically a head of state now. He'd made a life and career out of knowing more than others. Presumably he had his methods.

Across the dark living room, the Christmas tree's rainbow lights provided the only illumination in the house. He'd always wanted multi-colored lights, but Madeline had insisted on nothing but white. This was one of his little protests, even if the girls weren't going to open the presents under it until they got back from Tokyo on New Year's Eve. He started to worry, as he'd spent much time doing over the past few months, about what impact this would have on Evelyn and Christina, when something moved in his peripheral vision.

He glanced out the front window at a tiger prowling down the middle of the street, then down at Carl Sagan's *The Demon-Haunted World: Science as a Candle in the Dark* next to the laptop on the coffee—

Wait. What?

He jerked his head back to look outside again. Sure enough, there was a large tiger majestically making its way down the street, its shadowy orange and black body silhouetted by the red, blue, green, and yellow Christmas lights outlining the neighbor's house. Was this real or some kind of hypnagogic hallucination? Other than being a little drunk, he felt lucid.

Mofongo confirmed his sanity when she must have seen the same thing he did and growled, which was exceptionally rare. He'd always wondered if she would back him up if shit hit the fan.

"911, what is your emergency?" asked the operator. Darwin couldn't help but think she had a sexy voice. Should he ask her out? No, save it for tomorrow. It was probably against the law, anyway.

"Hi, this may sound crazy, but there's a tiger walking down the middle of my street."

"...I'm sorry, did you say a tiger?"

"Yes, a tiger. Like...the jungle cat." It seemed he was the first to call it in.

"Sir, have you consumed any alcohol or drugs tonight? You can be fined and jailed for falsely calling 911."

"No...well, yes, I had some wine, but not a lot." He'd drank a whole bottle and was currently working on a glass of scotch, but he was a big guy. Besides, it's not like it was against the law. Why had his pulse started to race?

"Are you currently in danger?"

"No, I'm inside."

"Alright, sir, please remain inside and do not approach the tiger. We'll send a car."

Darwin gave her his address and the tiger's bearings then hung up. What. The. Hell. He got up off the couch with a groan and walked through the empty house towards the back door. A twenty-two hundred square foot house felt awful big and lonely when you were the only one in it around the holidays. At least he wasn't entirely alone; he had Mofongo.

He walked out into the backyard and the cold of the winter

night. He didn't need to listen to that 911 vixen's warning to stay inside; it was fenced in and safe. Darwin grabbed a cigarette from the pack on the table by the door and lit it. He'd quit smoking along with grad school but recently fell back into the bad habit when the girls were with Madeline. It was a doubly dirty habit for (wannabe) doctors who should know better. Dammit Dar, you're falling apart.

Should he sell the house? He'd used all the money his dad left him for the down payment. It was the only savings they'd had at the time, and although he'd thought it was reckless, they *were* able to afford the mortgage with Madeline's salary. And it had appreciated significantly. The Lockhart's had been right about that. But it was also the only home the girls had ever known. So many memories. So much nostalgia. Could he live here without Madeline and keep his sanity? She had no problem letting him keep it; she'd only spent half as many nights here as him over the years and was ready to upgrade after the IPO.

Darwin thought of that riddle about how you can only run halfway into the woods because then you're running out. Maybe life was the same, and he had passed the halfway point. Maybe it wasn't an accident that our greatest aspirations and nightly outrageous fantasies shared the same word: dreams.

A rustling in the dark foliage rimming the backyard caught his attention. Probably just the wind, the sound of entropy. It was too damn windy in this city. How did the exotically colored bird of paradise perched in one of the trees feel about it? Maybe he should move back to Seattle, or get away from this damn wind and flee to southern California. Hell, he could put his dual American-Australian citizenship to good use and move down under if not for the girls.

He burned down the first cigarette surprisingly fast. He took a long sip of scotch, then grabbed and lit another. Not so rational now, are you? Chain-smoking degenerate.

A bomb went off in his mind, turning the world into dripping geodesics and fractals. What he saw put the rainbow Christmas lights and bewildering tiger to shame.

Chapter 13: Madeline

Wednesday, December 18th, 2019 — 3 hours of sleep

Fields of lavender in neat rows extended over rolling hills in every direction for as far as I could see. The scent was overwhelming. Blue jays and robins chirped pleasantly overhead, sometimes flying into each other and erupting in a burst of purple flowers that gently rained down. The temperature and humidity matched my body exactly, like being in a sensory deprivation tank. There was no boundary between me and the late afternoon, which went on even longer than the rows of lavender. I wonder if I'll ever get tired of that place. I can't believe most people spend no time at all optimizing the years of their lives spent dreaming.

Who needs time off from work when you can take a short vacation every night?

Madeline drew in a deep, smoke-filled breath. She exhaled, and the smoke danced and twisted itself into two pirate ships doing battle on the high seas of steam. A kraken emerged from the water and devoured them both, also taking with it any lingering sign of the cigarette she was smoking. Japan may have been something of a smoker's paradise, relatively speaking, but it wasn't allowed at the Tokyo Stasis Hotel, even outside on the roof. But that was no problem; no one gave her a second glance.

She and Darwin had quit smoking together, though they'd never been heavy users. It'd been more of a situational thing, either after drinking, sex, or both. She smiled, recalling the past hour she'd spent with a man who looked and acted *perfectly.* She may have technically still been married, but it wasn't technically infidelity.

The man wasn't technically real, after all.

He was a combination of several others. And she felt no guilt about these irreverent reveries, even if in many senses they were indistinguishable from reality. To think she once got legitimately mad at Darwin for cheating in one of her dreams.

"Would you like something to eat?" asked a waiter she hadn't noticed approaching.

"No thanks," she replied, holding up the nutrient shake with her good hand, "there's a meal's worth of calories in here." The waiter smiled and walked away. She took a sip of the shake. A few months ago it would have tasted like chalk but now resembled a delicious vanilla milkshake and could have tasted like anything she pleased. Ridiculous nutrient shakes were all she consumed these days.

The rooftop pool had been converted into a giant hot tub this time of year, and Madeline looked through the haze coming off it and out at the cold, bright winter day. She blinked for several seconds and when her eyes opened, a dragon emerged from behind the nearest skyscraper. But it was a far cry from the terrifying, blood-dripping variety she'd unintentionally hallucinated in the past. Instead it resembled the friendly, white and teal animated dragon from *Spirited Away,* the movie her daughters were watching in the suite downstairs.

Madeline blinked again, and cartoon dragons filled the

skyline, a whole flock, if that was the correct term for a group of such creatures. But she was not tempted to jump off the roof and ride one as it swooped by, as she suspected was Takayoshi Yamamoto's motivation on the night she met him up here. Her senses had been reliably fooled, but deep down her mind had not.

She blinked once more, shook her head slightly, and the dragons disappeared. She'd never thought of herself as having an especially vivid imagination, a quant as opposed to a poet, as they said in business school. But she was getting good at this.

The movie would end soon, and there was much to show Christina and Evelyn in Tokyo on their first trip out of the US. She also didn't feel comfortable leaving them alone in the room for more than an hour. Madeline got out of the hot tub, careful not to let the cast on her left wrist and hand—and more importantly, what was underneath—touch the water. She could have experienced most of the sensations of being in here without actually getting in, but there was still a reality premium to most things, at least at this stage. She'd also found that her risk tolerance had skyrocketed.

Madeline donned her robe, more out of a fading habit of modesty than the cold of the forty-five-degree air. She was about to head back down to the room when a man sitting against the wall on the far side of the pool, having a conversation with a waiter, caught her eye. His arms were out of the water with his elbows resting on the edge, giving a clear view of his muscular chest and a tattoo on one side of his exposed ribs (the Stasis had a liberal policy towards tattoos compared to many pools in Japan). The man may have been thirty feet away, but even through the water vapor, the tattoo's shape was familiar: a kind of dreamcatcher without feathers or beads, filled with skinless humanoid figures.

The device gave her no indication that her subconscious had started to come online and her mind was drifting off. She assessed the data from her other senses and let herself feel the true air temperature. As far as she could tell, she was not dreaming, and the symbol was not a hallucination.

Relax, Madeline. It was probably just the mascot for something she knew nothing about, like an eSports team. Or a new trendy tattoo, like the butterfly she'd once had on her pelvis that had been replaced by a laser removal scar. It was certainly no stranger than the torture device many Christians had inked on them. But something about it made her uncomfortable; sure, the sample size was only two (or three?), but they'd all been debonair men hanging out at *Suspended Animation Collection* hotels. She made a mental note to look into it later.

She moved her gaze up from the tattoo to the man's handsome face to see that he was staring right back at her, as was the waiter. The old Madeline would have immediately looked away in embarrassment. Instead she held his gaze and found herself in a staring contest. Five seconds passed, then ten. Madeline narrowed her eyes and pouted her mouth into an exaggerated, mocking glare, breaking the stern look on his face into a smile. He probably thought she was about to approach him, but she turned around and went back to the room.

Being single again was going to be fun.

She checked on the girls, then her phone, charging in the bedroom next to the headset device she now wore when sleeping. There was a missed call and voicemail from Doctor Magnusson. The man never stopped working.

"Hello Madeline, this is Doctor Magnusson. I hope you are

still managing to get by as well as you were the last time we spoke. I may have found a more permanent solution to your *predicament* and would like to discuss this with you in person as soon as you're back from Japan. Please let me know the earliest date and time that work for you. Happy holidays and take care."

Madeline stared at her cast, covered in Christina and Evelyn's colorful and inscrutable writing and doodles. What great PR. She wiggled her exposed fingertips and congratulated herself for coming up with a solution that hid both her ring finger and the lucid dreaming device Doctor Magnusson had given her.

Did she even want a permanent solution to her 'predicament' at this point? In many ways this new reality in which she had control over her senses like a visceral lucid dream was even better than after she'd first had the procedure done. It gave her even more of an edge, and she needed to be sharper than ever right now. But she couldn't reasonably keep the cast on much longer. Perhaps she could claim that she fell and rebroke her wrist, but she couldn't do that forever. A glove would be too conspicuous, too difficult to explain, and the headset version was a non-starter.

"Mom! I wanna get spirited away," said Christina. Her two daughters ran into the bedroom.

"Yeah, I wanna be friends with a dragon," added Evelyn. "But don't tell Mofongo."

"Well, I can't take you to the spirit world, but I can take you to some pretty cool places in Tokyo. *And*, one of them even has a dragon."

"Let's go!" the two girls said in unison.

"Alright, get your gear on. It's cold out there."

The girls began collecting the winter gear they'd haphazardly shed around the suite after their last outing. Someone knocked at the door. Strange, she had the do not disturb sign activated. She walked to the room's entrance and paused, then opened the door.

No one was there, the long hallway empty in both directions.

Chapter 14: Darwin

It took Darwin a few hours to understand what must have happened. There was something familiar about the thirty-minute, thirty-thousand-light-year rocket ship ride he'd taken after lighting that second cigarette. It was not unlike the peaks of the waves he'd ridden during the men's ceremony. Some of his fellow astronauts were even the same, except this time the planet-sized elephants were tigers.

Darwin had been dosed with DMT.

Someone had tampered high up the chain in the cigarette manufacturing process a while back. Smokers across the country had suddenly found themselves on similarly terrifying journeys. A handful had died. He recalled there had been a recall, but apparently no one had told the bodega around the corner, or they hadn't felt the need to participate. Various enduring urban legends dating back to the fifties told of psychedelic terrorists, Soviet spies, and the CIA spiking water supplies with LSD. While spiking cigarettes with DMT was smaller in scope, it was at least technically viable.

Darwin had managed to get some shuteye afterward but was unable to sleep late like he'd become accustomed to. Instead he found himself sipping an enormous cup of black coffee and watching the local morning news, clean-shaven for the first time in months.

"In this morning's top story, a tiger escaped from where it had been illegally kept inside of a home in Pacific Heights." Darwin spat out a sip of coffee, most of which landed on Mofongo, curled up on his feet. The dog gave him a brief look of mild annoyance, then ceased fighting gravity and laid her head back down with a grumble, otherwise unperturbed.

He'd completely forgotten about the tiger! It was real after all. Jesus, he's lucky it didn't attack him while he stumbled around like an idiot in the backyard.

The news anchor continued, "Footage from the home's security cameras show that the owner was mauled to death after letting the tiger out of its cage and attempting to ride it. A toxicology report is yet to be performed, but it's believed he was under the influence of narcotics. Fortunately, no one else was injured, including the tiger. The fully grown male cat was found and tranquilized in the nearby neighborhood of Laurel Heights and is being transported to an animal sanctuary where it will peacefully live out the rest of its life alongside other members of its species. Several other animals were also found illegally kept in the twenty-million-dollar mansion and are being similarly relocated. A few of the cages were open and empty but appear to have been recently used, leading authorities to believe their inhabitants may have escaped and still be on the loose somewhere in the city..."

What a world. Well, the past eighteen hours had certainly given him some good fodder for conversation tonight. And he was going to need it—Darwin had a date. It was his first first date since meeting Madeline more than a decade ago. He'd always hated them, answering the same questions and telling the same stories and jokes. He thought he used to have a few lines that consistently worked but could no longer remember them. If the recent conversations he'd had on dating apps were any indication, they'd surely have fallen flat anyway. He had no edge in the digital dating world like he'd once had in the analog one.

But Sephira was different.

She didn't seem like a bot or a sex worker, as was clearly the case with all the others who'd initiated contact with him. With no local single friends, he was at first into the idea of dating apps. But after a depressing few weeks of stilted text conversations, he'd been ready to give up on digital dating and give in to being the oldest guy at the bar. That's when Sephira messaged him.

Sure, there was still a chance he was getting 'catfished.' You had to be especially skeptical of things you want to be true. As one of his heroes Richard Feynman had said, 'The first principle is that you must not fool yourself—and you are the easiest person to fool.' But he and Sephira had exchanged a short story's worth of words over the past few days. If she wasn't actually a doctoral candidate in neuroscience, then she was awful good at faking it. She may have had a limited online presence but hey, so did he. And it would make Madeline jealous as hell if she looked anything like her profile pictures.

Sephira had made things easy for him, even proposing a date (today), a time (eight o'clock), and a place (the bar at the San Francisco Stasis Hotel). It could be a red flag, but it fit with her story that she was only in town for a few weeks to visit friends over the holidays. Darwin liked that she was assertive. Maybe that's just how girls from Cyprus were.

"You think I still got it, girl?" he asked Mofongo. She didn't even bother to lift her head and just let out another grumble.

"Whatever. You didn't know me in my prime."

Darwin was so nervous after getting dropped off out front of the hotel that he started to take a walk around the block. He was fifteen minutes early. He had time. But he regretted the decision when he rounded the second corner and found himself at the edge of one of the many tent cities that had sprung up around San Francisco in recent years. The *Suspended Animation Collection* hotel juxtaposed with such abject poverty was typical for what the city had become. Progressive politics run amok. Maybe it *was* time to sell the house and move.

Darwin was about to turn around and abort when he saw a familiar face in the darkness. It couldn't be. He glanced at his watch to ensure he still had time, then walked towards a figure slumped up against a trashcan covered in disturbing graffiti.

"Michael?" he asked as he squatted down to get on the man's level. The stench was hard to bear. A barely recognizable version of the successful author he'd met months ago looked at him with glassy, unrecognizing eyes but did not respond. It didn't make any sense. Michael had hosted the damn men's ceremony at his Larkspur mansion. He was California famous and the furthest thing from homeless. "What are you doing here?"

The man who Darwin was sure was Michael twitched a few times, then with shocking speed and strength for someone in their fifties, reached out and grabbed Darwin's peacoat with both hands and pulled him in close. "I am the devil, and I am in hell, which is right where I'm supposed to be," he said, revealing rotting and missing teeth. "Now get the hell out of here!"

Michael (the devil?) shoved Darwin backward, causing him

to lose his balance and splay out on the wet asphalt. Darwin scrambled to his feet, but the violence and yelling had caused some of the other vagrants to take an interest. He suddenly felt very out of place and took Michael's advice right away.

Rattled thoughts raced through Darwin's head as he rounded the corner and strode back towards the front of the hotel. Was Michael an addict? Perhaps he'd been to one too many men's ceremonies. Should he tell Preston? No, fuck that guy. What about Arlo? He didn't have his contact info but could presumably find it. Should he cancel the date with Sephira? No, it was too last minute to do so now.

Darwin took the elevator to the top floor, noting that this hotel followed the ridiculous superstition of 'omitting' the thirteenth. He checked his now-dirty coat and was glad to see there was still an open table next to the window. The benefits of grabbing drinks on a Wednesday. He tried to mentally shift gears, wishing he'd pulled the trigger on that drink he contemplated having at home to take the edge off.

His phone buzzed, which must have been Sephira; he'd added her to the tiny list of people exempted from Do Not Disturb. She was running ten minutes late, for which he was thankful. There was also another missed call from the unknown 206 Seattle number, this time accompanied by a three-minute voicemail. Darwin would listen to it later; he needed to get his head in the game and didn't need any further distractions tonight.

He was starting his second whiskey when Sephira entered the far side of the lounge and waved. She looked even better in person than her pictures online, causing a rush of imposter syndrome and nervousness that the lone drink he'd had was woefully insufficient to mask. These kinds of experiences were supposed to be behind him. What if she wanted to go back to his place—or hers—wherever it was? He still loved Madeline and grasped at the dim hope of reconciling with the mother of his children. Was it too soon to be dating? How far was he willing to go? Would he even be able to perform? He merely wanted to make Maddy jealous. She wasn't seeing anyone new as far as he knew.

Darwin silenced these doubts and got up out of his seat but became self-conscious of wearing slacks and a dress shirt. Sephira was in ripped jeans, sneakers, and a black leather jacket. Then one of the few good pieces of advice given to him by Balthazar came to mind: There's no such thing as being overdressed, nothing wrong with being the best-dressed guy in the room. He regained some confidence.

"You must be Darwin," she said as she approached.

"Sephira, nice to meet you in person." They exchanged a brief hug.

"Sorry for being late," she said as they sat down at the table.

"No worries. I hope you don't mind that I went ahead and ordered a drink." Shit, he should have asked if she wanted him to order her one. At least he didn't blurt out that he thought late people were rude and selfish.

"No problem at all. To be honest I had one while getting ready. I get a bit nervous on first dates."

"Me too." He neglected to tell her he hadn't been on one in twelve years.

"Sorry, one second," she said, then took her phone out of her purse, "I need to send one last text, then it's going on mute."

"You know, I didn't have a smartphone until I was out of grad school. I didn't even have the internet until high school." Was bragging about being old?

117

"People used to live their entire nasty, brutish, and short lives without antibiotics, too. No need to be romantic about it."

"Good point, and great choice of location, by the way, although this neighborhood isn't what it used to be. I've actually never been inside this hotel before. It's pretty swanky." Who says 'swanky'?

"I always stay here when I'm in San Francisco. The rooms are lovely."

Under the table Darwin tried to fiddle with where his missing wedding ring used to be. He placed his hands on the table, gulped, and said, "You didn't want to stay with your friends?"

"I'm told most people can't afford spare bedrooms around here. These beds are a lot more comfortable and private than sleeping on a couch. Two weeks would be too much of an imposition, anyway."

How could a grad student in her late twenties afford to stay here? The prices looked like they were in yen! And why wasn't she visiting family this time of year? Those were probably inappropriate questions so soon after meeting someone. He was about to bring up a shared interest instead when she answered both his queries and proved him wrong. "My father was some kind of hotshot financier. Possibly a criminal, actually. He left me enough money to do as I please."

Ok then. She was even more open and direct than he'd thought. He hoped there wasn't an expectation that he follows suit. Darwin said, "That's...great. Not that he's dead or was possibly a criminal. Mine is too. Dead, that is, not a criminal. What I mean is—"

"I know what you mean," she said with a disarming smile.

Time to pivot to that shared interest. "Does the sleep-assist technology built into the bedframes actually work for you? Low-frequency electrical stimulation has been shown to help some patients with chronic insomnia, but I'm not sure it would work for the average person, especially without wearing some type of device. It's an interesting marketing tactic given some are convinced it causes cancer."

"I've heard people report having vivid dreams when they stay here. Some even report having similar dreams," she said.

"Well, self-reported subjective anecdotes aren't exactly reliable, especially when people are primed to believe something beforehand. We're notoriously bad witnesses of our own experiences, and dreams are hard to recall in the first place. Unfortunately, sometimes in neuroscience these reports are all you have to work with."

"What if they weren't all you had to work with? What if you could read someone's mind?"

"I'm not sure 'mind reading' is the preferred terminology, but the field is indeed advancing rapidly."

"Let's see if you can read my mind right now, Darwin." Sephira stared at him with a blank expression on her face. Man, this girl was weird.

"You want me to guess what you're thinking?"

"It doesn't have to be a guess."

"Ok...um..."

"Nevermind, I'll tell you later. Show you, maybe. To go back to your question about if the sleep-assist technology works for me—I don't sleep much these days. I slept as much as possible when I was a little girl. Dreaming was better than being abused, but maybe that's TMI. Anyways, I've never had much trouble falling and staying asleep and have always been a vivid dreamer, so I can't really say if it affects me. I stay here for the other amenities."

"You don't sleep much, really? As someone studying neurophysiology, you should know how important it is." Was he giving a lecture now? Get it together, Dar. Saying the right thing was so much easier when he could take as long as he needed to come up with a response via text. He'd forgotten how hard it was to have a real-time conversation like this. So much for whatever edge he imagined he'd once had in the analog dating world.

The cocktail waitress showed up, giving him some much-needed time to collect himself and his thoughts. She asked Sephira, "Would you like anything to drink?"

"I'll have whatever he's having," she said, then looked at him provocatively, "and two shots of zivania."

"Zivania?"

"It's from Cyprus. Not many places have it. It's strong, but why not trade a little of tomorrow for tonight?"

"Two shots of zivania it is," Darwin said to the waitress. He didn't exactly have a busy schedule the next day.

"So, Darwin, you say sleep is important, and I understand that all animals, including single-celled organisms, engage in something resembling sleep. But why do you think we need it in the first place?" Sephira asked after the waitress left.

"Because we get sleepy, of course." She smiled. Nailed it.

"Ok that one was too easy. How about something more interesting—why do you think we dream? I may not sleep much anymore, but I still dream all the time."

She was a strange one alright. "As far as I know, we don't definitively know. Any other answer is speculation."

"Spoken like a true scientist. It's a shame how most of science has lost interest in dreams over the past few decades.

Tell me, are you a betting man?"

"It depends. The odds are always statistically against you in table games and slot machines, so they make no sense. Now, when it comes to poker or sports—"

"If you had to bet on one reason, what would it be?"

"What's the wager?"

"I'll tell you later," she said with a wink. Then she removed her jacket and hung it over the back of the chair. Underneath she wore a simple black tank top, which seemed wildly out of place for the time of year and setting. It revealed the lean, heavily tattooed arms he recalled from one of her pictures online. They resembled collages of fantasy and horror novel covers. It was difficult to think of something more unlike Madeline. She asked, "Are you ok?"

Darwin was confused at the question until she motioned with her head at his hands on the table, more specifically the watch on his left wrist. It was alerting both of them that his heartrate had spiked. Yikes.

"You know, I've lived my whole life without a smartwatch," quipped Sephira, making fun of his earlier comment. The waitress returned with their drinks before he could respond, saving him some embarrassment. "To new friends and new beginnings," Sephira said. Darwin wondered what kind of new beginnings she meant. They both took the shot. It burned, but he did his best not to let it show. She continued, "Hopefully that will help calm your nerves. Now, where were we?"

"You asked me why I think we dream."

"Ah, yes, but that's not entirely correct. I asked you if you had to bet—and we *are* betting, by the way—on one reason why we dream, what it would be. People tend to give different responses and reveal what they actually believe when they have

121

skin in the game."

"How are we going to decide if I'm right or not?"

"I'll decide. And remember—there may literally be skin in the game."

If not for the burgeoning effects of the zivania, he may have been a bit weirded out. Instead he was intrigued. He thought for several seconds, then said, "If I had to put my money, or more, on one hypothesis, it would be that dreams are an epiphenomenon. Nothing special, just a side effect of other processes that occur during sleep having to do with the consolidation of memory."

Sephira studied him in silence for too long, staring at him with dark, intelligent eyes, then said, "That's a very boring answer, Darwin. I think that maybe you haven't had the right kinds of dreams. Or maybe you have, but you just don't remember them."

Darwin presumed he'd given the wrong response and lost the mysterious wager. To build some street cred, he contemplated mentioning the DMT he'd accidentally smoked last night or the ayahuasca he'd intentionally consumed a few months ago, when she said, "I suppose you think consciousness is nothing but an epiphenomenon too."

Are these the kinds of things people discuss on first dates these days? They were really jumping into the deep end. Well, he knew she wasn't like the other women he'd met online over the past few weeks. He said, "We know almost as little about consciousness as we do about dreams. It's certainly possible it's nothing but an epiphenomenon, but I believe there's a strong argument it evolved via natural selection. It seems to exist in most animals, albeit on a continuum, and it's easy to see how it could bestow a survival advantage over mere automatons."

Again she paused and stared at him for much longer than any normal person would, said, "I would expect no other answer from someone named Darwin. I *do* think you're partially correct, but there's more to life than just passing on genes, you know, even if the process of doing so is fun."

"Your turn, then. Why do you think we dream, or that we're conscious?"

"I think—I *know*—that the only reason we're conscious is *so that we can dream.* More than that, it's the reason we're alive and why we evolved like we did."

"And...we have sex so that others can dream in the future?" Darwin speculated.

"In a sense, yes."

"I wonder if that's why we dream about sex so much," he said with a smile.

"Do you dream about sex a lot, Darwin?"

"Uh..."

"All sentient creatures dream, you know. From humans to birds to octopuses. And just like we have eyes so we can see, we have consciousness so we can—"

Darwin couldn't help interrupting. "But even if I accept the dubious premise that all sentient animals dream and that consciousness is a prerequisite, isn't it more likely that causality goes the other direction?"

"No."

"No? That's it?" he was getting exasperated.

"You didn't let me finish. The reason consciousness is subservient to dreaming and not the other way around is that most people—especially scientists like you, Darwin—have reality flipped upside down. They believe that physics results in chemistry, which results in biology, which results in sentience, which results in phenomena like dreams, and that things get *more real* as you move down the stack towards 'fundamental' particles. You—"

"Yes, I've read *Sapiens,* like everyone else. But those are artificial distinctions and—" She gave him that strange look again. He said sheepishly, "I'm sorry I keep interrupting. I'll stop."

"Thanks. A true gentleman. Where was I? Ah, you think you have it figured out, but 'experts' can't even explain what accounts for ninety-five percent of the matter and energy in the universe. They just call it 'dark.' I know your specialty is biology and not computer science, but to use an analogy to the latter—dreams aren't an algorithm within an application running on an operating system running on hardware. The stack is upside down. Dreams are the electromagnetism, the fundamental force, that makes the entire system possible. It's why the 'laws' of physics, chemistry, and biology don't apply in dreams."

Yikes. He hadn't gotten 'catfished,' but it was now clear why Sephira was the only woman he'd had any success with so far online: She was insane. Bonkers. Whatever—may as well give in, play along, and have fun until he finished his drink and could get the hell out of here. "And how do you know this is the case? Extraordinary claims require extraordinary evidence," he said, invoking 'Sagan's standard.'

"How do you know it's not the case? What if this," she motioned with her arms to everything around them, "is just a dream inside of reality, and you don't remember your real life right now like you mostly don't remember this one when you dream? I see you ogling my tattoos. They're scenes from my *real* life, so I don't forget."

Darwin was flabbergasted. He was about to explain how the burden of proof lies with those making unfalsifiable claims when Sephira continued, "I'll tell you how *I* know—because those who created the system showed me." She preemptively held up a hand as if anticipating his interruption. "But I do understand that someone else's 'self-reported subjective anecdote' isn't good enough for many people. Especially for people like you, Darwin. They need to read it in a peer-reviewed paper, or better yet, experience it for themselves."

This just kept getting better. Were there red flags he missed? Wading back into the dating pool was going to be harder than anticipated. "Let me guess—and like Christian fundamental-ists who get advanced degrees in biology or geology to debunk evolution or prove the Earth is only several thousand years old, you're getting a PhD in computational neuroscience and chronobiology to verify this theory is correct?"

"It's not a religion to me, like science isn't a religion to you. It's simply the way things are." Sephira stared at him in silence again, her external beauty now a glaring contrast to the lunacy beneath the surface. Then she cracked a smile unlike one he'd see from her so far, leaned forward, and whispered, "I'm fucking with you, Darwin."

Now it was his turn to wear a dumbfounded stare as he processed what she'd just said. Finally he asked, "You're serious...about not being serious?"

"Sorry, I have a weird sense of humor."

"When did you start fucking with me?" The combo of relief and alcohol kicking in was nice.

"Only recently. The bet is still on, for example."

"Um...did I win?"

"I haven't decided yet. In the meantime let's do another round of shots."

They ended up taking three more shots each of zivania. Darwin was amazed Sephira seemed less fazed than him despite being half his size. Then again, she was younger and technically still in school. Presumably she had higher tolerance, but why did his feel so low?

He hadn't needed to work too hard to avoid mentioning he had a wife and kids, which he didn't think was appropriate for a first date. Instead they'd spent most of the time discussing his experience studying and working for Doctor Huxley. Sephira had found his stories endlessly fascinating and tolerated his rants about the corrupting effects of research grants and academia's resemblance to a pyramid scheme propped up by grad students doing the work for tenured professors at far below market wages driven down by high-skilled foreign labor imported for precisely such a purpose. She hadn't even questioned that he was the one who'd actually discovered the Huxley procedure. Shit, Madeline hardly believed that. And Sephira's questions were surprisingly sharp for being new to the field. It felt good to have someone find you so interesting, especially when they looked like Sephira.

Darwin regarded himself in the bathroom mirror. Damn, you're getting old, man. Thirty-six going on fifty, with one foot in the cremation station. Well, growing old was a privilege, and given the night's events he was apparently still attractive enough. His glazed eyes suddenly reminded him of the disturbing encounter with Michael earlier in the evening. He'd completely forgotten. He promised himself he'd follow up on it tomorrow, not wanting to kill the moment's buzz.

A fancy matte-black business card on the counter with 'CCP' embossed in silver caught his attention. Something was written below the letters, but his blurry vision couldn't make it out. Should he pick it up to see who it belonged to? Nah, there was no upside. Stay focused.

He walked out of the bathroom, not into the top-floor lounge of the San Francisco Stasis, not into the bedroom of the house he'd lived in with his family for the past eight years, but into Sephira's hotel room.

Chapter 15: Madeline

Madeline marveled at the beauty of Shinjuku Gyoen National Garden blanketed in a thick layer of pure white snow. Tokyo rarely received more than a dusting and never anything like this. Even more atypical were the pink cherry blossom trees, fully bloomed in mid-December. She wished her daughters could see it all but supposed the *real* afternoon and park were nice enough without her whimsical additions.

She smiled at her two little munchkins bundled up in beanies, scarves, gloves, boots, and heavy jackets. They'd both outgrown or destroyed most of the winter clothes she'd bought them just last year and had filled in the missing pieces of their wardrobes on the first day of the trip's shopping spree. Madeline had let them pick whatever they wanted, and they were consequently covered in bright, uncoordinated colors and adorable cartoon animals.

Madeline's outfit was different. She wore only a light jacket for warmth. She could have worn a summer dress—or nothing at all—but didn't want to draw any more stares than normal. However, when she looked up from Evelyn and Christina to the path ahead, she noticed they were in fact being watched by two men sitting on a bench. She was used to being looked at by the locals, usually with smiles, but something about the stern looks on these two men's faces made her uncomfortable. She closed her eyes and shook her head to remove the snow and pink pedals. The two men remained, still staring at her and the girls from behind dark sunglasses.

It was the middle of the afternoon, and Japan had an exceptionally low crime rate, which was why she'd left her pepper spray and taser at home. But they were in a secluded part of the large park amongst evergreen trees, and it was also the middle of winter; no one else was around or could see them. She was probably being paranoid but decided to head back the direction they came rather than continue past the two creeps.

"I think we took a wrong turn. The greenhouse is back this way," Madeline said, taking the hand of each daughter that didn't hold a cone of bright green ice cream, temperature be damned. She turned them around and started to retreat but stopped when she looked up at the path.

Another man stared at them. His demeanor was akin to the two on the bench, but he stood in the middle of the walkway just ten feet in front of her.

Should she scream for help? Her survival instincts told her this was a bad situation, but other, less primitive instincts she'd acquired about living in polite society held her tongue for the time being. What if she made a scene about nothing? Evidently she hadn't lost all her inhibitions just yet.

But she might have missed her opportunity—a lawnmower or leaf blower started up on the other side of the trees, loud enough to partially drown out any cries for help. The timing couldn't have been a coincidence, especially in December.

"Miss Lockhart," came a man's authoritative voice from behind her, barely audible over the machine's drone, "we don't want this to be any more difficult than it has to." She glanced over her shoulder and confirmed her worst fears: The two men from the bench had stood up and now also approached her family.

She let go of her daughters' hands, put hers up in front of her, and stepped back with her right (dominant) foot in what to many looked like someone who didn't want to fight but was in reality the Krav Maga stance. Her hands were open instead of balled into fists to not look threatening, but with the additional benefit of being ready to throw a palm heel strike instead of a punch. The former could do more damage with less risk to her hand. Sure, there was a greater likelihood of killing the recipient, but that was the choice they made when initiating violence. Not her problem.

"I don't want any trouble, guys," she said as she began backing off the path so that all three of the men were in front of her to some degree. Now that they all stood, she could accurately size them up and doubted their bulkiness was only due to their outerwear. Given their mass it was conceivable she could outrun them, but Evelyn and Christina definitely could not. And one of the several ponds in the garden blocked their escape. "Girls, stay a few feet behind me," she ordered.

Christina said something that sounded like, "Mom, I'm scared."

"Madeline," yelled the lone man to her right, now also walking slowly towards her, "we just want what's under the cast. That's it." On queue one of the others produced a knife. To what, cut off the cast right here? Were they insane? And how did they know?

The closest man was now only two full paces from her but had stopped and crossed his arms over his chest as if trying to intimidate her while waiting for an answer. Fortunately

Madeline had spent much time on her footwork and knew the precise range of one of her kicks after a short hop: exactly where the man was now standing, flat-footed with his hands in no position to defend himself. Amateur.

With one fluid movement she turned to face him and pushed off with her back foot to jump forward. When her left foot planted, she was already starting to twist, deriving maximum power from her hips and whipping her right leg around like she planned to kick clean through him, because she did.

The startled man began to step back with his right foot, leaving all his weight on his left leg just as Madeline's designer bootie smashed into the outside of his knee. His leg bent in as if that was the direction his knee was supposed to bend, sending him collapsing to the ground where he writhed in pain. One threat had been neutralized. He'd probably never walk right again, but decisions had consequences, something she'd recently been painfully reminded of.

"Pow!" squealed Evelyn.

Madeline had done that a thousand times to a pad at the gym, but boy was it satisfying to do it for real to someone who deserved it. The next assailant would get it in the groin. She was pleasantly surprised at her composure—you never know if you'll remain calm and remember your training or devolve into total panic when shit hits the fan.

She whipped around to face the other two, who were now advancing more cautiously in fighting stances of their own. She was level five in Krav Maga and knew the best way to defend against both an assailant with a knife and multiple attackers (other than running), but also knew the odds were not in her favor. Combat sports were segregated by sex and weight class for good reason.

Madeline motioned with her head to where she'd dropped her purse on the ground and yelled, "Take my purse. I'll throw in all the jewelry I'm wearing too. Please leave us alone."

"You're making this difficult. We don't want to hurt you or your daughters. We just want the device."

"Get your own damn device." She would have happily parted with any of her valuables. No amount of money was worth endangering herself or her family. But the glove was keeping her sane, and she had a visceral reaction to the thought of letting them get close enough to manhandle her and the girls.

The two men continued to move towards her. She kept moving backward through the trees, keeping them several paces away. Never let your opponent get within striking range, especially if they're stronger than you or have a weapon. She desperately needed something to change the situation.

Madeline glanced down the path in both directions, past the bench and the man clutching his broken knee. Still no one. Shit. For all she knew there were additional goons—whoever they were—out of sight, keeping people away. There were no weapons to improvise in her immediate vicinity beyond two half-eaten ice cream cones. The cast would probably increase the force of her left hand, though it may break what was underneath...

Madeline looked behind her—she was almost to the edge of the pond. They said they wanted the device, and there was a better way to determine if that was true without letting them touch her. Scorched earth it is. Her new plan would also hopefully discourage them from other nefarious intentions.

The look on the face of the knife-wielding man hinted he may have guessed her decision, but it was too late. She turned around and knelt, picked up one daughter with each arm, and jumped into the frigid water. It was only a few feet deep, so she squatted down, keeping her hands submerged.

"It's not waterproof and now it's broken!" she yelled to the men on the shore over the sounds of her daughters' complaints and the machine's buzzing. "Are you happy now?"

The two men looked at each other and exchanged some words she couldn't hear. Then they walked back to the path, collected their fallen comrade, and left, ignoring her purse. The loud buzzing sound stopped.

Madeline waded back to the shore and out of the pond. Her adrenaline rush faded and was replaced by the miserable feelings of cold and wet. She felt terrible that Evelyn and Christina couldn't replace or neutralize the negative sensations like she could. Or could she?

In the same way she'd learned to alter her mind's reality over the past few months, she tried to imagine she was warm and dry, standing at the pond's shore on a hot summer day. Nothing changed. At first she thought the fight and chilly water had jolted her into a state of complete wakefulness, but then realized the trees were not the green and brown of winter or the pink of spring, but the fiery red, orange, and gold of Japan's famous autumn foliage. Some of them were literally on fire.

The device had indeed given up the ghost.

She wanted to find the nearest police officer and report the attempted assault but needed to get back to the hotel and the other device before she further lost control. She could wear a beanie for a few days if need be. She would figure out what the fuck just happened when she was thinking straight.

"Mom I'm cold," said a shivering Christina.

"I'm so sorry sweetie, but we had to get away from the bad men. We'll get back to the hotel as fast as possible, and then

I'll get us all some hot chocolate."

"Are we still gonna go see the dragon?" asked Evelyn.

"We'll see."

They speedwalked out of the park with squishy shoes, leaving a trail of wet footprints and people staring at them in quiet disbelief. Madeline tried to ignore the rapidly changing shapes of the clouds overhead but knew there was now a full-scale naval battle transpiring between dozens of old pirate ships.

Fortunately the Tokyo Stasis Hotel was only a few blocks from the gardens. They were there after fifteen minutes of tromping past storefront holiday displays and equally colorful pachinko parlors. Enough water had dripped off them on the walk back to minimize the scene and mess they made as they strode through the grand lobby and into one of the elevators.

"I think a number is missing," said Evelyn, tugging on Madeline's sleeve.

"What's that?" asked Madeline.

Evelyn pointed at the elevator buttons and counted, unnecessarily starting from the beginning. "One, two, three, four, five, six, seven, eight, nine, ten, eleven, twelve, fourteen!"

"Yes, you're right. Good catch! People used to think the number thirteen was bad luck, so they skipped the thirteenth floor. Lots of buildings still do it out of tradition."

"How do they skip it? Is there a hole in the hotel?"

"They don't really skip it. They just change the number thirteen to fourteen."

"But isn't the fourteenth floor just the thirteenth floor?" chimed in Christina. Darwin had taught them well.

"Yes, that's right. People are silly."

Madeline entered the suite. The maids had come in and cleaned despite the do not disturb sign. Very un-*Suspended*

Animation Collection of them, but not worth complaining about. She didn't bother to remove any of her damp clothing and went straight to the bedroom. When she saw the nightstand, the composure she'd found during the fight and maintained since shattered and was replaced by panic.

The other, headset device Doctor Magnusson had given her wasn't there.

Outside the window, over the park and above the skyline, the pirate battle was over. Both sides lost. A jet-black kraken had emerged from where the sun was setting and began to consume the horizon.

"I'm terribly sorry about that, Missus Johnston," said the front desk receptionist over the phone. "I'll speak to house-keeping and have them look into it right away."

"Thanks," said Madeline, trying to remain calm after tearing the room apart looking for the device. But the scene across the room and out the window made it difficult to do anything but panic. She rushed over and closed the curtains.

"But mom, it was such a pretty sunset," said Christina.

"I'm sorry honey. The light was hurting my eyes."

"When do we get hot chocolate?" asked Evelyn.

"As soon as you shower and change into dry clothes," replied Madeline, realizing she should do the same. She went to the bedroom and stripped, showered, and donned clothes more appropriate for the real temperature outside.

"Have you found anything yet?" she asked the housekeeping manager after being transferred.

"I'm sorry ma'am, but our shift turned over after your room was serviced. The woman who cleaned it already left and is off for the next few days. I called her but am yet to hear back. We'll let you know when we do."

Madeline hung up without saying goodbye. She made another call.

"Room service. What can we get for you, Missus Johnston?"

"Three hot chocolates with extra marshmallows. One with peppermint schnapps. Make it a double." She needed to take the edge off, and didn't alcohol disrupt dreams? Perhaps it'd help with the hallucinations.

"Right away."

"Thanks."

Madeline noted the time. It was only five p.m., which meant Doctor Magnusson would likely still be at his office in Bangkok and working if...he hadn't moved his practice back to the Bay Area now that the modified Huxley procedure was legal in the US. That's right, he'd called her earlier. Stay calm. She had trouble thinking straight but her experience from the past several years meant she could still instantly convert any two time zones in her head; it was midnight on the West Coast. She doubted Doctor Magnusson was the kind of person to be awake at such an hour but then recalled that—like her—he only slept a few hours each night. And he *had* given her his cell number in case of emergencies. If this didn't count, nothing did.

His phone rang once, twice, three times. Madeline began to lose hope. Halfway through the fourth ring, he picked up and said in a hushed voice, "Hello, Madeline."

"Doctor Magnusson, I'm so happy you answered. I'm sorry for calling so late, but it's an emergency."

"There is no need to apologize. I put my patients' health above *everything*, including my own well-being." Doctor Magnusson spoke as if he was trying to ensure someone else didn't hear, which was reasonable given the hour. Perhaps he was somewhere visiting family for the holidays, if he did such a thing. But something in his voice sounded off. It could have just been that she was literally going crazy. "I presume your emergency has to do with the predicament to which my earlier message referred. I've spent much time thinking about—"

"Yes, exactly. I'm glad you've put so much work into this and may have found a permanent solution, but I need something as soon as possible. Ideally today. The devices no longer work."

"I don't suppose the devices stopped working on their own?"

"No, I broke one and the other is missing." Why would he assume that?

"I see, I see. That is indeed...disturbing news. No need to explain further. I'm going to refer you to a facility in Tokyo that should be able to provide you with something to hold you over until you get back. I'll text you the name. They'll be expecting you. In the meantime watch out..." his voice was drowned out by what sounded like screeching tires in the background before coming back with a sense of urgency, "...take a double dose of the supplements I gave you and please *be careful,* Madeline. Take a taxi, preferably one not arranged by your hotel. Do not walk or drive."

"Thank you. But what do you mean? Why would—"

"I'm afraid I have to run." He hung up the phone.

Madeline replayed the conversation in her mind, and although it was like looking through a thick screen of smoke and water vapor, she was left with the conclusion that Doctor Magnusson had sounded scared. Thus she was relieved when a text came through a few minutes later from the doctor with the name of a sleep specialist. He was in the Shibuya district, open until six, and able to squeeze her in at the end of the day. She could make it if she left right away. Things might not be as dire as she'd thought.

Someone knocked at the door, startling her.

"Girls, get in the bedroom," commanded Madeline. They obliged without complaining, and she closed the door once they were inside. She slowly approached the suite's entrance then opened it a crack. It was room service with the hot chocolate. Damn, that was fast. Probably making up for the housekeeping snafu.

"Just leave it on the floor and I'll get it when dressed," Madeline said.

"No problem, ma'am," the man replied, though he lingered longer than expected. Madeline fished a thousand-yen bill from her wallet and handed it through the door's opening. "Thank you so much," he said before leaving. She opened the door and glanced both directions down the hall. Like earlier, there was no one. Did he run after dropping off the tray? How was he already out of sight? Perhaps he'd ducked into another room. Not worth worrying about right now.

"You can come out. The hot chocolate is here," Madeline called to Christina and Evelyn. "Now, mom has to go run an important errand that just came up."

"Is it because of the bad guys in the park?" asked Christina.

"Yes, it's related to that. I'm not sure how long it will take, but it's very important you be good girls while I'm gone. I don't have time to get someone to come watch you." Leaving them alone for up to a few hours was irresponsible, but all things considered it was probably safer for them to stay here right now. "No matter what, don't answer the door. If someone knocks just pretend there's no one home. We'll go get whatever you want for dinner as soon as I'm back, and in the meantime you can watch any movie you choose."

"*Spirited Away!*" volunteered Evelyn. Christina agreed.

"If you really want to watch that again, then so be it."

Madeline set up the movie and scoured the suite to ensure the girls would be safe in her absence while chugging her spiked hot chocolate. The drink tasted real enough, and the girls certainly seemed to enjoy theirs. When she'd convinced herself they'd be fine, she gave her daughters a prolonged hug.

"Mom why are you crying?" asked Christina.

"I'm not," replied Madeline, wiping a tear from under her eye. "I love you and I'll be back soon."

"What are you looking at?" asked Evelyn.

"Nothing, sweetie," said Madeline. She needed to get moving; her eyes already were, rapidly.

Madeline verified Christina properly locked the deadbolt behind her, standing on a chair to do so, and that the do not disturb light was activated, though apparently that didn't mean much around here. She took the elevator down and entered the crowded, festive lobby but stopped when she heard the piano player.

It couldn't be.

She longed for the device to warn her when hallucinations crept into her awareness, but she knew for herself it wasn't real after getting a better view; it was the man from her daydreams earlier, playing...

Dun, dun-dun-dun.

Flustered, she ignored him and strode through the rest of the lobby, outside, and past the lines of taxis and valets. She'd been given some advice about them by the doctor but couldn't quite recall what it was.

The rush hour traffic was at a standstill. Shit. The subway was probably the fastest way to get there, but the thought of cramming into the crowded metro was maddening. She double-checked the directions on her phone. It was only a half-hour walk if she cut through Yoyogi Park. She'd be there in time, and the cold, fresh air felt good. What had Doctor Magnusson said?

An indeterminate amount of time later, Madeline stood mesmerized beneath a canopy of blue Christmas lights. They happily obscured the starless night sky; she wasn't sure if its blackness stemmed from light pollution or something more sinister. Her breath materialized in front of her, then spiraled and transformed into fantastical and infinitely interesting shapes and scenes.

Someone bumped into her hard, causing her to realize she stood in the middle of a bustling holiday attraction. She should find somewhere out of the way. As Madeline sat down at a bench in the darkness, beneath a canopy of trees, she couldn't shake the feeling there was something she was supposed to do, or not do, but for the life of her could not remember was it was. It was like trying to recall a days-old dream.

But perhaps that's all it was...just a dream.

Chapter 16: Darwin

Darwin's fucking head hurt. So did his sinuses. He had a distinct memory of feeling something like this the morning after Balthazar had kept him up all night doing cocaine once in college. Never again. But what *had* happened last night? And where was he?

He sat up in bed and surveyed the empty hotel room. Fancy. Then he lifted the covers and looked at himself. Also fancy, but disheveled. He wore a wrinkled dress shirt tucked into wrinkled slacks that ended in his colorful, lucky socks. Ostensibly he didn't believe in luck, only probability, but even he had a few small superstitions that he told himself were just for fun. He also still wore his watch, which told him it was already eleven o'clock in the morning. Fortunately Mofongo had a doggy door to take herself out.

There was a note on the nightstand, written in perfect cursive. Darwin hadn't used cursive in twenty years. It read: 'Darwin, thanks for the lovely evening and stimulating conversation. Next time we'll skip the zivania. Hopefully your head doesn't hurt too much. I took off your shoes after you passed out. Nice socks. I wanted to remove the rest of your clothes too but resisted the temptation ;). I dreamt about you, by the way. You can guess what happened. Sorry for the disappearing act. This may sound crazy, but I had to check out and fly home on short notice. I'll let you know next time I'm in town and tell you the story then. -Sephira. P.S. I decided you lost the bet. Make sure you get enough sleep and keep thinking about it. Next time it's double or nothing.'

Various jumbled scenes from the prior evening flashed through his mind, like someone cut up a film reel into different sized pieces, discarded half, and reassembled the rest in random order. The zivania explained the headache, though he didn't remember having enough to feel as shambled as he did. And maybe he was getting sick, which would explain the insane pressure in his sinuses. It *was* that time of year. The note brought back parts of their conversation, like the silly bet and discussion about dreams, but everything after the second shot was blurry. He certainly didn't remember coming back to her room but was glad nothing had happened now that he was sober.

Would he have gone through with it? Could he have in that state? He wasn't sure he could have forgiven himself. Blackouts were terrifying—a friend on the football team in college came out of one to find himself in a jail cell and facing a manslaughter charge. Got into a fight and killed a guy. Didn't remember a thing and spent ten years in prison. Ruined his whole life.

Darwin donned his shoes and jacket, took a piss, blew his nose. He was somewhat alarmed to see blood come out, but at least it was from the latter, not the former. He took the elevator down to the lobby. The Christmas decorations were over the top and impressive. He must not have noticed them the prior evening because he was so nervous and distracted from—

Michael!

His pace picked up as he exited the hotel and headed to the back of the building. It was a gray morning and would probably start raining any minute. He rounded the corner, expecting to confront the same abject scene from his memory, but there was nothing of the sort—no tents, no discarded needles, no human feces. No Michael. But there *was* one person who looked like they might be able to tell him where he'd gone.

"Excuse me, officer," said Darwin as he approached the parked SFPD car. He felt a little silly with his wrinkled shirt and pants, unkempt hair, and dried bloody nose, like some kind of walk of shame.

The officer saw him, then rolled down the window and asked, "What seems to be the problem?"

"There was a homeless camp here just last night. Do you know what happened?"

"The city cleared it early this morning. There are more storms and cold weather in the forecast, not to mention all the complaints from the neighbors."

"What happened to the people who lived there?"

"Some get escorted to various places. Shelters, hotels, hospitals, jails. Others just wander off."

"Alright, thanks."

"No problem. Merry Christmas," said the officer, rolling up her window as the first raindrop fell on his head.

Darwin resigned himself to figure it out later. For now he needed to get home, shower, and nap. He felt like he hadn't slept at all.

The scorching air shimmered above the golden dunes that extended to the horizon in every direction. The sky was pure blue except for the angry, white-yellow sun. Fortunately the freight train Darwin rode atop was moving at such a speed that it created a light breeze. It reminded him of the Mauritania Railway, the backbone of the Sahara, that carried the longest and heaviest trains in the world over four hundred miles for twenty hours from the iron mines to the Atlantic coast. What an adventure that had been.

But this wasn't exactly like that. Come to think of it, Darwin didn't have the slightest idea where he was. He still wore his wrinkled slacks and dress shirt, but nothing was familiar aside from that. Well, he may have been lost and sweating, but at least his head and face no longer hurt.

A billowing tower of smoke rose a few hundred feet ahead. The black snake of the train wound through the desert in the other direction for as long as the featureless dunes, which weren't quite golden now that he took a harder look. The right term to describe their color failed to come to mind.

He seemed to be the lone rider on top of the freight cars—the lone person anywhere—and made his way forward towards where the passenger cars likely were. The cars' tops were open but filled to the brim with what felt like small, tightly packed rocks, covered by ash-colored tarps. They were also close enough that he could jump from car to car.

Darwin took the first few cars slowly and carefully, then got the hang of it and worked up to a light jog. But as he neared the locomotive, he began to doubt the train included passenger cars at all. The sun's position told him it was around the middle of the afternoon, and he had no idea how many hours remained in the journey. For as hot as it was now, it could get below freezing overnight in the desert, and he didn't want to spend it outside on the top of a moving train.

And what was this train moving, by the way? The cargo

underfoot felt and sounded different than anything he'd encountered when on a similar adventure during the year spent traveling before grad school. Maybe it would give him a clue as to where the train was going. He knelt and unfastened the tarp from one corner, then stumbled and almost fell off the train when he pulled it back and sunlight sparkled on what was beneath.

Diamonds. The entire car was full of diamonds, cut and polished to perfection and scintillating in the bright desert sunshine.

He scooped up a handful, letting most fall through his fingers, then examined those that remained in his palm. They seemed real. He often complained that diamonds, more expensive by weight than plutonium or heroin, were nothing but compressed carbon, obnoxiously overvalued by an industry built entirely on marketing and a greedy cartel that artificially restricted supply. But he'd begrudgingly educated himself and shelled out a significant portion of his life's savings at the time to buy one for Madeline because that's what she wanted and it made her happy. He'd even paid extra for one created from captured carbon instead of mined. He knew a high quality rock when he saw one.

His heart started to race—the cargo of all the dozen cars he'd crossed so far had felt the same. He refastened the tarp, resisting the urge to pocket the fortune contained in just one handful, and jumped to the next car ahead of him. When he lifted the tarp, he was surprised to find not diamonds but the deep green of emeralds. He repeated the process for the six cars remaining between him and the engine. Sapphires. Rubies. Amethyst. Opals. Topaz. Jade. Each car was nearly overflowing with a different gemstone. What the hell kind of train was this?

His excitement turned to fear when he understood the implications of the train's value. It was worth trillions of dollars, setting aside the catastrophic effect on price such a massive influx of supply would have. Shouldn't there be security? Surely he wasn't supposed to be here.

The locomotive's horn startled him, so loud it reverberated in his bones. He lost his balance and stumbled over the edge, taking with him jade worth many thousands of dollars. Darwin twisted as he fell and extended both arms, barely catching himself on the side of the car, where he hung by sweaty hands. He looked ahead, past the black engine, and was confronted by a new problem even greater than the threat of the train's security or falling off and being marooned.

It was either a mirage, or the desert wasn't nearly as vast as he thought.

A wall of iridescence extended from the sand a few hundred feet in front of the train, up past the horizon, and into the sky forever. Behind it was...what? He couldn't tell. It was distinct from the heat haze above the dunes in the other directions. And there was no tunnel, either. The train was heading right for the (solid?) wall at full speed.

The horn screamed again, rattling his brain but not his grip. He pulled himself back up on top of the car and had to make one of two mutually exclusive choices: run forward to the engine to try and somehow stop this behemoth or run backward to get away from the impact, if that's what was indeed about to happen. It would be impossible to materially reduce the train's speed before reaching the shimmery barrier. Best to put as much space between himself and the crash site as possible.

He was at a full run when the train's horn sounded a third time. Out of curiosity he stopped and turned to look forward.

There were about twenty cars ahead of him now. The tower of black smoke had almost reached the wall. End of the line.

From this distance Darwin would see, feel, then hear the impact. He definitely didn't want to wait for the second one. He glanced at the sand rushing by ten feet below and was thankful it sloped downward, away from the tracks. He looked forward again just in time to see the first freight car buckle and start to rise at a crazy angle. He jumped and orchestrated something of a clumsy roll when he hit the ground.

The crash was even louder than the horn and continued for ages as each car in the endless train smashed into the one in front of it. After crumpling to various degrees, the cars veered left, right, or up to expend the remaining energy before further crashing and extending the cacophony. The final sound was billions of tiny, colorful gemstones raining down from the sky.

Darwin found himself sitting in the shade. The car he'd jumped from had barely crumpled then went straight vertical, its rear coming forward to form a right angle with the tracks. It balanced precariously on its face, blocking the sun behind it, then began to creak and lean in his direction. Not good given how close he still was to the tracks.

The car was much longer than it was wide, so he moved parallel to the tracks, hoping it meant a shorter distance to get out of its way. Scrambling through the thick, baked sand was difficult, but he soon emerged from the shadow and into the sunlight a moment before the car slammed into where he'd just been, showering him in yellow-green stones that looked like peridot.

Darwin's labored breath was now the only sound as he surveyed the outrageous scene of destruction and magnificence that extended in both directions. Most of the cars had fallen off the tracks in one way or another. Many had tipped over. An extended rainbow of glittering gemstones carpeted the ground. They were technically only mineral crystals or rocks with primarily aesthetic value, but it was difficult not to be captivated.

Then the sky drew his attention away from the ground; the sun was sinking towards the horizon at an alarming pace. The Earth usually rolled away from its star at about a thousand miles per hour this close to the equator. Darwin wasn't sure who or what to thank for relativity—god? Einstein? The universe itself?—and that we can't feel the planet spinning, but the sun's current movement implied the Earth's rotation was accelerating, possibly at such a speed for the centrifugal force to exceed the planet's gravity and fling everything off into space. But all he felt was the declining temperature as the sun disappeared behind the dunes. It seemed some laws of physics and thermodynamics still applied, while others did not.

Darwin's suspicion that he may have been on a different planet and maybe in a different universe was confirmed when the sky turned starless and so dark it looked Vantablack, the darkest human-made substance, which used vertical nan-otubes to trap light instead of reflecting it. But he could still see, which brought his attention back to the ground and the rainbow of light emitted from the glowing, scattered gems. They created a miles-long river of polychromatic light following the railroad tracks, segmented into colors based on what type of jewel each car carried but with some overlapping and mixing into new hues.

And it wasn't just the gemstones from the train that shined—all of the sand faintly illuminated the night. He could make out the dunes' outline in the distance against the complete absence of light behind them, like negative silhouettes. He picked up a handful of still-warm sand and examined it flowing through his fingers, each grain a different shade. It seemed comprised of much smaller and less radiant versions of the jewels carried by the train.

A sound behind him broke the silence. He turned to find the first living thing he'd seen since arriving here: a translucent, bioluminescent sidewinder snake slithering towards him in the relative darkness. The desert life must have been coming out to hunt now that the temperature had cooled. Darwin scrambled to his feet and followed the rainbow road towards where the engine had hit the strange wall, glancing over his shoulder every several steps to ensure he stayed far ahead of the serpent.

He expected to find a gruesome scene as he approached the destroyed locomotive—surely the driver hadn't survived the crash. But instead he found no signs there had been an engineer at all. Perplexed, he went to examine the barrier with which the train had collided. It was like walking up to the edge of a flat world. The glowing sand abruptly ended in total darkness. He extended his hand into an invisible wall that felt like glass, no longer iridescent in the sunlight, but much stronger; the train hadn't caused any cracks or dents whatsoever.

A similar sound to the sidewinder snake caught his attention again, only it was farther away and getting much louder. He turned around to see that the winding river of gems and light was now flowing away from the edge of the world. In the distance was a growing vortex of sand into which the jewels were falling, taking their light with them, as if one of the sandworms from *Dune* was about to emerge.

The vortex expanded at an accelerating rate in all directions.

Darwin frantically searched for something on the wall to hold onto and avoid getting sucked down, but it was as smooth and featureless as it was inscrutable. Gems, sand, ruined train cars—the entire world—was now flowing into the whirlpool and disappearing into nothing. Darwin slid down towards the darkness where he was sure he'd be crushed, suffocated, or both. For this was not a world at all, but an hourglass whose time had run out.

And so had his.

Darwin had had some crazy, anxiety-ridden hangover dreams in his day—Sunday nights after bachelor parties when going through minor withdrawal symptoms. But never any that seemed that real. He was disappointed the nap hadn't done anything to alleviate the pain in his head and face, but at least he was no longer tired. He actually felt remarkably refreshed for only having dozed off for one hour on the dot.

He had no new messages, which wasn't surprising, except there was a voicemail from the prior evening. That's right; he'd forgotten. He absent-mindedly pressed play, expecting to hear the intro of some recorded or rehearsed sales pitch and immediately delete. Instead he sat up in alarm at the familiar sound of the voice.

It was Doctor Gregory Huxley.

But while his voice was familiar, the tone and cadence were unlike anything Darwin had heard from him in the thousand hours they'd spent conversing.

The message's content was even more disturbing.

Chapter 17: Madeline

The light changed, and the waves of people crossed the street and crashed into each other like The Great Wave off Kanagawa. Despite being enveloped by a sea of humanity, Madeline was alone in the boat and about to be capsized by the rogue wave. Hadn't she always loved the anonymity and loneliness of Tokyo's crowds? She didn't know. There was very little she knew at this point.

It could have been early morning, or late night, or high noon. In a way it was all of these things; the time of day changed whenever she blinked. A different scene awaited her each time she opened her eyes: bright winter sun, neon flashing lights against a dark sky, or something in between. She'd tried keeping her eyes closed but now made her blinks as brief as possible and kept her eyes open until the last tear evaporated and they felt about to bleed.

Anything was preferable to what was emblazoned on the inside of her eyelids.

The world around her looked like Shibuya Crossing, Tokyo's Times Square, but she wasn't sure. She'd tried asking the apparition of the faces in the crowd many times where she was, but it was as if they all wore the expressionless masks of geisha. She'd given up. Besides, what good was knowing where you were if you didn't know where you were from or going? It was as if all the thousands of dreams she'd had over the past several months, intentionally or not, had equal standing with reality. It was hard enough to tell what was real in this crazy city. Her life on the true plane of existence was now but one gossamer strand in an enormous, entangled web.

Madeline tried to keep the concept of a web out of her mind as her eyes began to burn. She needed to blink soon and knew who—or what—awaited her. She decided to try a different strategy: a deeper, intentional blink that would hopefully let her go longer before the next one. She gathered her resolve and closed her eyes.

They were getting closer.

She snapped her eyelids open and found it was now night. The city had taken on a cyberpunk aesthetic, like the Neo-Tokyo of *Akira*. Bright, colorful signs conveyed disconcertingly specific messages to her in a mix of English and Japanese. But one half of the sky was not dark. The Mount Fuji in the background of The Great Wave, inexplicably visible through a gap in the towering skyscrapers, now resembled something more like Mount Doom. It spewed an inverted cone of lava and ash, flickered with lightning, so that the picturesque volcano and its plume created a terrible hourglass.

And Madeline was no longer the only person who saw it.

The streets, like the volcano, erupted into chaos. She instinctively fled in the opposite direction of the mountain but found it difficult to keep her balance. At first it seemed the stampede of people was so great that it shook the very ground, but then the road buckled, and a fissure appeared under where a few unfortunate people at the wrong place and time did the opposite. Windows shattered—it was an earthquake. Madeline kept to the middle of the street in an attempt to avoid the broken glass and other debris shedding from the buildings but soon recognized that wasn't the only danger of death from above.

Scoria, ash, and fire began raining down from the sky. Events had turned so horrible so fast it almost didn't seem real, but the smoke that stung her lungs and eyes felt authentic enough. She was forced to blink, but at least the scene inside her eyes was no longer any more terrifying than the outside world.

It was close to daylight when she opened her eyes, but the illumination only made things worse. It highlighted just how much blood was in her vicinity, how much ash in the sky. A burning, car-sized boulder smashed into the street a few dozen feet ahead of her. The convincing scene of fiery gore and destruction left in its wake dispelled any remaining thoughts that this may have been some grand illusion.

Madeline was in a catch-22; she could take shelter from the falling wreckage, but only at the risk of getting crushed in a collapsing building, which were now plentiful. She was saved from having to make such a fateful choice by the distant pyroclastic flow racing up the street. Remaining outside meant she'd end up like the corpses of Pompeii, or worse.

She frenziedly searched for somewhere to take cover from the approaching wall of death and saw someone across the street waving at her. It was a gentle movement, like one would make to another who expected to see them. A gap in the smoke, snowing ash, and stream of panicked strangers rushing past gave her a better view of who it was. Perhaps there was a good reason why this man was the only person to take any notice of her.

It was Elias Sultana.

Seeing him under different circumstances would have caused one of many emotions, none of them relief. But something about his calm demeanor and familiar, handsome face amidst such utter pandemonium gave her hope. She looked up to ensure there were no imminently falling rocks, down the street to wait for a gap in the people hopelessly trying to outrun the mix of blistering gas and lava moving hundreds of miles per hour, then sprinted across the trembling street.

By the time she got there, Elias was holding a thick door open for her, and without hesitation she went inside and down the few stairs. Elias followed her in, then closed and secured the door. People outside banged on it, begging to be let in, but they were soon drowned out by the sounds of bells and whistles and the clinking of thousands of tiny metal balls.

It was the distinctive cacophony of a vast pachinko parlor.

A few dozen of the colorful, flashing machines were occupied by people who seemed to have no idea that something resembling the biblical end-times was happening just outside. How could they? The ground didn't shake, and the tsunami of fire that must have already consumed everything overhead apparently didn't penetrate the arcade at the end of the world. The room was smoky, but here the source was the cigarettes being prolifically smoked by the parlor's patrons. And, somewhere amidst the burning tobacco was a hint of another familiar scent that further helped her relax: lavender.

"Take a seat, Miss Johnston," said Elias in his unique accent, holding out a blue basket filled with chrome. "Or is it Lockhart now? Either way, your first five hundred balls are on us."

She didn't know what to say other than 'thanks' as she sat down at the nearest open pachinko machine. But she didn't feel like playing. She was exhausted now that the adrenaline was fading and yearned to do nothing but close her eyes and rest. Elias had removed his jacket, and underneath it wore what appeared to be the same dress shirt as last time she saw him, with the sleeves similarly rolled up. On the flexed forearm offering the basket of tiny metal balls was the dreamcatcher tattoo. Madeline smiled resignedly, shook her head, closed her eyes. She should have known.

The scene that awaited her wasn't unlike the one she left behind. Inscribed on the inside of her eyelids was a cosmic, knotted web. A kind of dreamcatcher, she now supposed. Flayed, humanoid creatures gradually struggled and crawled their way through the strands towards her with mechanical movements. She opened her eyes and blinked rapidly several times, turning the scene into a kind of stop-motion animation lit by a strobe light. It was as she suspected: In between blinks these strange beings went into a sort of *suspended animation*. They would surely make it to her with her eyes shut for an extended period, but she no longer had the strength to keep them open.

Madeline closed her eyes and gave in to sleep.

Chapter 18: Darwin

"Let me get this straight," said the officer, "an exotic, beautiful young woman lured you to her room in one of the nicest hotels in the city and performed a very expensive and in-demand medical procedure on you against your will?"

"I know it sounds crazy," said Darwin, becoming more and more flummoxed. Falling into a honey trap was embarrassing enough without this treatment. "But yes, that's essentially what happened."

"Sounds like I need to get on these dating apps," said the other officer. They both laughed. "I got a friend who mortgaged his house to have that procedure done. And what exactly was the pretense for your meeting this...Sephira...in the first place?"

"It was a date." They looked unconvinced. It probably sounded like an escort service.

"To confirm—you're married, Mister Johnston?"

"Technically yes, but we're in the process of getting divorced. Well, maybe. The date was just exploratory. But that's not important."

"If you say so."

"Sephira, or whoever else may have joined her, didn't just perform the modified Huxley procedure," said Darwin. "I think they may have applied radiation to cause additional changes. It took effect immediately."

"So...a kind of modified, modified Huxley procedure?"

"Yes."

"And why do you think she—or they, whoever they are—would go through the immense trouble of doing such a thing?"

"I'm not entirely sure, but I do have an idea. Listen to this." He placed his phone on the table in speaker mode and played Doctor Huxley's voicemail. Darwin had to admit it sounded like a rambling madman, not unlike how he probably sounded. The two officers listened with raised eyebrows.

"Darwin, it's Greg. I didn't want it to be like this. No, not like this. I wanted to talk, to hear your questions, to help me figure it out. You always had the most insightful questions. In all my years teaching you were my brightest student. So bright. I'm sorry how things turned out. So sorry. I offered to list you as a co-author, but you balked, then walked. You knew how things worked. Always the idealist. But things are not ideal, especially now, which is why I'm calling.

"I don't know how or why they did it, but I do know what they did. Irradiated my brain. The effect is...troubling. Very troubling. We knew—*you* knew—of the danger to those who'd undergone the procedure. Iatrogenesis. Now I'm in danger, including from myself. Mostly from myself. Others are likely in danger too, including you, I think, because of your knowledge. So much knowledge. I suspect they'd rather let us kill ourselves than trigger murder investigations, but I don't know their limits. Be careful, and wary of going to the police in your own investigation. They warned me, like I'm warning you. They're probably watching. I know they're watching me, monitoring my accounts, my old phone. Just leaving this message could get me killed. I'm tired, Darwin. Too old for this. I just want to sleep. Be wary of sleeping, too.

"Now, the important question—who are they? I have my suspicions, yes. I've encountered them before, over the years. The dream harvesters. The sandmen. Dreams and oneiromancy have played a role in nearly all major religions, but not like this. I never imagined they had such resources, like this. I can't stand to dream any longer with this imagination, but I'm just so tired, like there's sand in my eyes, and I don't have the resources to stay…" Several seconds of silence followed, then the sound of soft snoring for several more until the message ended.

The two officers looked at each other. One asked, "Whose voice is that?"

"Greg. Sorry, *the* Doctor Gregory Huxley," said Darwin.

"The guy who invented the procedure?"

"Actually…I invented it, but he was my advisor."

"Are you a doctor, Mister Johnston?"

"No. Well, I almost was."

"What did you say you do for work?"

"I'm not currently working. I'm a stay-at-home dad."

"Right. So you aren't a doctor, and you haven't been to one, but you know the procedure was performed on you because you invented it. Forgive my skepticism, but you sure don't look like someone who underwent brain surgery last night."

"It's endoscopy. They go in through the nose so there's no scar. My nose has been bleeding all day. I tried to get ahold of Greg after I heard the voicemail, but his phone was off. Is off. Then I came straight here." Darwin started to regret his order of operations. Maybe he should have followed his initial instincts and gone to the ER instead of making an appointment for tomorrow.

"Mister Johnston, if we were to give you a drug test right now, what would it show? And please keep your eyes focused on us."

"What? Why would..." Darwin's pulse and mind began racing. It was likely he had been drugged the prior night, which could corroborate his story. But then he remembered the tiger. And the spiked cigarette. How long did DMT stay in your system? He'd also taken some of Madeline's leftover Vicodin from the medicine cabinet after getting home from the hotel. It was technically illegal to take without a prescription, but he was in so much damn pain. And what was that sound? It was like a freight train whistle. He'd had bouts of tinnitus before but never anything like this. It made his head throb even more and made it impossible to think straight. "Do you guys hear that?"

The officers looked at each other again. "Did you drive here today, Mister Johnston?"

"No, I took an Uber."

"How about this—you go home, get some rest, then make an appointment to see a doctor. Leave us your information along with that of this Greg fellow, and we'll look into it and get back to you if we find anything interesting."

Darwin was glad for the chance to end the interrogation he'd led himself into and get away from the two skeptical cops and whatever that damn sound was. He wrote down the information, thanked them for their time, and tried calling Doctor Huxley again once he was out of the station.

"We're sorry, you have reached a number that has been disconnected or is no longer in service. If you feel you have reached this recording in error, please check the number and try your call again."

Fuck. What was he going to do? He needed a plan.

It was the middle of the afternoon, but the clouds were already growing dark. It was only a few days until the winter solstice but still, the sun shouldn't set at three. Maybe the sky was just dark with a coming downpour. He needed to get home before that started. It was a thirty-minute walk, but the cold, fresh air would do him good.

Several houses already had their Christmas lights turned on, shining like radiant gemstones in the dim light. Darwin fixated on them until a car's horn—louder than a bomb—startled him back to his surroundings to find himself standing in the middle of the road. He awkwardly held up a hand in apology and retreated to the sidewalk. Get it together, Dar.

The horn's echo finally stopped ringing in his ears when it was overtaken by the wail of an approaching siren. It was soon followed by other sirens in the distance, creating a kind of catastrophe symphony in surround sound. Darwin covered his ears with both hands and turned to watch a firetruck approach, its lights flashing like the glowing rubies and diamonds from his dream. The blue-shifted soundwaves increased in pitch unbearably until the engine zoomed by and the Doppler shift flipped to the other end of the spectrum, stretching out the frequency and lowering the siren's pitch.

The truck continued straight for several more blocks before making a right. Darwin tried to guess where it was going and looked ahead from where it had turned. A column of smoke rose in the distance, swirling upwards and blending in with the dark sky. After staring at the smoke for a few seconds, he realized the fire must be disconcertingly close to home.

A block later he'd broken into a jog, and he covered the last five blocks of the journey at as close to a full sprint as he could muster. His watch warned him that his heartrate was dangerously high.

As he passed the other houses on his street, a new sound overwhelmed that of the sirens' echoes, his labored breath, and his heavy footsteps: the roaring of fire.

Darwin stopped and stared in disbelief at the inferno that had utterly engulfed his house. Initially he was too shocked to act, but then he snapped to and frantically scanned the small crowd assembled. A conspicuous absence caused whatever adrenaline he had left to get dumped into his system: Mofongo.

Even from the curb the heat was intense, like the angry sun of the hourglass desert. Even the men in protective gear battling the blaze kept their distance. But Darwin threw caution to the scorching wind and attempted to run past them and into the house. He was forced to retreat when a blast from the garage—the extra propane tanks?—knocked him to the ground, where he rolled wildly to extinguish his burning coat.

Hopeless and helpless, he rose to his knees in the driveway, pulling out what remained of his singed hair, and watched the flames lick the approaching night. The thick tendrils of smoke were the color of Vantablack, so dark that they looked two-dimensional.

He no longer heard anything at all.

Chapter 19: Madeline

There is no way to escape, no respite from thinking. The brain is always on, always active, whether awake or asleep, although the line between the two has blurred beyond recognition. Dreamless sleep is what I long for more than anything. A chance to truly rest.

Is there an alternative? Yes, I suppose there is. A state entirely devoid of brain activity. But is it within my control to achieve? What if...no, don't think like that. Don't give up or in. As someone, though I don't remember who, once said: Think of the perseverance and resilience of non-human animals in the face of unfathomable hardships. Bide your time. Avoiding ruin is paramount in game theory. Quitting the game entirely cancels all possible future upside. You must survive.

You never know what the next spin of the wheel will bring.

Chapter 20: Darwin

Darwin knelt and picked up a handful of warm ashes. Which of his family's possessions did they use to be? He let them run through his fingers like he'd done with the sand in the dream that for some damn reason he couldn't shake from his mind despite how long ago it seemed and how much more important his present concerns were. Reality was now the implausible nightmare, and his time in *this* world was running out.

The rain had helped extinguish the blaze, and the firefighters had saved the neighboring houses. Darwin's home, his family's home, was not so lucky. He doubted anything was recoverable. He wandered along the outskirts of the charred remains of his life, beyond the investigation's perimeter. He suspected the pain in his head and face had spread, but at the moment he was numb. Pockets of smoldering embers and a few flashlights illuminated the dark husk of the house. Every additional minute they spent digging, he feared they'd come across the burnt skeleton of a dog. He wiped his hands on his already destroyed slacks.

"Mister Johnston," said a faint voice.

Where was he going to go? What was he going to do? The house was insured, of course, but this new chapter in his life was truly starting from a blank page. And Darwin was writing with a pen low on ink.

"Mister Johnston," said a louder voice. This time it came with a strong hand on his shoulder and caught his attention. He looked up into the face of a fireman who was older and wiser than the calendar-type guys who'd manned the hoses. It was the fire investigator who'd interviewed him earlier. The entire day had been filled with questions.

"Sorry, my hearing is still recovering from the blast," said Darwin.

"No problem. As I told you earlier, that was a brave thing you tried to do. Stupid, but brave. We've done a first pass and haven't found any remains. None of the neighbors I interviewed remember seeing, um…"

"Mofongo, like the Puerto Rican dish. We let our youngest daughter name her after a family vacation. They're delicious. You should try one if you haven't."

"Yes, Mofongo. It's possible she escaped through the doggy door and then the burning fence. If she's scared or injured she could be running or hiding. I've seen pets come back days later."

"Thanks," said Darwin, reminding himself not to get his hopes up.

"I also found this," the fire investigator said, holding up a safe. The outside seemed unscathed enough that presumably the contents were undamaged. He *had* paid extra for some level of fire protection. "The fire is still under investigation, so I can't let you take it with you unless I see what's inside."

"Sure, no problem." Darwin used his ash-stained hands to enter the combination. He opened the safe to reveal a Glock-17, a full clip of ammo, two passports, and five thousand dollars in cash. He forced a sheepish smile at the investigator.

"What are you, a secret agent?"

"I'd tell you but uh..."

"It's probably better you don't finish that sentence."

"Right. Any idea how the fire started? Was it the Christmas tree? I left the lights on but wasn't gone that long and—"

"The fire is still under investigation, so I'm not able to disclose any preliminary thoughts on cause or motive."

"Motive? You mean it may have been arson?" Doctor Huxley's message came to mind. Darwin thought he'd already completed a blackout on the bingo card of negative feelings but discovered there was still an open square.

"We investigate every fire as if it could be. I'm not able to share my thoughts with you at this time. I'm sure you understand."

It dawned on Darwin that he was technically a suspect. He asked, "Why would I burn down my own..." before further re-alizing that he couldn't have been the first estranged husband to burn down, or hire someone else to burn down, the family home for insurance money. Best to stop pushing the issue.

The fire investigator continued, "I do have one more ques-tion—do you know anyone who drives a black SUV? One of the neighbors reported seeing one parked out front shortly before the fire broke out."

"Um...no, I don't think so. No."

"Thanks for your cooperation. We're going to seal off the scene, call it a night, and come back and continue the investigation first thing tomorrow morning when there's more light. We should be able to hand the property back to you after that. Do you have somewhere you can go tonight? Someone you call? We can give you a ride if need be. I'm afraid your car was ruined, along with everything else in the garage."

"Yeah, I'll figure it out, don't worry."

"Ok. Once again, I'm sorry for your loss, Mister Johnston. Try and get some sleep if you can. We should be able to release the property back to you around lunch tomorrow."

Darwin walked out to the street and past the remaining fire engine, police car, and handful of lingering gawkers. At least the media truck was gone, and the ambulance had left empty. His injuries were minor enough to be treated at the scene, and no one else was harmed. No other person, that is. Should he call Madeline to tell her and the girls? What time was it in Tokyo? Simple math was impossible. Best to wait until tomorrow when he'd have more answers. Hopefully she wouldn't find out from another source before then.

At first he thought he was wandering aimlessly, admiring the Christmas lights that shone like the jewels in the dream that HE COULD NOT GET OUT OF HIS HEAD. Every few blocks he got the strange sensation of being followed, or thought he heard a sidewinder snake slithering up behind him. But when he looked over his shoulder, he saw only wet, empty streets.

After about thirty minutes he understood where he'd been subconsciously heading. Darwin wasn't sure why he was going there. Maybe the day's events had made him wary of asking for help from the authorities. Maybe he wanted to be alone and have time to think. Maybe it was because his good friends were either out of town visiting still-living families for the holidays or had moved out of San Francisco over the past several years in a kind of diaspora to places they could better afford to start and raise families. Or, just maybe, Preston owed it to him.

He walked up the steps to the small townhouse his soon-to-be-ex-brother-in-law kept in the city. It was ostensibly a place to crash after late client dinners and meetings instead of 'boozing and cruising' forty-five minutes or more down to Palo Alto only to turn around and come back the next morning. Darwin didn't doubt it was used for that, and although he'd never seen any evidence, he'd always wondered if it was also used for other, more clandestine meetings. He pretended to stoop down and find the hide-a-key, then whipped around to catch whoever he was sure was spying on him.

A dog, standing in the darkness at the bottom of the stairs and looking up at him with something between trepidation and expectation. On further inspection, his dog. Mofongo must have confirmed it was him at the same time because her tail started wagging like he'd never seen before. Darwin knelt as she bounded up the stairs. He could not remember the last time he cried. Even the separation from Madeline hadn't spurred the kind of overwhelming emotional response to bring him to tears. But they streaked down his dirty face as he embraced an uninjured Mofongo.

The day was still a complete disaster, but it wasn't quite the raging dumpster fire he'd thought. Many of his incinerated possessions had held sentimental value, but the only thing that truly couldn't be replaced was sentient life. He reminded himself of this as they entered Preston's tastefully furnished pied-à-terre. It had presumably never had a dog in it, much less a sooty, soggy mutt, but that was too damn bad for him.

Darwin bathed Mofongo and took a shower himself, after which the bathroom resembled a crime scene. Then he changed into some of Preston's clothes. They were a little tight on him but nice. Expensive, no doubt. He mostly still looked like shit—the singed hair and eyebrows didn't help—but felt a lot better, like he could think straight. His hearing was almost back to normal and no longer filled with the incessant echo of

167

freight train whistles. He was still wide awake, which he now assumed stemmed from the modified Huxley procedure. He remained upset it had been done, of course, and the further changes alleged by Greg, if true, were indeed troubling. But he had to admit that from a scientific perspective, it would be fascinating to obtain first-person experience of undergoing the operation he'd discovered.

He picked up his phone to call Madeline and tell her what had happened now that Mofongo was safe. There was a missed call and voicemail from an unknown number. He pressed play.

"Good evening, Mister Johnston," said the voice of one of the two officers he'd spoken to earlier in the day, a lifetime ago. "This is detective Crouch. I hope you're feeling better. We looked into the call and message you received from Doctor Gregory Huxley. I'm sorry to tell you like this, but he died last night. In San Francisco. I don't know how close you two were, but I'm sorry for your loss. We'd like to have you come back down to the station to answer a few more questions sometime in the next couple days. Feel free to give me a call back at this number when you get a chance. Thanks."

Whatever little relief had blossomed in Darwin wilted. Yes, in one way or another he'd wished for Doctor Huxley's death countless times, but never seriously. Now that it had actually happened, he felt...he wasn't sure. It didn't help that the man had taken to the grave any further suspicions around who had messed with his brain and why, and that they were presumably the same people who had messed with Darwin's in the same way.

He ran to the window and scanned the street, then closed the curtains. He begrudgingly admitted to himself that Preston had in fact been right: Scary shit was going on, and much of it seemed related. Darwin was stuck in some kind of web, and he fucking hated spiders. He had a few pieces of the puzzle, and they fit together, but he still had no idea of the overall picture.

Darwin brewed a large pot of coffee and sat down at Preston's desktop computer, thankful he could sign in as a guest and didn't need to try and guess his password, and prepared himself for a grad school-level research binge.

Chapter 21: Madeline

Unlike Earth, with a comfortable axial tilt of twenty-three degrees, the planet is angled at precisely ninety degrees, knocked over by a collision with a massive asteroid early in its life. This event also created the planet's three moons, which stabilized its axial tilt and share its rotation perpendicular to its star. With its poles in the same plane as its solar system, they spend half of each year drenched in sunlight or darkness. Each solar day lasts an entire year. They are one and the same. Sunrises and sunsets span the equivalent of a month on Earth.

Although the planet has a similar axial tilt to Uranus, it's approximately the same size and distance from its star as Earth is from the sun. The seasons and storms are extreme. The equator is encased in ice all year (and day). The temperature fluctuations are too intense for green plants like those on Earth to evolve. Thus there is no photosynthesis or analogous process to convert carbon dioxide into oxygen. Life on the planet utilizes an alien chemistry, and its circadian rhythms have evolved to play these extended, semi-annual notes of light and darkness...

When Madeline felt as if she was actually standing upon the planet's surface and looking up at a sun that remained fixed in the sky for months, when it seemed as real as the contents of a lucid dream, she blinked hard and went back to sitting in a chair at a pachinko machine. She held the new world between her thumb and pointer fingers and examined it, then dropped it into the tray when she was satisfied. The machine accepted it, as expected. She was surprisingly good at worldbuilding now that she understood the ropes. It was as if she were describing places that already existed and she'd visited.

She carefully pulled back the spring-loaded lever, trying to exert precisely the same amount of pressure as last time. She'd tried the other types of machines in the arcade, but this variety gave her the most control. She let the lever go and the tiny, richly imagined planet launched over the field of play. Gravity took over, and it arced down and began haphazardly bouncing through the hundreds of brass pins, cups, and other obstacles towards the bottom, like a vertical pinball machine.

Madeline's excitement grew as it remained in the center of the field, above the target pocket. It bounced off one last pin, and she smiled as it disappeared into the same hole as the previous world/pachinko ball she'd created, which had been one giant concentrated animal feeding operation where billions of humans were efficiently raised and harvested by smarter, more powerful (but not less cruel) creatures.

The machine made a series of noises like a robot orgy. The bright digital screen played a seizure-inducing animation involving adorable animals, oversexualized girls of indeterminate but questionable age, and exotic fruit. The plot seemed different than last time and was equally inscrutable, but it ended in the same way: with a spinning slot machine wheel. Displayed next to it was the result of the wheel's spin from her previous ball: a dreamcatcher.

At first the wheel spun too fast to discern its contents, but it slowed down after a few seconds, and Madeline could make out the icons as they scrolled by. The number six, a cartoon dragon, a pair of dice, the symbol for Yen. The wheel had almost slowed to a stop now, and her pulse quickened. A diamond...a snowflake...a dreamcatcher.

The wheel stopped.

More robot orgy noises and flashing lights proceeded. Just one more to go. Madeline was yet to win a jackpot but had seen others do so. Aligning three of most symbols resulted in many more pachinko balls and a climax of light and sound. But once, just once, someone had aligned three of the dreamcatchers. The machine had immediately turned itself off, and Elias—always Elias—smiled and escorted the player to the elevator at the back of the parlor, never to return.

The only other way to hypothetically gain access to the elevator was to trade in fifty thousand pachinko balls at the prize exchange counter. However, in her indeterminate amount of time here, no one had come close to accumulating that many. Most people instead traded in smaller amounts for temporary pleasures like cigarettes and alcohol. The three-dreamcatcher jackpot seemed like the only way out. To where? She did not know, but it must be preferable to either the arcade or the hellscape outside. It was her singular motivation.

An entire world covered in the valleys, forests, and meadows of Yosemite National Park, but five times the scale. Granite cliffs abruptly rise at close to right angles to heights greater than Everest. Streams, still comprised of liquid water at such altitudes because of the high atmospheric pressure, crash over the precipices and rain down into the vales below. Light from an orange dwarf star bends and reflects off the waterfalls' mist, resulting in a sky crisscrossed by rainbows...

Standing in a grove amidst trees taller and stouter than most skyscrapers, Madeline felt the thick, damp air of her creation on her skin. She took a deep breath and held it in. Imagining sights never seen before was easy, but dreaming up a new, un-smelled scent was a challenge. Instead she used one readily available to her—that of a verdant forest on a hot day. But how was it that she knew this? Why could she vividly recall the sights, sounds, and smells of a place such as Yosemite while having no specific memory of being there herself? It was as if she'd learned concepts from reading a dictionary or encyclopedia; she understood the universe but could not place herself within it.

Madeline did not have too long to ponder these mysteries because she heard something trampling through the valley floor, heading her direction. Fallen branches as thick as her waist were being snapped like twigs underfoot, plants weighing dozens of pounds brushed aside as if they weren't there. When she'd imagined that everything in this place was five times the scale, she'd meant it. Like when dinosaurs roamed the Earth, the climate was warm and the air rich in carbon dioxide, allowing life to grow and grow...

The room-sized bushes at one side of the small clearing parted. The head of a school bus-sized bear appeared and stared at her with brown eyes the size of basketballs that looked remarkably like those of...who? On what animal's eyes had she based these? She couldn't recall but didn't have time to dwell on the question.

The bear fully emerged and sauntered curiously towards her. Madeline didn't want to wait around and see if its curiosity turned into something else that tempted it to make use of its forearm-length incisors or sword-length claws. She closed her eyes and opened them to once again find herself sitting in front of the same machine in the pachinko parlor at the end of the world.

Two dreamcatchers down, one to go.

Once again she examined the world held in her fingers, then dropped it into the machine. She had a sense of what was happening now: The world was being inspected by the beings who had reached her the first 'day' here, whenever that had been. She'd taken to calling them dream crawlers, though she lacked the precise word to describe how they moved. Exactly what they were now inspecting the world for she didn't know—habitability? creativity? originality? something beyond her understanding or comprehension?—but whatever it was, the new world passed the test, and the lever was loaded.

She launched the ball into play, where it started to follow a nearly identical path to the past two. Madeline tried not to get her hopes up—there were too many random variables; surely this was a game of pure luck, not skill. And even if she earned another spin of the slot machine, there were dozens of icons. The probability was minuscule. But she couldn't help holding her breath as the ball continued its bouncing path downwards.

Her eyes went wide when the tiny planet disappeared into the pocket she'd aimed for, and she didn't blink while watching the incomprehensible sequence of vibrantly colored pixels, ultimately resulting in the whirling wheel next to the two dreamcatchers from her previous spins. In her peripheral vision the other nearby players had taken notice and were also watching. The cacophonous arcade seemed eerily quiet.

The number six, a cartoon dragon, a pair of dice, the symbol for Yen, a diamond...a snowflake...a dreamcatcher...a little black bomb with a lit fuse. Her heart sank. It had been stupid to get her hopes up. The secret to life was properly managing your own expectations. The machine played a song and animation that suggested it was disappointed in her but spat out a few hundred balls as a consolation prize.

Madeline used them to get a drink.

Chapter 22: Darwin

"It doesn't rain blood. That doesn't make any sense," Darwin said as he double-checked the soles of his shoes. He was truly talking to himself now that he'd dropped Mofongo off at her ridiculous doggy hotel—complete with canine-approved programming on the TVs—for an indefinite amount of time. He hadn't made a reservation, and they were allegedly full over the holidays but said they always had space for his good girl. It just happened to be in one of the suites. At that price of course they did.

Unfortunately, talking to himself was far from the craziest thing he was doing.

He continued speaking, loud enough to be heard over Metallica's 'Enter Sandman.' His heavy metal playlist helped keep him awake. "The only way that much blood could fall from the sky is if many animals, or one enormous one, like a dragon, were bleeding in the sky. It's not real. Be skeptical. Use reason and rationality."

He finished his ninth cup of black coffee for the day, mixed with a little whiskey. Alcohol interfered with REM sleep and dulled the hallucinations but was also a depressant; it was a careful balance to strike. He squeezed several hydrating drops into each eye, then slapped himself across the face. Damn, that was harder than he'd meant, but he felt lucid enough for the journey ahead. He shuddered at the thought of falling asleep again and ending up in a nightmare anything like the one from his first night at Preston's almost a week ago. He was still recovering. He would much rather return to the hourglass desert than the horrors of that literal hellscape.

Doctor Huxley had been right: Be wary of sleeping. Definitely a bad idea. So much for personally enjoying the benefits of his invention. Darwin now had a hypothesis for how certain types of radiation applied to a brain that had undergone the modified Huxley procedure could result in the symptoms he was experiencing. He even had an idea for fixing it, but not the resources to test it out.

Darwin had learned that the doctor had been right about a lot over the days he'd been holed up in Preston's apartment doing research. You could sure get a lot done when you didn't sleep. Dropping off Mofongo before the doggy hotel closed was the only time he'd left. He hadn't even been to the hospital, the police station, or back to what remained of his home. He was likely a suspect for both murder and arson at this point, but that wasn't among his top three concerns. No, he was more concerned with slipping into something like a perpetual bad DMT trip, a powerful organization likely wanting him dead, and—most of all—that his family was in trouble; his wife and daughters were missing on the far side of the world.

He'd also had an erection for more than four hours, but he'd just have to live with it for now.

The Tokyo Stasis Hotel had insisted his family wasn't there and couldn't infringe on their customers' privacy by providing any more details. It only confirmed Darwin's suspicions given what he'd learned. There was some truly insane shit on the

177

internet, but he'd assembled enough of the puzzle to discern the picture it created. It felt good to do intense directed research again with the goal of helping others.

He declined to call Madeline again because it was an *idempotent* operation; it yielded the same result no matter how many times it was performed: voicemail. Repeating the same action over and over again and expecting different results was allegedly the definition of insanity, and although that was clearly not the actual definition nor what one would expect with many operations, Darwin assumed he presently fell into the insane category. He scowled as he recalled the conversation he'd had with Vipul earlier.

"The answer is still no," Vipul had said. "Now, I have a lot of work to do."

"It's Christmas Eve," Darwin had said.

"I don't celebrate Christmas. And for once no one is bothering me. Except for you."

"Plea—"

"I'm the chief technology officer of a soon-to-be public company, not some dark web hacker."

"It's not going to *be* a public company if the CEO mysteriously disappears right before the IPO."

"Listen, Darwin, I care deeply about Madeline, personally and professionally. I do. We've worked closely together for the past five years. My future is tied to the success of this company. I owe her a lot, all things considered. But she told me she wanted to unplug for a while to spend some quality time with family over the holidays before the final sprint to the Nasdaq, which is a perfectly reasonable explanation for not getting back to me. And, it's none of my business, but I get the sense something's going on between you two and I don't want to be in the middle. It's strange you don't have shared accounts or access to any of her individual ones. If you truly believe she's missing, then go to the police and solicit their help."

"Can't you just give me her password so I can check if she reused it on other services and see if there's anything suspicious? Didn't you used to work in cybersecurity?" Darwin in fact knew that Vipul had been exiled from his prior company and the industry for hacking their main competitor, though it was a sensitive subject. Madeline gave him a chance when no one else would.

"The term 'cybersecurity' is a decade out of date. Everything is connected to the internet now—it's just security. And we don't even store passwords, only hashes. I couldn't give it to you if I wanted to."

"What?"

Vipul sighed. "With contemporary computer architecture, there are essentially one-way functions. They're trivially easy to perform in one direction—to generate output from input—but it's computationally unfeasible for even the most powerful computers to reverse engineer the input from the output. Cryptographic hash functions fall into this category. They take input of any size and generate a string of alphanumeric gibberish that's unique in almost all cases. When someone sets their password, we run it through a hash function and only store this useless output to minimize risk if it's compromised. Then, whenever someone enters their password to log in, we run it through the same algorithm and verify that the output matches. Besides, she's my boss. Her system privileges are just as high as mine, plus she has two-factor authentication set up, like every sane person."

"What happens if you use the output as the password?"

"It's not idempotent. The hash would be different." Vipul sounded exasperated. "Are you even listening to me?"

"I'm sorry but I'm not familiar with that term."

"Idempotency is…"

In the present moment, Darwin ruminated on how frustrating it was to be an expert in some domains of science and an amateur in others. He'd long ago lost the argument with Madeline that computer science wasn't really a science. The technology underlying the modern internet was almost unfathomable, indistinguishable from magic.

He had tried contacting 'Sephira' too—he doubted that was her real name—but unsurprisingly she never texted him back. What limited online presence she'd once had was gone. She hadn't been fucking with him after all, at least in some respects. Bitch.

Circadian Capital Partners, however, was a different story. When he'd come across the initialism in his research, another image came back to him from that night at the San Francisco Stasis Hotel. It was nothing but a matte black business card with 'CCP' in silver, but it was enough. And it was the reason why he opened the passenger side door to place his handgun in the shotgun seat of his brother-in-law's Volvo SUV he was 'borrowing.' Presumably Preston wouldn't need it in the near future. If Darwin made it through all of this, he'd have to thank the man. They were even now.

He stopped when he saw what was already sitting in the passenger seat: the gun. Darwin then realized his hands were empty. Right—he'd taken the weapon with him to drop off Mofongo, just in case. Being anywhere near a firearm was dangerous in his present state, but not as dangerous as he believed the CCP to be. Keep it together.

Darwin started the car, and the opening notes of Slayer's 'Raining Blood' blared from the speakers, momentarily paralyzing him with fear. Too coincidental. Not real. Act on rationality, not emotion. He turned off the radio and sat in silence in the dark garage for a few minutes. Had he gone his entire life up until recently without being in any real danger? His ancient ancestors would be proud. Now he needed a Christmas miracle, and although he thought both Christmas and miracles were nonsense, it *was* December twenty-fifth as of a few hours ago.

He reminded himself that you have very little control over what happens to you in life, only how you respond. If something is out of your control, then it's not worth worrying about, and the same goes for things that *are* in your control, as long as you have a sensible plan, right? And free will is just a delusion held by those who don't understand the underlying science, right? Easier said than done, especially after staying awake and staving off nightmares for the better part of a week. How condescendingly he used to give such advice.

Darwin slapped himself one more time and shined his phone's flashlight into his face. Light therapy was a proven way to hack your circadian rhythm, and his was bottoming out. He needed to open the garage door before the accumulating carbon monoxide from the running car made it all-too-plausibly look like he took the easy way out. Mere minutes could cause loss of consciousness and death. It happened by accident all the time to those with legacy gas-guzzlers.

He opened the garage door and carefully drove out into the drops of what thankfully looked like plain old water falling from the night sky. Going just twenty-four hours without sleep caused cognitive impairment equivalent to a blood alcohol content over the legal limit. Darwin knew better than anyone that drowsy driving killed more people than drunk and high driving combined. Including the whiskey he was effectively wasted at this point. At least it gave him some courage.

In the rearview mirror a parked car several blocks down the street turned on its headlights. The vehicle pulled out and began following him.

Chapter 23: Madeline

"...reporting today on a Christmas tragedy, a fatal head-on collision on 101 South in the early hours of Christmas morning. The identity of the driver who caused the wreck has been released, and the news sent shockwaves through the Bay Area. The blood alcohol limit of prominent neurosurgeon Doctor James Magnusson, a recovering alcoholic, was almost four times the legal limit as he drove the wrong way up an offramp and onto the freeway. Doctor Magnusson was a pioneer in the recently approved but still controversial modified Huxley procedure, whose inventor died just last week under what many have called suspicious circumstances yet to be ruled a murder or suicide. Authorities are withholding the identity of the other vehicle's driver until they can contact family members, but police escorted them to a hospital where they remain in critical condition..."

The newscaster's words sounded uniquely distant, like the audio equivalent of looking the wrong way through a telescope or pair of binoculars. But they were enough to trigger something in Madeline and pull her out of her trancelike state. She felt an overwhelming sense of something resembling déjà vu as if the words' contents were supposed to be important to her. It was like being told that someone she knew had died but not feeling anything in response, so she ended up with an abstract sense of guilt instead of visceral sadness.

Madeline's eyelids fluttered open to see Elias Sultana standing nearby and watching the news on his phone, a mischievous grin on his face. What a strange thing to smile about. A phrase popped into her mind: 'You'll never make the news if you waste all your time watching it.' But she didn't know from where it came.

When Elias noticed her watching, he put the device away and gave her a slight nod. The hand that hadn't been holding a phone held a basket of pachinko balls. He looked at it and seemed to ponder something for a few seconds, then extended the basket towards her with a smile and said, "Here's another five hundred, on us. You're doing great work here, Madeline. You're surprisingly good at this."

She accepted the basket mechanically without saying 'thank you,' although the gift would save her countless hours of mental toiling. Elias nodded one more time and walked away. Madeline stared at the glittering basket, thinking. The mirror-like Pachinko balls reflected the flashing rainbow lights of the parlor and reminded her of...Christmas. Huxley. Magnusson. There were other names associated with these. Combinations of syllables that represented concepts with profound meaning. They were on the tip of the tongue of her mind.

She ignored the myriad distractions around her and focused. She crawled through the webs of associations with the words. Christmas...Huxley...Magnusson...Christ...Christina! And Evelyn. And Mofongo and the others. Even Darwin. Their faces came back to her, the crests of great waves in a flood of memories and tears. There was no need to try and hold them back, no shame or embarrassment about crying openly;

some non-trivial percentage of the patrons at the parlor were weeping at any given moment.

Madeline had remembered, but her grasp of the dim memories of her past life, her real life, was precarious. Already they were beginning to slip away. How could she hold on? Then something else came back: her dream journal. That was it.

She needed to write it down.

Part 4: Deep Sleep

One week later

Chapter 24: Darwin

"How would you like to live an extra ten years?" asked the comically cliché doctor wearing a white lab coat and stethoscope from the TV. "And I'm not just talking about a decade of decrepitness tacked on at the end of life, but another ten or fifteen percent of all ages, from your twenties through your golden years. The modified Huxley procedure will let you do precisely that, by safely reducing how much you need to sleep. Think of what you could do with all that extra time! And, with an additional four or five hours each day available to work, we're confident it will pay for itself in no time. It's a *no brainer.* It's also why Circadian Capital Partners is offering special financing. What better way to ensure you accomplish this new year's resolution, and every one going forward? What are you waiting for? Visit—"

The TV turned off, and a familiar voice said, "Happy New Year, Darwin. Welcome back." Darwin barely recognized the speaker through crusted, squinted eyes. He tried opening them wider, but the fluorescent lights were painfully bright. The speaker continued, "They said you'd be coming to any minute. This may be shocking for you to hear, but the year is 2045. The singularity is here, and you've just woken up from a simulation of the past."

What? Scenes and related sensations that seemed suspiciously like real memories started coming back, but Darwin yearned for them to be something, anything else. What if it had all just been some kind of terrible dream? But any illusions were dispelled when he went to raise his hand to block the light and found it handcuffed to the bed. And not in a good way. Maybe there was no good way to be handcuffed to a hospital bed.

"Just kidding. It's 2020, and everything is fucked."

Darwin's eyes somewhat adjusted to the brightness, giving him a better view of the man now standing by his bedside. "...Preston?" he asked. It hurt to speak, but Preston's presence was strangely comforting.

"Good, you recognize me. And from the look on your face it appears you remember some of your actions before the accident." Oh, that's right. "You're lucky we're still technically family."

Darwin took in the collection of tubes coming out of different parts of his body, some more comfortable than others. "How... what?" he croaked, hoping his eyes conveyed the rest.

"You've been in a medically induced coma for a week. You were on a ventilator, which is probably why it's hard to talk. You went into cardiac arrest and straight up died on the way to the hospital, but they brought you back. We've gotta discuss what that was like when you're up for it. They had you under therapeutic hypothermia in the hopes of preventing or minimalizing brain damage. Initially we thought it didn't work and weren't sure you'd be all there when you woke up. *But*, on further inspection, it seems the brain damage you *do* have is unrelated. They said it might have already been present, which I told them makes perfect sense. As far as I'm concerned you were never all there to begin with. For example, what kind of person gives Maddy and me the level of shit you did for undergoing the modified Huxley procedure only to go and get it done himself months later? No need to answer. It was rhetorical.

"Anyways, other than the heart attack and brain damage, you're remarkably ok. You suffered minimal injuries in the crash, though your face was smashed by the airbag. You look bad, man. Fortunately you were in one of the safest cars on the road. I wish I could say my car was equally fortunate to have had you in it."

A week! Darwin began to panic. If he'd spent a week dreaming, he was lost beyond redemption and facing a fate worse than death: dying as a stranger to his family, friends, and self, like his grandfather after a ten-year bout with Alzheimer's. Then he remembered he was an expert on this subject and relaxed a bit. General anesthesia was unlike being asleep, when the brain was just as active as while awake. Patients under anesthesia or other kinds of medically induced comas didn't dream, and their brain state—or lack thereof—was closer on the spectrum to death, which apparently he'd also undergone.

So, that was it, eh? No light at the end of the tunnel, nothing. He'd always bravely espoused the belief that such was the case, but it wasn't very comforting to be able to say 'I told you so' on such a matter. He'd been under for surgery a few times before and knew what it was like (or not like). But deep down somewhere in his skeptical mind, he'd held out a glimmer of irrational hope that something entirely different happened when a human's brain stopped due to death, even if he didn't extend that charity to other sentient animals below some arbitrary cutoff point. He would much prefer to go to a happy place in the sky forever or respawn in the simulation as a dog living at a winery.

Maybe he was a little more concerned about dying than he thought.

But Darwin had bigger concerns than what happened (or didn't) after death. He now recalled enough of what had transpired in the days before the accident to understand his priorities. He looked at Preston and asked, "Madeline?"

Up until now Preston had been his usual, relaxed self, but his demeanor changed. "No one has heard from her in two weeks. She left the girls in their hotel suite to go run an urgent errand, and that was the last anyone remembers seeing her."

One of the machines hooked up to Darwin beeped. "How are they?" he asked, trying to sit up, but the handcuffs and tubes limited his range of motion.

"Don't worry, they're fine. They figured out how to order room service and movies and didn't leave the room for a week. Ran up a hefty tab. Those are some resourceful girls you're raising. I suppose they do have fifty percent Lockhart genes. When they didn't show up for a scheduled brunch on Christmas morning, Madeline's friends got suspicious and found their room number. I bought them flights back to San Francisco, and they've been at our place since Saturday. *Someone's* gotta take care of them. I picked up Mofongo too. Quite a full house we've got with my parents in town."

"Thank you." He felt a tumultuous mix of relief the girls were safe and dread Madeline was still missing. She'd made him watch enough true crime over the years to know that it usually meant only one thing if someone was gone for more than a few days.

Preston must have noticed him trying to look around the

hospital room because he said, "Your daughters aren't here, but there *is* an officer outside. I didn't want them to see you like this and wasn't sure what you'd be like when you came out of the coma. More importantly, you and I have some urgent shit to discuss."

Darwin stared, wondering how much Preston knew. How much did *he* even know? He raced through his fragmented memory, trying to reassemble the pieces he'd fit together before the accident, when a nurse entered the room and said, "Mister Johnston, glad to see you're awake. How are you feeling?"

"Don't let him tell you he's a doctor," Preston inserted before Darwin could respond. "It's not true, and he definitely doesn't know what's best for him."

The nurse scowled at him.

"I feel ok," Darwin said. "How—" he was interrupted by a coughing fit. The nurse handed him a cup of water. "How soon can I go?"

"In a hurry, are we? Legally, I have no idea. Medically, it depends on your progress over the next few days. You're relatively young and in good shape, so hopefully muscle atrophy shouldn't be too much of an issue and you won't need physical rehab. The stent we put in seems to be working like it's supposed to." She checked the various equipment and monitors surrounding Darwin, then said, "The doctor will be in a little later. In the meantime just press this button if you need anything."

"She's cute," Preston said as soon as she left. "Getting down to business. I'm confident I can get them to drop the charges for breaking and entering and grand theft auto given I'm the aggrieved party. But all I can do for illegally transporting and negligently discharging a firearm is post your bail and make an introduction to my attorney. Highly recommended, by the way."

"Thanks." Darwin's actions sounded a lot worse when put into those terms, but the cuffs still seemed a tad extreme and unnecessary. While his wrists hurt, his throat felt a bit better. "Is it really breaking and entering if you use a key?"

"Happy your sense of humor is coming back. I've actually already arranged your bail but haven't pulled the trigger because I thought having an armed guard outside your room while you were in a coma was for the best. However, I'm not sure *why* I thought that and am hoping you can help.

"Moving onto more serious crimes, it sounds like you're a suspect for both arson and murder. You haven't been officially charged, but ghosting the authorities then stealing a car and driving towards the airport with a gun doesn't look like the behavior of an innocent person. You had quite a week, man. I'm sure you didn't burn down your house or kill your former advisor, just like I'm sure you had your reasons for the crimes you did commit. In fact, I assume it's all related, including the change in Madeline's behavior over the past few months and ultimately her disappearance. And, Darwin, I assume you have some hypotheses as to *how* it's all related."

Darwin's head ached as more details came back. One of the machines connected to him beeped in what sounded like a warning.

Preston said, "Sorry, maybe this is too much to spring on you right after waking up from a coma, but my baby sister is missing. I'm trying to take care of a five-month-old and my two nieces while keeping this out of the media. Tomorrow was supposed to be my first day back from paternity—"

"Keeping this out of the media...what?" Surely media attention could do nothing but help in a missing persons case. Then understanding dawned, and Darwin continued in the loudest voice he could muster, "You're worried about the optics for the fucking company? About your investment?" The beeping's cadence increased.

"I'm worried about the optics for Madeline and her future. You should be too."

"She's not going to have a future if we don't find her! It's been two weeks. She's probably dead by now!" The beeping accelerated further, like just before the drop in one of those techno songs.

"Calm down, Darwin. Don't die on me again. I—and more importantly, Madeline—still need your help. You and I are *both* missing pieces of the story."

Darwin focused on slowing his breath and heartrate while glaring at Preston, coaxing him to continue.

"There are a few large, publicly accessible dream databases. They're used for scientific research, like if you want to see if men or women dream about sex more often. Spoiler—it's men. They're probably also used by dream enthusiasts and other weirdos." Darwin failed to see how this was relevant. He was the one who'd told Preston about it, years ago. The same thing existed for psychedelic trip reports. "And, as is the case with many kinds of websites, there are shadier—some would say better—versions on the dark web. For example, a database of dream journals whose authors thought they were private but were then hacked into or otherwise stolen. The data is more authentic and intimate without people's real names and some of the most embarrassing or disturbing details removed. Reading them feels voyeuristic. I actually—"

"Get to the point."

"Last week Madeline's dream journal appeared on the 'Dream Punx' site. Some of the info *is* redacted, presumably to conceal the details of her abduction, but you'll know it's really her when you read it. Or, at least it *was* her. The most recent entry is from yesterday."

Another tumultuous mix of feelings filled Darwin. It again included something resembling relief but now also confusion. He was still trying to process the data when the doctor knocked on the open door and asked, "Mind if I interrupt?"

"Just one minute, doctor," Preston said, turning back to Darwin. "Jesus this guy looks like Clooney. What kind of hospital is this? Anyways, I'll be back tomorrow morning. Get some rest. Sleep on it. Hopefully you're feeling better and have had time to process everything by then. In the meantime I'll get you uncuffed and your phone, passport, and gun back. I'm proud of you for finally listening to me. I'm also working on getting you permission to leave the US while out on bail, which I hope will be expedited given your wife is missing in Japan. Don't even think about checking yourself out and fleeing the country before then. I've got a hundred grand on the line."

Twelve hours later Darwin stood in the dark, damp hospital parking lot. The sun would rise in a few hours. It was frigid in his thin gown, and he shuddered at the memory of pulling out the catheter himself. The upside was that the premature exit he'd made over the past ten minutes combined with the cold had jolted him awake. He'd spent the night up until then resisting the overwhelming urge to drift off, ignoring the creeping phantasms in his peripheral vision. Falling asleep was just too risky, but he couldn't go on like this much longer.

Darwin only had one move left, and he should have made it sooner. It was the lowest branch in the decision tree. He needed to secure his own oxygen mask before helping others. From what he'd read in Madeline's dream journal, she was going to need all the help she could get, and he had an idea where and how to find it. At least his destination was on the way to Tokyo.

He sighed as he scrolled through the contacts in his phone. He could partially make out his reflected face in the bright screen; he really did look like shit, which was appropriate given that's precisely how he felt. Darwin called a number for the first time in years. It picked up after less than one full ring.

"Chuckieeee. I was starting to think this day would never come."

"SFO. As soon as possible."

Chapter 25: Madeline

Another unknown day of an unknown month in an unknown year. I'm not sure how many hours I slept for last night, or any night, or even when *it's night.*

Like the casinos of Las Vegas, the parlor is always open and there are no clocks, windows, or other ways to mark the passage of time. My own 'sleep' schedule is far from a reliable ruler. And there's nowhere to lay down other than the floor, though that seems discouraged, so I doze in a chair. At least there are bathrooms. They're by the prize exchange counter, where I can use pachinko balls to buy food and drinks, though I rarely feel hunger or thirst.

The prize counter is also where I can buy freedom.

Elias's actions confirmed that it was *Christmas at some point in the discernable past, though I can't be certain whether that was weeks, months, or years ago. I spend much of my time in a state of semi-lucid dreaming, and Darwin once told me that even though some dreams may feel like they go on for days, most only last minutes in 'real' time, like the opposite of the time dilation experienced near a black hole. My watch hasn't worked since I was tricked into coming here, whenever that was, and there's little difference between being asleep or awake. There's only one stage in my sleep cycle now. My circadian rhythm only plays one note: the clinking sound of steel and brass.*

But I suppose that's not entirely accurate. These aren't ordinary metallic pachinko balls, even if they make the same sounds. I quickly burned through the first five hundred I was given. I'd never played before and wasn't any good. Pachinko is like a more boring, less skillful version of pinball. There are several types of machines with various themes and slightly different mechanics. All you control is the spring–loaded handle that launches the balls into the top of the playing field, where they bounce off various objects and either land in one of several pockets—in which case you win more balls and potentially a spin of the slot machine wheel—or fall all the way down and disappear into oblivion. The balls are everything in pachinko—the bet, the game pieces, and the prize—and in this *arcade, they're even more than that.*

Because on closer inspection they aren't simply game pieces, although I suspect they're indeed part of some bigger game with higher stakes; they're miniature, diverse worlds. And you can't purchase more, which is the entire point and business model of other pachinko parlors. The only way to get more is to create them by dreaming up new, unique planets. That *is the point of this place. Pachinko is just a means to an end, and we're just slave labor. Fortunately, although I don't seem to have any control over the parlor itself, I have close to godlike powers when creating new balls. Sometimes—*

Madeline stopped writing mid-sentence and looked up towards an unfamiliar sound. One of the other patrons had snapped. It wasn't the first time, but it was the most violent outburst yet. A Japanese man in his fifties who had only 'recently' arrived had picked up a chair with both hands and was smashing it against a machine, presumably to get at the balls inside. His first swing had cracked the screen, and he was at the apex of his windup for the second. His mouth was open, and he appeared to be screaming, but Madeline heard nothing from him despite being only ten feet away. However, this wasn't surprising; none of the patrons could talk to each other, only to an Elias.

Across the floor, an instance of Elias had recently arrived for his 'shift' from the elevator at the back of the arcade where the overseers came and went. He sauntered towards them. The patron had gotten in five good swings and done considerable damage, though he hadn't freed any balls by the time Elias arrived.

Now that he was only a few feet away, Madeline noticed something different about him; every Elias always wore the same outfit, except now there was one difference: a glove-like device on his left hand and wrist. A twinge of déjà vu hit Madeline—she used to have one very much like it. She'd have to write that down too, but right now she, like the other patrons, was focused on the confrontation between the two men.

But the outcome was predetermined. She'd seen it before. The Japanese man opened his mouth again in a silent battle cry and charged Elias with the chair held over his head. Before he closed the distance, she heard a whoosh of air followed by three loud crashes, then saw Elias dodge the swing, grab the back of the man's head, and smash it three times into one of the machines. It was like the audio was out of sync, sound faster than light. Weapon or not, resistance was futile, as if Elias knew what you were going to do before you did it.

Two other men, apparently undeterred by what they'd just witnessed, rushed Elias from opposite directions. When they got within several feet, he held out his hands and they collapsed, catatonic, like he had a goddamn superpower.

Elias propped up the dazed, bloodied man who'd wielded the chair and walked him to the parlor's front door through which Madeline had come in. His hands occupied with the stumbling patron, Elias kicked open the door to reveal a sliver of something resembling the sixth circle of hell from Dante's *Inferno*. Elias threw the man out, like a bouncer tossing someone from a club. He strolled back to where the other two men still lay stupefied and dragged them to the door. They stared with unresponsive, glassy eyes as they were tossed into the flames. Elias then continued his measured stroll around the room. Some of the other patrons exchanged grim glances, then all went back to playing, worldbuilding, or sleeping.

Madeline shifted focus back to her notebook. Her phone had been absent since arriving, but the rest of her purse's contents were intact, including a pen and small notebook that had taken over from the online dream journal she could no longer access. There were now a few dozen entries, but that in no way gave her any indication of how long ago she started writing. Until recently the notes were comprised of bits and pieces of what she remembered about her old life, which she read through whenever she began forgetting. The newer entries had shifted to information to remember about her new life, as sometimes even her short-term memories were blurry.

She was about to continue writing to once more discourage her future self from attacking Elias when the sound of faint, frantic banging joined the hullabaloo of hundreds of out-of-sync animations and metallic clinking. Madeline tried to ignore it. It wouldn't last more than a few minutes. She couldn't remember exactly how many people had been cast out the front entrance, either because of failed attempts at violent resistance or simply giving up and refusing to play anymore. But they always tried to get back in. More and more new patrons were stumbling in, increasing the parlor's occupancy, but no one exiled ever got back through the door.

It reinforced her conviction that the only way out was to buy or win her way into the elevator, no matter how long it took.

Madeline had almost given in to despair early on but was now determined to beat this sick game and bring retribution to its creators. More importantly, Elias had accidentally shown her there was still a real world outside, somewhere, and that it contained the people from her memories. Her family. Hate and love were each powerful motivators on their own, but together they provided an endless source of energy. And as someone wise had once said, though she could not remember who: (S)he who has a 'why' to live for can bear almost any 'how.'

Besides, the situation could be worse. Playing pachinko and dreaming up new worlds wasn't the worst existence. Darwin spent much of his free time doing the latter by choice. She'd realized that's where many of her ideas came from: reading (and heavily critiquing) his science fiction.

She took a deep drag from a cigarette and surveyed the parlor around her. The faint banging sound had stopped. A pretty young woman walked to the now-broken machine. She grabbed the recently exiled man's basket and dumped the pitiful few balls it contained into hers. The woman had quite a stash, even more than the ten thousand or so Madeline estimated she'd accumulated.

That gave her an idea.

Chapter 26: Darwin

Approaching at night in a helicopter, the *Arianna* (or whatever it was called now) reminded Darwin of the drone footage he'd seen of Burning Man. A neon carnival amidst a sea of blackness, and in this case the dark literally *was* a sea instead of a desolate, dusty plain. No doubt it contained similar levels of group sex and drug use.

But Darwin was grateful for the latter. His headphones sat in his lap, and the sound of the chopper's blades overhead combined with the wind from the open doors made staying awake during the ninety-minute helicopter ride easy. That had not been the case on the five-hour flight in the Gulfstream from San Francisco to Hawaii. Fortunately Balthazar owned the plane outright, and thus it was stocked with the highest quality stimulants money could buy. So much for 'never again.'

"Hell of a way to kick off the roaring twenties!" Preston's voice, audible even over the helicopter's blades, reminded Darwin that he wasn't the only one to partake. "Livin' the dream! Woohoo!"

Darwin had planned to go straight to the private airport at SFO after discharging himself from the hospital, but his conscience got the better of him. The CCP had killed Doctor Huxley—Doctor Magnusson too, apparently—and had tried to kill him once already. He couldn't take off on such a dangerous escapade without first seeing his family. Not after what they'd been through. And he'd had several hours before the plane was ready, anyway. Why he'd thought he could sneak into Preston's house to see Christina, Evelyn, and Mofongo without being otherwise noticed was beyond him. It had been an idiotic idea, but then again, no doubt he was certifiably insane at this point.

And so, in exchange for a bag of supplies and not reporting him to the authorities for breaking the terms of the bail Preston had posted, Darwin had agreed to let him come. So far he didn't regret it; it'd taken longer than anticipated to get here, even via private plane and helicopter, and it'd been nice to have company. They'd had time to further fill each other in on the past few weeks and flesh out Darwin's hypotheses. Seemingly outlandish conspiracy theories made for great conversation in their present state. And Preston had been able to confirm what was just a hallucination, like the gremlins on the wings. But Darwin was concerned that his attitude towards Preston's company would change when they finally arrived.

The chopper slowly descended towards the helicopter pad at the back of the massive ship, which looked as long as four football fields laid end to end. It was easy to make such a size estimate because there was an almost full-sized soccer field on the deck for comparison. When they were eye-level with the ship's navigation bridge, Darwin noticed the huge flag flapping from a pole at the top, above the complicated-looking antennas and illuminated by two floodlights. The flag was royal purple with a vaguely familiar golden symbol in the middle.

Preston hit Darwin on the shoulder and motioned for him to

put on his headphones. He obliged and Preston said, "The flag of New Libertatia!"

"It looks like a flag for the artist Prince."

"That's the symbol for the country's cryptocurrency."

Darwin wasn't surprised. He'd introduced Balthazar to Prince in college, and he'd taken an immediate liking. They were both small in stature, and Balthazar had been a prince himself at the time. But that wasn't the only thing Darwin had introduced him to; how much of all this was ultimately his fault?

The helicopter landed and Darwin removed his headphones as the blades slowed. He took a long sip to finish the last of his foul-tasting water and get a boost of energy before what lay ahead.

"Take it easy on the coke, man," said Preston, sniffling. "Don't forget you died of a heart attack a week ago. Just because you can't inhale it through your broken nose doesn't make it less effective."

Darwin had half-expected Balthazar to greet them on the pad and was surprised to be instead met by an enormous man in what looked like a fashionable hazmat suit. "Mister Johnston and Mister Lockhart, right this way," he said, motioning for them to follow. Darwin and Preston glanced at each other, then shrugged and obliged, carrying their bags. The outside air was comfortable and humid, though the breeze reminded Darwin of the approaching storm. Even through his broken nose, he smelled the sea.

The helicopter pad and surrounding area were separated from the rest of the ship by a wall of shipping containers stacked five-high. The only way to and from was through a kind of tunnel. When they arrived at the barrier, the man in the biohazard suit said, "Please leave your bags here and proceed to customs and immigration. The process takes about thirty minutes." Darwin was confused; it's not like there was a line.

Darwin and Preston again looked at each other and shrugged, then handed their bags to the man. He carried them towards the shipping container next to the one they were to enter. Its door opened and a ghostly blue light emanated from inside. At least they didn't have to go through that one.

Inside the main tunnel another person greeted them in a similar biohazard suit, this time a woman. "Good evening, gentlemen. I'm Doctor Goodspeed. I need to draw some blood from both of you to be analyzed while you shower and your clothes are disinfected."

"My clothes are dry-clean only," said Preston, looking concerned. He was dressed to impress.

"We aren't going to wash them. We're going to expose them to ultraviolet radiation. It's germicidal, and though it can cause colors to fade over time, one session won't have an effect. Only the higher end of the UV spectrum is ionizing." Preston still looked hesitant. "You're welcome to take the helicopter back to the island, but this is the only way into New Libertatia."

So, Balthazar was still a hypochondriac, thought Darwin. What other option did they have? After showering in the surprisingly luxurious facilities inside the shipping containers, they were given back their clothing and bags, which had presumably gone through the same UV treatment. Doctor Goodspeed greeted them outside the door on the other side of the tunnel. She no longer wore a hazmat suit but a black, low-necked cocktail dress and what looked like several hundred thousand dollars of jewelry. She was one of the most beautiful women Darwin had ever seen in person. But of all people Preston didn't seem to notice.

Doctor Goodspeed said, "Both of your blood tested positive for several interesting substances, but nothing we're concerned about here."

The man they'd left their bags with also no longer wore a hazmat suit but a kind of royal purple military dress uniform. He held up Darwin's Glock and said, "I'm sorry Mister Johnston, but you can't bring guns into the country. You'll get it back when you depart. Don't worry, you won't need it here."

Some libertarian paradise this was. "Ok," Darwin said.

"Man, you really have changed," said Preston without looking at Darwin, "But he's right. Technically this is the safest country in the world."

Doctor Goodspeed said, "Please let me see your passports." They handed them over and she added a stamp resembling the flag of the 'country,' including brightly colored ink. "Welcome to New Libertatia."

"Thank—"

"Chuckie!" came a faint voice. Darwin looked past the doctor and understood what—who—had been distracting his for-now brother-in-law.

Preston glanced at Darwin and said, "Chuckie? Ah..."

Balthazar strode towards them, wearing a suit that belonged on the cover of *GQ*. Maybe he *had* worn it on the cover of *GQ*. Darwin held out a hand when Balthazar was several feet away, but his old roommate bounded the last few steps then jumped up and hugged him. Fortunately Darwin outweighed him by over fifty pounds and kept his balance despite how unstable he felt.

When they separated Balthazar looked at him and said,

"Wow, you look like shit."

"Good to see you too. And yes, I'm aware. I also feel like shit, especially after going through that." Darwin motioned towards the wall of shipping containers blocking off the helicopter pad.

"My apologies. I guess you can say I...run a tight ship. Soon—"

Balthazar was interrupted by Preston laughing. He continued the moment he stopped. "Soon to be ships. But this is a closed ecosystem so I have to take precautions. Have you heard about this new coronavirus in China? They're trying to keep it under wraps. But it's going to rock the world. I already took some enormous positions. It's insane how much money I'm going to make when it blows up. I'll be richer than Mansa Musa."

"I've been a bit more focused on personal health concerns recently," said Darwin.

"That's right. But stop worrying. Our healthcare system is the best in the world. You won't believe the kind of talent I attract by offering the opportunity to work free from regulations. Permissionless innovation. I'm confident we're going to cure aging before it really affects our generation."

"Speak for yourself," said Darwin. Balthazar didn't look to have aged since college.

Balthazar said, "Ben Frank got a lot right but also said nothing is certain except death and taxes. Well, I already opted out of taxes and am working on death. And if the doctors can solve that, I'm sure they can help you. It won't cost you anything, either—we have a single-payer system, as in I pay for everything."

Preston erupted in laughter again. Balthazar continued, "For now, that is. We plan to get into medical tourism down the road. Anyway, I passed everything you sent along to the team. They're excited and will be ready for you first thing in the morning. Hopefully there's time to operate before the waves get too big."

"I don't suppose you mind sharing a few of those positions you're taking to profit off this virus?" asked Preston with a smile. Balthazar frowned and looked at him, seeming to notice his presence for the first time. Preston extended a hand and said, "Sorry, Preston Lockhart, Bleeding Edge Capital. I'm a huge fan of your work. It's great to meet you, though I'm not sure of the proper etiquette when greeting a tzar." He was like a kid meeting their hero. Balthazar may have only been five foot six, but he was a giant in Preston's eyes. He'd finally met someone who liked to hear themselves talk as much as he did.

Balthazar perfunctorily shook Preston's hand and said, "I know who you are. We run a thorough background check on everyone before we even let them in the helicopter. As long as you're still legally related to this guy just call me Balthazar or tzar." He ignored Preston's other question and turned his attention back to Darwin. "You arrived in the middle of an extended New Year's party. I made the whole week a national holiday. Do you want to dive in? It'll take a full day to give you the tour. And I'd rather do that in daylight when you're feeling better."

"I don't really feel up for partying, but Preston you should go ahead if you want."

"No way brother, I'm not leaving your side."

"Then let's head to my office and catch up. Leave your bags and Ahmed will bring them to your rooms," said Balthazar, starting to walk backward with his arms stretched out towards the shipping containers, cranes, wind turbines, and other giant machines covering the deck. "The back fifth of the ship, everything behind the bridge, is used exclusively for operations and logistics. Loading and unloading supplies and people and whatnot. The boring but vital shit too many countries don't spend enough resources on..."

Darwin indeed found it boring as Balthazar rattled off dozens of precise figures and described in detail how his burgeoning utopia literally stayed afloat. Well, the fact that Balthazar relished such minutia presumably accounted for some of his success. They reached the base of the tower that spanned most of the ship's width. Darwin assumed it had once been painted white, but it was now covered edge-to-edge in a sprawling, colorful mural depicting what looked like a dramatized version of the country's founding. Christ.

Balthazar's info dump continued, "...our day-to-day operations are entirely powered by solar, wind, and waves. They're abundant this close to the equator and trade winds. We only use diesel for moving the ship to go in for supplies or maintenance. You know I hate driving demand for oil as much as anyone. I'm actually in early negotiations to go nuclear. But let's just say—"

The doors to the elevator at the bottom of the tower opened, and Darwin was shocked to see a familiar face. He began the process of reality testing, using all the rationality he could muster to determine whether or not it was a figment of his imagination when Preston said, "Arlo! What are you doing here?"

So, it was real; Arlo, the facilitator from the men's ceremony, was somehow standing right in front of him on the *Arianna.* He didn't look surprised to see them as they greeted each other, but the man's calm demeanor was such that Darwin doubted anything could rattle him.

"Arlo recently arrived to lead ceremonies and do coaching for some of our citizens, myself included," said Balthazar. "Start the new year off right. Help us see things from different perspectives. He's one of the best in the business, like everyone here."

"I can vouch for that. I've attended four ceremonies that he's facilitated in Marin County over the past few years," said Preston. "Darwin even came to one."

"No shit?" said Balthazar, looking at Darwin. "I'm glad you finally decided to live a little."

"You are all too kind," said Arlo, taking turns looking kindly into each of their eyes. "It is such a pleasant surprise to see you, Preston, Darwin. Perhaps we can find some time to catch up while you are here. I would love to learn about the new developments in your lives."

"You enjoy the view from up there?" asked Balthazar. "It's tall enough to see over containers stacked ten-high above deck."

"The officer of the watch required my services," replied Arlo.

Balthazar asked, "Why don't you join us and we can all catch up together?"

"I sincerely appreciate the offer but am afraid I must retire to the dreamworld for the night. I have much work ahead, and the festivities of the New Libertatian libertines are a bit too exuberant for me. Darwin, you look like you could use some rest too. Goodnight, and sweet dreams."

They got into the elevator and the doors closed. There was something or someone Darwin had wanted to ask Arlo about, but he couldn't remember. Whatever, he'd figure it out later when his more pressing concerns were alleviated.

The elevator ascended, the doors opened, and Balthazar said, "This is where I single-handedly manipulate the global economy. Well, a small team and I. Pretty fucking cool, huh?" Complicated navigation equipment filled much of the spacious, deserted bridge, but one end had been converted into a plush office. The back wall—the only one not comprised of windows—was covered in numerous pictures of Balthazar looking debonaire in *Fortune, Fast Company, Aquapreneur*, and a dozen more publications. It seemed he'd had the cover of every magazine he'd ever been on blown up and framed.

'Balthazar Abadi: The Man Who Stared into the Abyss Until It Blinked.'

'The Tzar: Genius, Reckless, or Both?'

'Balthazar's Bizarre Bazaar.'

'Founding a Company Is Cool, but What About a Country?'

Ridiculous. Darwin turned his attention to the other three sides of the space. He had a two-hundred-and-seventy-degree view from up here and estimated he could see about fifteen miles before the Earth's curvature obstructed his sight. The nearest landmass was Hawaii, but they were more than two hundred miles away, outside major shipping lanes and the territorial waters and exclusive economic zone of the United States. The moon was less than half full and itself obstructed by rain-filled clouds.

It was a dark night on the open ocean, and Darwin shuddered at the idea of falling overboard.

The only light came from the *Arianna*'s deck below and the bioluminescent sea serpent, half as long as the colossal ship, swimming alongside. But because no one else had commented on it and the fact that sea monsters (at least of that size) weren't real, he ignored it as just another hallucination. It still gave him an eerie feeling.

"You get internet out here?" asked Darwin.

"We have our own dedicated satellite. There's a huge receiver right above us and a local network set up across the ship. Just got it upgraded a few days ago. Have you not paid any attention to the moves I've been making?"

"I've been busy raising a family, sorry."

"Then let me enlighten you. This is the *Arianna*," said Balthazar, motioning out the front bridge windows at the radiant deck below.

"I can't believe you named her after that girl who dumped you in college," said Darwin.

Balthazar let out a single sharp laugh. "And she's yet to reach out to me. Can you believe it? But that's actually a common misconception. The ship was already christened. And it's bad luck to change the name. Though it did factor into my decision to buy her. Of course I could have bought a new ship and named it whatever I wanted. But it's kind of my thing to take advantage of a good value when I see one. Plus I put all the money I saved and then some into modifications. They're a bit...extreme.

"Now, like her namesake, the *Arianna* may not be conventionally beautiful. But she does have a great personality and a fascinating past. She was the largest container ship in the world when built. Three hundred feet longer than the Eiffel Tower is tall. Much bigger than any of my ex-family's gaudy yachts. Hypocrites. She's even bigger than their oil tankers. She was built in France but in her former life was owned by a Swiss company and registered in Panama. She sailed over a million miles, moved over two million containers—I estimate a few hundred were full of illegal narcotics at the time—and burned around two hundred and fifty million gallons of fuel. Nearly single-handedly influenced the planet's climate. She was taken by pirates twice, first off the Horn of Africa and then off the eastern shore of the Philippines. For complicated legal reasons she was set to retire twenty years early and make a one-way trip to the world's largest ship-breaking graveyard on the beaches of Alang, India. But I swooped in and saved her from such a sad fate."

"Wow, you really do your due diligence," said Preston.

"What's to stop her from being taken by pirates now?" asked Darwin. "She's quite a catch and all alone out here in the middle of nowhere."

"As I mentioned, the modifications are a bit extreme. We're a peace-loving country but do have a small military of former special forces. Anyway, there are currently eighteen hundred and thirty-six people on board, including you two and excluding the six who left on the last bird out before the tropical cyclone hits. You picked an interesting time to finally visit. It looks like most people are currently enjoying the party before the storm out on the soccer field. I hope to qualify for the 2024 Olympics, by the way. But the *Arianna* is lonely and getting a bit crowded. I was about to buy a cruise ship and anchor it right alongside. But this virus will crush the cruise industry so I'm waiting to scoop one up on the cheap later this year. Triple our population and expand our choice of staterooms beyond converted shipping containers. I'm considering rolling out an e-residency program like Estonia in the interim. We've already had more than half a million people apply for citizenship. Those here right now are an exclusive group."

"You really think the virus is going to be a factor outside of

China?" asked Preston. "No one at my firm is concerned."

Balthazar looked at Darwin and said, "The important thing to remember when talking to a venture capitalist is that they're in an industry where they only need to be right ten percent of the time. It colors their thinking about everything. Now, smart people can draw different and even opposite conclusions from the same data. Happens all the time. It's the basis for markets. But they're usually wrong if they come to a different one than me. That's essentially how all of this is funded. It's why I moved out here in the first place. Get out of the same information bubble as everyone else and avoid being overly influenced by their opinions. Prevent me-too investments. But relocating to what was at the time international waters also had other benefits."

"I thought the idea of international waters being a lawless paradise is just a myth," said Darwin.

"Always the myth-buster. The high seas comprise half of the Earth's surface. And you're partially correct. The laws that apply to a ship in international waters are those of the country where it's flagged. It's why so many are registered in freedom-loving and forward-thinking—some would say shady—places. The *Arianna* was flagged in Uruguay, where basic human rights like drugs, gambling, and sex work are legal or decriminalized. Technically, however, any country can prosecute a serious offense on the high seas under 'universal jurisdiction.' But that won't happen if you're committing victimless crimes. I had several heads of state on here at the time and believe me—they weren't going to prosecute shit."

Preston laughed his fanboy laugh again.

Darwin had almost forgotten about his long list of troubles, but something about the recent encounter with Arlo still unnerved him. Whatever memory the facilitator had nearly triggered was important, a missing piece of the puzzle. He said, "Man, what a small world seeing Arlo on board."

"It *is* a small world, Chuck. I know you didn't ask—you've never asked, which I find deeply offensive, by the way—but that's exactly why I founded this country. Back in the day if you didn't like the place you were born you could strike out into unknown, unclaimed lands and live as you please. Now *all* the world's land except the poles has been claimed. Sure, you can pull an Elon and dream about starting an extraterrestrial colony. But that's ten or fifteen years away, at least. And you have to bring your own atmosphere. Mars is even more inhospitable than Antarctica, parts of which are the closest terrestrial analog. I've been. It's terrible. The Antarctic Desert is bigger and drier than the Sahara, my old backyard. By the time you can get a ticket off Earth and at the rate this place is heating up it'd make more sense to move down there."

Balthazar was pacing around the bridge now, gesturing wildly with his arms to punctuate his points like he was giving a presentation on stage. No doubt he'd given such a presentation many times before.

"So, everyone is born into this one hundred and ninety-five nation-state lottery. And the worse ticket you get, the more difficult it is to trade it in for a better one. Passport inequality is an overlooked and unaddressed injustice. You're trapped. I thought I was lucky and won the lottery. Born into royalty in an oil state. A bonified prince. And then *you* turned me onto New Atheism and into an apostate," Balthazar said as he pointed at Darwin with double finger guns.

It was difficult for Darwin to parse the myriad negative sensations swirling around in him by now, but one of them was definitely guilt. Maybe that was the real reason he'd resisted his friend's overtures all these years.

Balthazar continued, "But I don't blame you for getting me exiled from my family and fortune. They're the ones who insisted I get a Western education, after all. But I was disowned, a man without a country. Stateless! That should have made me freer than anyone. But it was just the opposite. The US took me in as a refugee and offered to grant me citizenship, for which I was grateful, but the income tax laws are such that you could live and work abroad and *still* have to pay US taxes. On top of that, you have to pay an exit tax even to renounce your citizenship if your net worth is over a measly two mil.

"So, I started looking into my options. Of course I was aware of microstates like Singapore, Vatican City, Malta, and Monaco. But then I learned about micro*nations* like Sealand, Operation Atlantis, Minerva, and the Glacier Republic. Self-proclaimed independent countries. Hundreds have existed over the years. Even today there are at least sixty-eight spread around the world. But what differentiates one from the other? How do you turn a micronation into a microstate?"

Balthazar paused as if waiting for an answer. Darwin and Preston just glanced at each other and shook their heads. He went on, "I won't bore you with details of the declarative vs. constitutive theories of statehood. But the takeaway is that you become a legitimate state the same way you turn any made-up thing like a law, currency, or religion into something real—recognition. You just have to get enough people to believe in it. That's all. 'Real' countries are accepted by other 'real' countries. But shit, even China isn't officially recognized by every member of the UN. Over thirty don't recognize Israel, including my old home. Many legacy micronations set up shop in land either claimed or disputed by existing countries, which creates challenges to recognition. Hence why seasteading in one way or another was the best option.

"New Libertatia is now formally recognized by eight other countries. Admittedly they're on the shadier side and their leaders are primarily interested in our financial laws. We're going to be like a combo of the Cayman Islands and Switzerland before they started getting soft. But it's a good start and a lot to show for a few years of work. Now the hedge fund is a sovereign wealth fund. And yours truly is once again royalty. I could have made myself a prince—that's where the term 'principality' comes from, by the way—or even a king. But I've already been a prince and there are plenty of kings around. I'm the only tzar in business."

"Why the name New Libertatia?" asked Darwin.

"Libertatia was an apocryphal utopian pirate colony in seventeenth-century Madagascar."

"I'm surprised you didn't call it Libertaria," said Preston.

"Having our citizens called 'Libertarians' would have been confusing and not entirely accurate."

Preston said, "Fair point."

"But enough about me. Don't get me wrong, I love talking about myself. I could do this all night. But your life seems to have finally gotten interesting and I want to hear all about it," said Balthazar. "I know that's why you're here and it's not to see your old college roommate or take me up on my other offers. They still stand, by the way. We don't care that you never finished your PhD. Legacy credentials aren't important here. You can jump to the top of that five-hundred-thousand-person list and pick up your research where you left off with all the funding you need. This can be your HMS *Beagle.* Shit, you're basically already working with the 'dream team.' Just wait until you meet them tomorrow, see the facilities, and experience the work they do firsthand."

Preston looked at Darwin with shock and said, "You've had a golden ticket to join New Libertatia and never cashed it in?"

"Up until recently I liked my life very much, thank you," replied Darwin. "And this isn't everyone's idea of paradise... plus I couldn't spend that much time away from the family."

Preston said, "I mean, I appreciate your commitment to raising my nieces, but working here would be a dream."

"Just to be clear, Preston—you will never work here," said Balthazar.

"I kind of assumed that," said Preston, dejected.

The stimulants Darwin had ingested earlier had worn off. "Could we turn on more lights in here?" he asked.

"Sure thing," said Balthazar. "Do you want some coffee? We've got a few of the best baristas in the world on board, though they're probably zonked out of their minds right now."

"That's ok," said Darwin. "Have you heard of Circadian Capital Partners?"

"CCP? Third-rate fund. More of a family office that primarily invests the wealth of a few rich families. Old aristocratic money, European style. It's fitting they share an acronym with the Chinese Communist Party, though they should add a 'C' and go by CCCP—they're so bad at allocating capital they may as well be the Soviet Union."

Preston laughed.

"Technically CCP is an initialism, not an acronym, because you pronounce each letter separately. Acronyms are said as one word, like NASA or LASER," said Darwin, unsure why he was wasting precious energy on such trivialities.

"Classic Darwin. Never change. Last I heard CCP is getting into medical financing and some 5G shit. Low margin telecom equipment and whatnot. Sounds like they're desperate. I believe their name popped up in one of the articles I read about those ridiculous 5G conspiracy theories when researching our own network upgrade. Millimeter wave is even lower frequency than infrared. It can't harm anyone."

"Not all conspiracy theories are necessarily ridiculous," said Darwin.

Balthazar appeared comically surprised. "You're the very last person I expected to hear that from. You're the one who convinced me of any sufficiently large group of people's utter inability to keep an important secret for any length of time, at least in the modern age. What, you believe they're some evil organization out to get you?"

"Almost no one is evil, at least in their own mind," said Darwin. "They often think they're doing god's work. And radiation doesn't have to be ionizing to have an effect. For example, the US military's Active Denial System for crowd control uses microwaves as a kind of heat ray. And the most likely cause of the 'Havana syndrome' experienced by US diplomats in Cuba and China over the past few years is a kind of pulsed microwave energy weapon."

"Invisible weapons? This must be good!" said Balthazar. "Should I get us some tinfoil hats?"

"Actually, something along those lines might end up being useful," said Darwin. Balthazar raised his manicured eyebrows.

"You should go back to the beginning," said Preston, "like you did on the flight over."

"Ok," began Darwin, "six months ago, unbeknownst to

me at the time, Madeline underwent the modified Huxley procedure..."

"Well, shit," said Balthazar.

The sun was rising, turning the clouds stretching across the unobstructed horizon numerous shades of green, from forest to neon. Not real, thought Darwin—the atmosphere scatters light on the shorter end of the visible spectrum. Ignore.

Balthazar continued, "Boy am I glad I never underwent that damn procedure, unlike most of the people here. Don't need to. I follow the Uberman polyphasic sleep schedule, like Da Vinci and Tesla. I nap for twenty minutes every four hours. Getting all your daily sleep in one session only came in with the industrial revolution, along with wage slavery."

"As an expert in sleep disorders, I'm not even going to respond to that," said Darwin. "Can we stay focused?" What should have been a one-hour story had taken...he wasn't sure. All night, apparently. His perception of time's passing was distressingly warped, though hopefully not for long. At least the conversation had helped keep him awake and distracted from the phantasmagoria.

"Sorry, I tend to digress. But digressions are often where the good stuff is," said Balthazar. "Anyway, so the executive summary is that Circadian Capital Partners is part of a cult that worships beings who live in the dream realm. And they're trying to turn the world into some kind of dream machine or dream farm to expand their empire?"

Darwin hesitated for a moment, then said, "Yes."

"And they've experimented with different methods over the years, like proliferating DMT usage and the subsequent hallucinations, which count as dreams to these kooks. But

219

now they're focused on getting as many people as possible to undergo the modified Huxley procedure, then further modifying their brains using electromagnetic radiation so they're essentially dreaming all the time?"

Darwin hesitated twice as long, then said, "Yes."

"And after testing on vagrants in the forgotten places of the world they moved on to the early adopters of the procedure. Or, to use your words—people who 'dream big'?"

Darwin answered right away this time. "For fuck's sake, yes. And they're killing those with the means to discover or remedy what they're doing. But I don't know why they're holding Madeline."

"Ho—ly—shit! I love it. The saying 'I'll sleep when I'm dead' must have special meaning for these people. I'd say it's insane they *actually* believe that. But it's no crazier than what fundamentalists in all major religions believe. Talk about a unique investment thesis. I was already short Stasis Hotels along with the rest of the travel sector but am going to lever it through the roof. I'll take positions against CCP's other significant investments too. We're going to need some airtight supporting material before we go public with this. It's supposed to be a holiday and most of them will be hungover as hell but I'll get my team to start looking into it today before the squall rolls in and potentially disrupts our internet. Red sky at morning, sailors take warning," said Balthazar, nodding out the bridge windows to the east.

At least the sun was indeed coming up, thought Darwin, even if the light he saw was on the wrong side of the color wheel. Looking out over the *Arianna*, he could now discern a park, even larger than the soccer field and complete with dense trees swaying in the wind. The party had finally ended, and the New Libertatians gone to get however many hours of shuteye they needed. The ship's deck was empty except for those who looked to be battening down the hatches and overseeing the reeling in, stacking, and securing of the solar panels that Darwin now saw floated in a black field around the ship. The whitecaps farther out made him nervous, but they couldn't quell the growing optimism that his most pressing concern may soon be alleviated.

Balthazar wiggled his computer's mouse, and the screen-saver of electric sheep jumping over a fence disappeared. He said, "Look at that—the email you sent with all your notes for my medical team is already open. Strange, I don't remember leaving it that way. But I'm way overdue for my nap and don't feel so hot. Hmm, the internet is down too. That shouldn't happen until the storm is upon us. Must be a bug in the new network. The team who installed it is still on board. I'll have them look into it ASAP. Anyway, the surgeons should be ready for you in about a half-hour. I live all the way on the risky end of the efficient frontier, but—"

"Concentrate to get rich, diversify to stay rich," interrupted Preston. Evidently he'd awoken from the extended nap he'd taken while Darwin re-recounted his tale.

Balthazar just shook his head and continued, "But are you sure you're ready to be the first patient to undergo an experimental brain surgery? I get that it's your idea and you're in bad shape. And don't get me wrong—the onboard team are experts in the modified Huxley procedure and are some of the best neurosurgeons in the world. I actually tried to get Magnusson to relocate here from Thailand. Almost had him too before they legalized the procedure in the US. Guess moving back there was the wrong decision for him. Anyway, this isn't just endoscopy. Are—"

Balthazar was interrupted again, but this time by a massive explosion on the deck below. Based on the other two men's reactions, it was all too real.

Chapter 27: Madeline

A Venus–like planet, perpetually enshrouded in a layer of dense clouds dozens of miles thick. Its inhabitants, though intelligent, have never beheld the sun, stars, or any celestial phenomena. They never had a reason to look up, and the spark of wonder never ignited...No.

A rogue ice world without a star, wandering the titanic void between solar systems. The planet itself is barren, frozen, and devoid of life, but the tidal forces it exerts on its lone moon keep the vast subterranean lunar oceans warm and liquid. The seas are salty and dark, except for the glow emitted by their inhabitants... No.

Madeline had a hard time concentrating on worldbuilding. She was running out of ideas. More importantly, she no longer needed more balls. Instead her focus was on the young woman named Sakura walking towards her on the way back from the bathroom. As Sakura turned down her aisle of pachinko machines, they caught each other's eyes and gave the slightest of nods. This was it.

Madeline's heart raced as she stood and picked up her heavy bucket of balls. There was no need to carry with you any more than you intended to spend at the prize counter—Elias had made it clear that the penalty for stealing another's balls was being cast out into the place where there was weeping and gnashing of teeth.

But Madeline intended to spend every last one of hers. And then some.

She tried to act normal as she strode across the parlor and into the women's bathroom. She entered the last stall. Sitting on top of the toilet seat was a bucket fuller than hers with a note on top, written on a torn-out page from her notebook. In shockingly hard to read, handwritten Japanese, it read, 'Best of luck, Madeline. Your courage is inspiring. Please don't forget about us.'

The parlor's patrons were unable to talk to each other—it was like being unable to cry for help in a dream—and the situation was set up to foster an everyone-for-themselves mindset. They had a collective action problem. But Madeline had found a few women who were lucid and willing to pool resources to purchase someone's freedom in exchange for a promise they'd find a way to rescue the others from the outside. That is, *if* outside was where the elevator led. Naturally, as had been the case for much of her life, Madeline was the de facto leader and the one chosen to undertake such an important and risky endeavor. It wasn't clear what the parlor's policy was on sharing, but she thought it best to keep their plan clandestine given the stakes.

She picked up the other bucket, giving her just over fifty thousand pachinko balls. She briefly marveled that all the worlds held in her hands represented only a tiny fraction of the hundred billion or more planets in the Milky Way. Madeline walked out of the stall, out of the bathroom, and set the two buckets down on the prize counter. The Elias behind the counter did not seem surprised, despite this being the only time someone had accumulated so many balls since Madeline had been there.

He gave her a strange smile and said, "Right this way, Madeline."

Elias led her across the floor, the eyes of the hundred or so patrons now in the parlor upon her. He swiped a key card to open the elevator doors, then extended his arm and said, "After you."

Madeline entered the elevator, followed by Elias, and the doors closed. There were about two dozen buttons, each numbered thirteen, followed by a city name. She scanned them—Honolulu, New York, Tahiti, Mexico City, Athens, Bangkok, Hong Kong, Tokyo, Sydney. She'd traveled enough and was a loyal enough Stasis Hotels customer to understand that the cities were those with a *Suspended Animation Collection* property. Interesting.

Elias said, "Great work, Madeline. Let's take you home."

He pressed the button for '13 – San Francisco.' Nothing happened, as far as she could feel. Several seconds passed before the doors slid open to reveal...another sprawling pachinko parlor, full of patrons.

"After you," said Elias again. But Madeline didn't move. Some people would have despaired, but escalating anger consumed her. Elias was on her right, facing the same direction. She balled her fists and stared straight ahead, visualizing stepping forward then hitting Elias with a—

"Spinning hammerfist," said Elias, finishing her thought for her. "Please don't do anything rash, Madeline. For your own sake. I know—*I know*—you are thinking about trying to harm me, but I assure you it would not end well. I've cast others out for following such a train of thought as far as you did just now. We knew about your plan with Sakura and the others. They'll be most disappointed and discouraged that you didn't come back for them. We consider that a win. You're very clever, Madeline. I hope you aren't too clever. Your harvest has been particularly bountiful. We'd like you to stay with us a while longer."

So, it was just like it had appeared when other patrons tried to fight back—somehow, Elias could read her thoughts. It wasn't exactly a surprise given how the process of validating new pachinko balls worked; those in charge of this place could see into their minds. The inner sanctum had been breached. How could she possibly resist? How could she even come up with a way of resisting if those thoughts were also exposed? She felt violated, naked.

Madeline glared at Elias, trying to determine if even now he snooped on her ruminations, but he wore the same inscrutable half-smile as always. Infuriatingly, once more he said, "After you, Madeline."

She tried to keep her mind blank, if only to deprive Elias any voyeuristic pleasure from peering into the citadel. She wished she'd taken more than a passing interest in the meditation fad that had swept her old world, sometime in the indeterminable past. The ability to completely clear her mind would have been welcome under the present circumstances.

As she surveyed the San Francisco parlor, she was surprised to see someone she vaguely recognized—that author Darwin was obsessed with. Michael something. She didn't really care; her anger was turning to despair, like she'd felt after first arriving. She now knew where the elevator led, or didn't. Elias had taken her pen and notebook, and soon she'd forget all that she'd worked so hard to remember and become just another zombie, like so many of the others.

"Let's go, Madeline," said Elias, a hint of edge now in his voice.

What had Michael's books been about that had so intrigued Darwin? Something about them seemed relevant. There had been a stack of them on the bookshelf. She could visualize their covers. Atheism. Panpsychism. Psychedelics. Free will. That was it. Yes, she remembered now.

"Madeline, please," said Elias. It sounded like his final plea and warning.

But Madeline did not exit the elevator. She reached out, pressed the close button, and the doors slid slowly shut.

Chapter 28: Darwin

"WHAT THE FUCK!" screamed Balthazar, jumping up and down as the bubble of fire reached the bridge level and began turning into black smoke. Darwin and Preston just stared in disbelief, mouths agape.

An ear-splitting siren then drowned out Balthazar's profanity. Within a few minutes there were water cannons and a fully outfitted fire crew battling the growing blaze in the middle of the ship. Darwin winced, feeling the still-recovering burns he'd suffered when his own house had burned down not long ago.

But what Balthazar said once his initial shock and rage subsided stirred a worse feeling. "It looks like the blast came from near the medical center...some of the team would have already been there preparing."

Darwin had stood up to watch the scene below but now had to sit to prevent his legs from giving out beneath him. Was this really happening? It seemed impossible but could not be merely bad luck or a coincidence. It had to be related. People had just died because of him, and now with no solution to his condition in sight, he would likely join them soon.

A tall Scandinavian man wearing pajamas and a captain's hat rushed into the bridge, closely followed by another man who turned off the local alarm. They both looked half-asleep, half-drunk. The captain surveyed the damage below and said in a thick Norwegian accent, "Ve need to set sail for Havaii. Even if ve contain the fire ve'll need repairs. If ve can't salvage the ship ve vant to be as close to shore as possible for a rescue operation of this magnitude."

Balthazar scoffed. "Sven, I may not technically be the captain of this ship. But I'm the tzar of this country. I am *not* abandoning her. I'll sleep with the *Arianna* in a watery grave if I must."

"Maritime tradition is that the captain is the last one off, not that they never leave," Sven replied.

"Call it a New Libertatian tradition, then. Besides, a rescue operation won't be feasible until the storm passes. And given the cyclone's size I prefer to take my chances on the bigger boat." The waves below already dwarfed the lifeboats rimming part of the ship. "Those lifeboats may be unsinkable but they'd be tombs by the time this squall was done with them. And I'm well aware of the catastrophic and ironic danger of fire at sea. But we have the best firefighting equipment money can buy. We'll get it under control."

The wind carried the flames to the edge of the park, where the closest palm trees lit up like torches and provided additional fuel for the conflagration. Two of the water cannons seemed to be firing at each other instead of the blaze. Sven said, "Heading vest vill also get us into the storm faster. Perhaps the rain vill help."

The western sky was filled with dark thunderheads, the occasional flash of lighting, and the gray blur of distant torrential downpour. But Darwin was barely paying attention. How much longer could he stay awake? Could he afford to take another nap? The urge to sleep could be stronger than extreme hunger or thirst, even more powerful than the desire to alleviate pain.

Sven said loudly and slowly into the radio, "Mayday, mayday, mayday. This is country *Arianna, Arianna, Arianna.* Call sign bravo, alpha, mike, foxtrot—"

"Sorry to interrupt, captain, but there's no signal going out," said the man at the other set of inscrutably complicated controls.

"Vhat do you mean?" asked Sven.

"I don't know of a more straightforward way to say it."

"That doesn't make any sense. There's no vay the blast, even of that size, impacted the radio," said Sven. "Vhere is the officer of the vatch?"

"Good question," said Balthazar. "I haven't seen Leif all night. But we can worry about that later. John, you're the chief engineer of this ship. Head up to monkey island and figure out what's up with the radio."

"On my way," said the other man (apparently Chief Engineer John) as he got up and left the bridge. He poked his head back in and asked, "Do you guys hear that?"

"The sound of New Libertatia's destruction? Yes I fucking hear it," said Balthazar. John took the hint and left again. Balthazar continued, "So our satellite and long-range radio communications are down. The local mesh network should still work fine. But we're stuck talking to each other until one of the two gets fixed or we get closer to shore. How long will that take?"

Sven said, "Ve'll likely have to reduce our speed given the storm, but I think ve can make it in around twelve hours."

"Ok, let's go," said Balthazar. "Presumably we can at least

keep the fire from reaching the engines at the back of the ship. What could cause an explosion like that? Could someone have accidentally—"

"It wasn't an accident," said Darwin quietly. Everyone's attention turned to him. "None of this is accidental or coincidental."

"You think someone did this intentionally?" asked Balthazar. "That would be a declaration of war against New Libertatia!"

"They must be here," said Darwin. "Or have been here."

"Who? Are you talking about the CCP? You think some fucking family office is trying to sabotage the highest-returning fund of all time? We've thoroughly vetted every single person on board."

"I spent all night explaining how it's not a family office, but one wing of a sprawling and sophisticated international cabal," said Darwin. "And they're interested in much more than returns."

Sven's walkie-talkie crackled. John's voice asked, "Do you guys see that?"

"You're going to have to be more specific. Ve see many things. Vhat's the status of the antenna?" replied Sven.

"To the east, coming up alongside the ship," said John.

Darwin had a sinking feeling, one he increasingly feared he'd experience literally, when he looked to the east and saw nothing but dark waves and forest green clouds.

John said, "Now it's coming across…"

Something person-sized plunged by the windows. It had only been visible for a moment, but from the blur of colors matching those he'd just seen worn in the bridge, there was no doubt it had been John.

231

Darwin ran out to the open bridge wing and had what felt like an acid flashback to Rick Larson leaping from one of the Golden Gate Bridge's towers; former Chief Engineer John had not made it to the water, if that had been his intention, though from the bridge's height it wouldn't have mattered. Darwin looked up to where he'd jumped from, and it was clear even to him that all the various antennas were now useless. He reentered the bridge and was surprised to find Preston visibly shaken given how unconcerned he'd been when someone he knew personally had done something similar. Odd.

"Sven, get the ship moving and call another engineer to look into the radio antennas," said Balthazar. "I'm going to talk to security. Something fucked is happening. Darwin, come with me. If you're right and the same people who are after you are after all of us then perhaps you can provide some insight. Preston...I guess you can tag along."

Darwin and Preston followed Balthazar as he strode out of the bridge, down a level of stairs, and into what appeared to be the security command center.

It was empty.

But the large room was still filled with movement. A few of the screens were black or scrambled, but the dozens of others showed various strange and disturbing scenes from around the ship.

Dancing flames, which to Darwin were bright blue, and not just at their base.

A hallway filled with smoke and stumbling figures.

A group of people on the deck who looked as if they were being attacked by invisible birds of prey. One disappeared over the edge.

Someone bashing their face against a bulkhead until they

went limp and dropped to the ground.

"Why aren't we moving yet?" asked Balthazar, looking up at the ceiling towards the bridge. Then he sat down at the computer and changed the screens' view to what must have been the engine room. At least it *used* to be the engine room. Darwin wasn't sure what one was supposed to look like, but presumably it shouldn't have been littered with debris and covered in blood.

Balthazar ran both hands through his jet black, slicked-back hair and said, "The cameras should have automatically alerted security to anything anomalous. We can play back what happened but—"

Preston jerked violently. Darwin and Balthazar looked at him.

Preston said, "Guys, I really don't feel so good." It was almost surprising to hear his voice given how unusually quiet he'd been. Come to think of it, had Darwin's brother-in-law blinked at all since awakening?

"Welcome to the club," said Balthazar. "It's not exactly exclusive."

But the look in Preston's unfocused, rapidly moving eyes made Darwin understand just what was happening. He asked, "You can't shake the dreams you had during that nap, can you?"

"No, I can't. It's terrible, man," replied Preston, looking down and shaking his head. "When I close my eyes I see...How can you tell?"

"Because you—along with everyone on this ship who underwent the modified Huxley procedure—are now in the same boat as me," said Darwin. "And stuck on this boat with us."

"I was with you guys all night. How could that possibly have

233

happened?" asked Preston.

"The new network we installed..." whispered Balthazar. "I knew they didn't look like network engineers. Is that even possible?"

They sat in silence for several seconds, digesting the truth and implications of the situation. Then Balthazar's radio crackled and Sven's voice said, "Tzar, you must come see this."

"Shit, not Sven too," said Balthazar as he stood up and raced out of the room. "He's one of the few who hasn't had the procedure done!"

Darwin and Preston followed him up to the bridge, where they found Captain Sven looking through a pair of binoculars into the distance. But even with the naked eye, Darwin could see what he was talking about: two black boats and a black helicopter on the horizon, heading right for them.

"I assume that isn't someone responding to our Mayday call," said Balthazar. He seemed calmer now, accepting of the situation.

"The engine von't start, and I can't get ahold of the first or second engineers," said Sven.

"Unsurprising. The engine room was sabotaged and whoever was there killed," said Balthazar evenly. Sven's pale face went even whiter.

"So we're trapped on a broken, burning ship in the middle of the Pacific with no way to communicate, an incoming storm, and almost two thousand crazy people. And now there are fucking pirates—or worse—coming for us?" asked Darwin. It was insane how fast things could change for the worse.

"Buckle up, Chuck."

Part 5: REM Sleep

One second later

Chapter 29: Madeline

The details of a conversation Madeline had had with Darwin on several occasions shined out of the past's haziness, like a lighthouse in the fog.

"It's not that I don't believe in free will. That doesn't put it strongly enough. I *understand* that free will doesn't exist," Darwin had said. "Belief implies some level of uncertainty is plausible, which is why people say they believe in astrology—deep down they know it's nonsense. I also don't believe the Earth is round, humans are adversely impacting the planet's climate, or two plus two is four. They're simply facts I comprehend and acknowledge, even if some others don't."

"Is this an elaborate excuse for forgetting our anniversary?" she'd teased.

"Even if it's technically a mitigating factor, I'm still sorry. And even if free will *did* exist, I would have had no choice but to marry you." Good save. He'd continued, "I'm serious though. Very few people who study the relevant subject matter like neuroscience or physics—even philosophy—are 'metaphysical libertarians,' or those who believe in what most people think of as free will. It's a fitting name because it's basically a prerequisite for being a political libertarian, and like political libertarians, they haven't really thought it through."

"Is this about Balthazar again?"

Ignoring the question, Darwin had said, "For example, name a non-human animal."

She'd paused for a moment then said, "A mini horse."

"Great choice. Now, what other animals came to mind, and why did you choose that one in particular?"

"I also thought of dogs, presumably because Mofongo is curled up on my feet, under the table and dreaming. I suppose I chose mini horse because Christina won't stop talking about the one she met at school yesterday."

"In what sense were you free to choose one of the thousands of animals that didn't bubble up out of the ether in those few seconds? Could you really have chosen a wildebeest, even after seeing millions on our honeymoon? Or a pangolin?"

"What's a pangolin?"

"Exactly. It doesn't change anything that you can explain why those specific animals popped up and you chose the one you did. They popped up because of who you are and the experiences you've had. But you don't have freedom over your genes *or* your past experiences, which are just the culmination of subatomic particles following the laws of physics in a series of deterministic or random reactions stretching all the way back to the big bang, and maybe before that. There's no room for top-down causation. 'Choices' are just emergent phenomena.'"

"Please don't share this line of thinking with the girls any time soon."

"I'll give you another example. Open your hand and hold it out in front of you, palm up." She'd obliged. "Now, at some point decide to close it into a fist."

Madeline had waited a few seconds and then—at a moment

she had to admit was entirely random and somewhat mysterious to her if she paid close enough attention—closed her hand. She'd said, "You're going to ask me why I decided to close my hand at that exact moment and if I was really free to close it at a different time. I get it—you don't know what or when you're going to think until the thought arises."

"And if I'd been monitoring your brain activity, I could tell before you when you're going to do it. There are well-known experiments showing that your brain commits to a decision before you're consciously aware of it. We can predict when and how you're going to act. More than that, if I electrically stimulated your brain in the right way, I could decide for you when to close your hand. Our thoughts, decisions, and actions are the result of electrical pulses and chemical reactions. The technology to manipulate them externally is improving exponentially. In a sense I can already control your thoughts. For example if I tell you not to think of a pink elephant, you'll almost certainly think of a what? But soon this will be possible using other kinds of signals..."

In the present moment, whenever it was, Madeline supposed the fact that out of all possible memories, this one bubbled up to the surface was yet another example of her lack of agency. But she was nonetheless grateful. She remembered how the conversation had ended.

"So what, the choices we make don't matter because we're automatons and don't actually make them?" she'd asked. "That's depressing."

Darwin had said, "Ironically I find it freeing. The only reasonable course of action is to eat your cake and have it too. Don't—"

"Don't you mean 'have your cake and eat it too'?"

"The saying originated the other way before it got corrupted. It's about making a tradeoff between two mutually exclusive choices. It makes more sense to say you can't eat something and then still have it afterward."

"Fine."

"As I was saying—the takeaway is not to regret your past decisions and to be quick to forgive others for theirs. None of you could have done otherwise. But you can still learn from the past, and for all intents and purposes act as if you *do* have free will. Your choices *do* matter, and there *is* a neurophysiological difference between voluntary and involuntary action..."

"I'm glad to see you smiling again," said Elias in the elevator, smiling again himself. "But either you walk through the elevator door onto this floor, or you get thrown out the front door into something worse than oblivion."

Madeline said, "You know, Elias, if that really is your name—in a way the entirety of the universe and past have conspired to determine what I'm about to do next."

Chapter 30: Darwin

"Don't ships like this have panic rooms for pirate attacks?" asked Preston.

"You've lost your mind if you think I'm going to forsake my countrymen and women and hide like a coward," said Balthazar. "Which, technically, I suppose you're in the early stages of doing. But with no help coming we'd end up starving or burning to death in there. Our only option is to fight. We have more than sufficient weaponry to defend ourselves. However, my concern is fielding enough people to use them."

Balthazar strode over to his office and grabbed a microphone from his desk. When he spoke it came from everywhere at once and sounded like the voice of god. "Citizens of New Libertatia! Our time has not been long. But our darkest hour is already upon us. The forces of evil have conspired against our great nation in a diabolical attempt to take the freedoms we cherish. But the strongest steel is forged in the hottest fires!"

Balthazar paused, glanced at the group in the bridge, and mouthed, 'is that true?' then continued, "No help is on the way, so we must help ourselves. Our enemies are already among us. They have sabotaged our communications equipment, sabotaged the engine, the heart, of our dear *Arianna*, and sabotaged many of our very minds. But they have not sabotaged our spirit.

I believe the three men and one woman who installed the new network are responsible for these despicable acts. I'd prefer they be taken alive. But I understand if you kill them on sight.

"Now, if you've undergone the modified Huxley procedure then you must understand that—like the Party's final, most essential command—you may have to reject the evidence of your eyes and ears. Take refuge in the rooms at the fore of the ship, away from the fire. I can't imagine you would do so at a time like this, but it's essential you do not sleep, or you risk slipping further into madness, becoming a further danger to yourself and others. If you are of sound body and mind then you must—"

Several bullets smashed into the bridge windows. Darwin, Preston, and Sven all hit the deck, but Balthazar didn't flinch. Apparently the windows were bulletproof. Darwin hadn't noticed how thick they were until now. Balthazar set down the microphone, a determined, angry look now on his face, and fetched a large matte-black case out of one of the mahogany drawers. He opened it by scanning his fingerprints then extracted the biggest, meanest-looking gun Darwin had ever seen. It was half Balthazar's size. Well, it was reasonable the strict 'no guns' policy didn't apply to the tzar.

The other three men got to their feet as Balthazar donned headphones, draped a sash of ammo over his shoulder, and purposefully walked out onto the nearest open bridge. He rested the rifle on the railing, took aim, and fired off several dozen rounds in an automatic, deafening burst aimed somewhere in the sky. He then fired another several-second burst aimed at the water. The empty shells fell and clinked onto the metal walkway, and even from this distance the spray was visible where their former contents hit the sea.

241

The helicopter and boat he'd fired on banked and changed their angles of approach. Something that sounded faintly like cheering came from the deck below.

Balthazar walked back into the bridge a second before another round of fire hit the walkway where he'd just been standing. He set the gun on his desk, pulled his ear protection down so the headphones hung around his neck, and flashed them a brief smile. Then he picked up the microphone and said, "If you are of sound body and mind then you must use any means necessary to battle the blaze and the attackers. Do not let them board the ship or the helicopter land. Most importantly, take care of each other and remember—you're fighting for more than just your lives. Long live New Libertatia!"

Cheering again came from below, followed by someone yelling, "Man overboard!"

Preston quietly asked himself, "What is happening right now?"

Several more bullets hit the bridge windows, adding to the spider web patterns of cracks. Everyone flinched but Balthazar, who said, "It's level eight. It should hold. For a while. I've made it publicly known that the *Arianna* can defend herself. If they're approaching and firing at us this brazenly they must have also sabotaged our primary defenses. It'd be a suicide mission otherwise. The cameras in the armory are down so I suspect those already on board got to it, along with all or most of our security team. They'd all undergone the modified Huxley, anyway. Fortunately I understand the principle of diversification."

Balthazar set down the microphone and extracted two handguns from the rifle case, handing them to Sven and Darwin.

"What about me?" asked Preston.

"Darwin seems to have learned to live with his crazy. But you need to head to the rooms at the front of the ship with the others." Balthazar turned to Darwin and Sven. "We can use the water cannons against the boats. But that chopper is going to kill us. Literally. Our best option is to bring it down or at least keep it at bay with Lakshmi here until it's forced to refuel." He patted the rifle on the desk. "The few years I spent in the military before going to university were mostly for propaganda and morale purposes. But I *did* learn a thing or two."

"You named the gun after your other college girlfriend?" asked Darwin.

"I'm sure you can understand why."

"Vhat if they have missiles?" asked Sven.

"Then we're fucked," said Balthazar. "You know better than me this isn't a damn battleship. But I assume they intend to keep as many of New Libertatia's assets and citizens intact as possible."

"Can't ve surrender and pay them vhat they vant?" asked Sven.

"First, we don't negotiate with terrorists," said Balthazar. "More importantly, you haven't been looped into what the rest of us know. Like Darwin said—they're likely after much more than just money. Now, go lock the elevator. Those already on board are no doubt on their way here to eliminate the only real threat to their friends."

On cue a loud bang and the crackling of gunfire came from somewhere below. Darwin almost threw up. Not so boring a life anymore is it, Dar? He would have given anything for his most pressing concern to once again be what he was making the girls for dinner. Sven rushed to secure the elevator, but

Darwin couldn't bring himself to move.

"I wager billions of dollars every day," said Balthazar, recognizing his hesitation and looking him in the eyes. "Emotions only degrade performance. This is no time for fear or mourning. We can do that later if we survive. This is a time for action. Protect my flank!" He donned his headphones, then with some effort picked up Lakshmi and took up his position at the entrance to the open bridge near his office.

Darwin managed to say, "Preston, I think you're stuck—"

The impossibly loud sound of Balthazar firing dozens of more rounds drowned out the rest of his words. Darwin beheld the gun in his hand. Here he was again, except now he'd almost certainly have to use it. He'd always been reluctant to give Balthazar credit for much of anything, but his words made sense. It was the kind of advice Darwin would have given someone else while sitting in an armchair in perfect safety. He could only control what was in his control, and the rush of adrenaline and hyper-alertness helped suppress the daymares. He chambered a round, ready to see what kind of a man he really was.

Then Captain Sven's head exploded.

Sven's gore-filled captain's hat landed at Darwin's feet. His headless, still-tall body continued standing erect for several seconds, then collapsed to the floor. But what—who—stood twenty feet behind where Sven had been, at the door to the open bridge and with an assault rifle aimed right at Darwin, was equally shocking.

Sephira smiled.

Darwin was sure this was the last moment of his life and that he was about to die for the second time in as many weeks. But he found he wasn't scared despite the murder he'd just witnessed. He felt disconcertingly calm. Maybe it was the dire state of his mind and memories, but his life did not flash before his bloodshot eyes. He thought very little of anything and waited for the end to come.

But it did not.

The cacophonous sound of Balthazar firing an extended burst paused and was replaced by return fire hitting the bridge's exterior. Into the brief silence that followed, Balthazar yelled, "Motherfu—," and began shooting again, oblivious to what transpired behind him.

Sephira kept her right hand on the rifle's pistol grip and trigger, bracing it against her shoulder. She removed her gloved left one from the handguard and held her finger up to her mouth, signaling Darwin and Preston to be quiet.

Darwin again looked down at the gun in his hand, held uselessly at his side. No chance he could make use of it before ending up like Sven. Sephira motioned with her head for him to throw it on the ground, her expression growing colder at his hesitation.

Would he effectively kill all of them by giving up the weapon? Was it better to go down fighting, or to at least give Balthazar a chance to do so? No—presumably they wanted them alive. Even a small probability of survival was preferable to certain death. Darwin motioned with his head back towards Balthazar and then shook it, hoping to convey a plea not to kill his friend.

Sephira nodded once.

What else could he do? Darwin tossed the gun several feet in front of him, towards where Sven's body lay. Before it hit the ground, Sephira adjusted the rifle to aim past him and fired two shots in quick succession. Lakshmi's cries ceased.

"Get on the ground!" Sephira commanded, moving carefully

towards them.

Preston obeyed, but Darwin remained standing, staring ahead. The world began breaking apart into Platonic solids with increasing numbers of sides—tetrahedrons, cubes, octahedrons, dodecahedrons, and finally icosahedrons, with twenty faces of identical shape and size. Each one showed the butt of Sephira's rifle coming towards *his* face.

Chapter 31: Madeline

The smug smile fled from Elias's face and was replaced by a combination of fear and confusion. Madeline hadn't realized it, but as she'd been walking Elias's thoughts down one path, she'd subtly adjusted her stance; she now faced him with her knees slightly bent, her right foot behind the left.

He hadn't realized it either, his mind probably still occupied by a pink elephant.

With a movement perfected through thousands of repetitions, to the point where she could do it *without thinking*, Madeline drove her back foot into the ground, twisted her hips, and extended the palm of her right hand straight out in front of her with all the limited strength she had. It wasn't enough power to take down someone Elias's size in one blow, but the explosion of blood told her it'd broken his nose, leaving him stunned and exposed for several seconds. It'd also caused him to take a step back—right into perfect range for kicks to the groin and side of the leg, which sent him to the elevator floor, where an indeterminate number of head stomps ensured he would never again need the device on his wrist and hand.

Madeline pulled the device over her hand and strapped it onto her wrist. It didn't feel exactly like she remembered. A different or newer model, perhaps. But it was familiar enough.

She blinked hard, and when she opened her eyes, the pachinko parlor began dissolving one pixel at a time. When all she saw was blackness, she grasped that something was on her head. It also felt familiar, like the other device Doctor Magnusson had given her for sleeping. She pulled off the contraption to reveal a room at a Stasis Hotel's *Suspended Animation Collection* property. Elias lay on the floor in front of her, dead.

A great wave of dread washed over Madeline as she took a closer look at the bloody pulp of a face.

The man wore the same clothes as Elias and was of similar build and ethnicity, but she was pretty sure the person she'd just killed wasn't him. If only she'd held off on those last few stomps. Madeline racked her brain, trying to remember what Elias looked like, but it was difficult to picture despite the myriad recent interactions she'd had with him in the parlor. Had he ever been there at all, or had her mind just projected his face onto all the overseers?

Breathe, Madeline. Do not regret—you couldn't have done otherwise. This man, whoever he was, had kidnapped her, possibly worse. Fuck him. She had to figure out what the hell was happening and how to help herself and everyone else trapped in that nightmare.

She used the device to alleviate her anxiety and the weakness from hunger and muscle atrophy. Just like riding a bike. She also numbed the pain from stiff joints and what felt like bedsores. Lastly she blocked the terrible smell that must be coming from her; she wore the same outfit she'd had on for as long as she could remember and apparently hadn't showered. At least it seemed she'd actually been using the room's bathroom.

Her immediate needs taken care of, her first inclination was to sprint out of here as fast as she could. But what if this dead stranger had armed colleagues between here and the exit, wherever it was? She wasn't sure how many 'Eliases' there were. Next she thought to call 110 (Japan's 911) from the phone by the bed, but she'd just killed someone and more importantly didn't know for sure where she was. On further inspection the room had no windows, and the phone was probably monitored or blocked from calling externally.

She raided the dead man's pockets and found nothing but a hotel key card—no ID, no phone, and unfortunately no gun or other real weapon. Shit. She explored the rest of the room, trying her best to ignore the corpse.

On the desk was her journal, along with the torn-out pages with the notes she'd written. Next to them was a computer running some complicated application she didn't recognize. Half the screen was black, the other half filled with a dozen or so different colored lines. It definitely needed some design work. She noted the laptop was connected to Wi-Fi instead of a hard line. She closed it and chose to bring it with her as evidence, along with the device that had been on her head and the bloody one still worn by the man she'd just murdere...killed. In self-defense.

There was disappointingly little else of interest in the room. It was pretty similar to the rooms she'd stayed in so many times, with woefully few weapons to improvise. A broken glass from the minibar would have to do. She discovered her Chanel bag, but her phone was nowhere to be found.

Madeline's first few steps had left bloody bootprints on the carpet. How long did she have until someone noticed this man was missing and came looking? It was growing increasingly difficult to remember her life in the parlor, but she thought this particular 'Elias' had only recently shown up for his shift. Potentially she had hours, but what if their exit from the nightmare had created some kind of alert? She needed to move.

Madeline hid the body in the shower and cleaned up as best she could, under no illusion it would buy her much time if someone entered the room. With her bag under her left arm and the five-inch shard of edged glass in her right hand, she carefully opened the door and peered out into the hallway.

It looked just like the Tokyo Stasis Hotel. She noted the number on the door: 1334. If this was the Tokyo Stasis, then the elevator should be down to the right. But the normal elevators in these hotels didn't even *have* a thirteenth floor, if that was indeed where she was. A dedicated elevator to and from this crime scene was too risky. Presumably her captors were still concerned about the prospect of dying in a fire and there were stairs somewhere. They seemed a safer bet.

She snuck out into the hall and slowly closed the door behind her. When she approached the end of the hall, she heard two men conversing around the corner, coming her direction. She pulled the dead man's key card from her pocket and tried it on the nearest room, hoping her intuition was correct.

The door's lock flashed green. She silently entered the hotel room, closed the door, locked the deadbolt. The inside of the room was the same as the one in which she'd woken up. A woman on the bed wore the same headset contraption that was in Madeline's bag. On closer inspection she also wore the same clothes, had the same hair, the same face...no...

The device informed her she was hallucinating. Madeline blinked hard, and the person changed from herself to a young Japanese woman. It was hard to tell with the smart sleep mask, but did she recognize the girl from the parlor? She briefly considered waking her up but thought better of it—who knew how she'd react, and she couldn't risk alerting the guards.

Then Madeline noticed the computer.

It ran the same application as the one in her room, but half the screen was not black; it showed the lively pachinko parlor, although it wasn't quite like Madeline remembered. It was like someone else's low resolution version or interpretation. The different colored lines next to it weren't straight; they looked like biosignatures.

It couldn't be. This technology didn't exist. Unless...the parlors' patrons were only given a shared structure and the modified human brains did the heavy lifting. The program wouldn't need to accurately simulate reality. It was less a brain-computer interface than a *dream*-computer interface. She wasn't an expert, but it seemed plausible.

Madeline understood now how she hadn't questioned the strangeness of her predicament. She'd just accepted it as-is, like in a dream. How much of the nightmare had been her vividly dreaming mind filling in the gaps, adding details to the program's suggestions?

For a terrifying moment Madeline feared she was still in another level of a shared, simulated dream and would never know. Hadn't Darwin said that in a way life was a waking dream, with our brains extrapolating, interpolating, and pattern matching from limited sensory input? Stay focused, Madeline. She could deal with the existential crisis later when she was out of here.

With her ear to the door, she heard the two men's voices pass and continue down the hall. Was one of them familiar? No time to find out.

When they were out of hearing range, she unlocked the

deadbolt and paused, turning to look at the woman on the bed. Should she take her with her? Could she? There must have been more than a hundred rooms on this floor, not to mention those at all the other *Suspended Animation Collection* hotels. There were too many people to help all by herself, one by one. She needed to get herself to safety first then help everyone from the outside, like she'd discussed with Sakura and the others. Madeline made a silent promise to the woman that she'd come back, in one form or another, then slipped out into the hall.

This time she encountered no one, and her heart fluttered when she saw the red exit sign at the far end of a hall and the device gave her no indication it was a hallucination. She broke into a run, slowing when she reached the door. It wasn't locked.

She opened it and froze—standing directly in front of her was an Elias. Whether or not it was *the* Elias, she couldn't be sure. They stared at each other, both surprised, but Madeline acted first and noted he was standing at the top of a flight of concrete stairs. She shoved him as hard as she could. He fell backward, tumbling down to the landing, where he lay motionless, his body bent at an impossible angle.

Madeline followed him down the stairs, but in a manner that wouldn't result in mortal injury. She glanced at him as she ran by. Was he dead? No time to check. She continued running down flight after flight of stairs. It was like she'd assumed—a dedicated stairwell that went from the ground floor to the thirteenth, with no stops in between. She paused when she reached the bottom, not wanting to be surprised again.

She eased the door open and found...no one, just an empty hallway. She ran down it, past several closed doors, and after a few turns saw what she hoped was the final exit.

This door she barreled through to find herself in the cold Tokyo winter air. She'd been in the Tokyo Stasis Hotel after all and was now in an alley beside it. Neon light spilled in from the street. The heavy door closed and locked behind her. It was difficult even to tell it was there. A glance at the sky told her it was early morning. The land of the rising sun would soon live up to its name. She ran out to the main street, ready to put as much distance between the hotel and herself as possible. Then she stopped. Something was missing. *Someone* was missing.

Christina and Evelyn.

Where were they? She racked her brain and found a high probability memory that she'd last left them in her suite at this goddamn hotel, with strict instructions not to leave. But when was that? Everything in sight was still decorated for the holidays; it couldn't have been that long ago. Even if there was only the slightest chance they were still up there, she couldn't forsake them like she'd just abandoned so many others. It was an insane thing to do, but then again, she was insane. And it was the last thing they, whoever they were, would expect.

But there must be security cameras. She needed to alter her appearance. Unfortunately the designer stores were all closed at this hour, and the only nearby place she knew would be open was the all-night convenience store one street over.

"Good morning. Happy new year," said the clerk at the front desk in Japanese.

"Good morning," Madeline replied. So, it was around new year. She bought a matching *Pokémon* shirt, jacket, and hat using cash from her bag, then changed in the bathroom and left her clothes behind. It wasn't Burberry but it would do.

Back out in the cold early morning air, Madeline gazed up

at the Tokyo Stasis and counted thirteen floors up from the street.

It resembled any other floor.

The windows had a mix of open and closed curtains, and the lights were off in most of them. Unsurprising given the hour. What had she expected, a windowless band around the building, or for their criminality to be in plain sight?

She reentered the hotel, fully aware it was a questionable idea. There were more people than she'd expected in the lobby, some of them clearly wasted; it must have been a weekend. On her way towards the elevators, she gave a brief nod to the young man behind the front desk. Surely not everyone who worked here was in on such a diabolical scheme.

Once in the elevator she swiped her skeleton key card, pressed the button for the fiftieth floor, and watched the numbers climb. Was it her imagination, or did it take slightly longer to go from twelve to fourteen as it did to go between other floors? It was impossible to tell in the high-speed elevator.

The lift glided to a stop. She half-expected to see Elias waiting for her when the doors opened, but all that awaited her was an empty, tastefully decorated hallway with abstract paintings of what loosely resembled colorful sleep spindles on the walls.

She tried to manage her expectations as she approached the room where she'd left her daughters, once upon an unknown time. Even the device couldn't fully calm her nerves as she stood outside the door and listened. Nothing.

She used the key card on the main lock and eased open the door, somewhat dismayed there was no deadbolt, which she was pretty sure she'd ensured the girls used. The room was occupied, but even in the dim light from the cityscape outside the windows, she knew that it wasn't by the girls. If—when—she found them, she would never again let her two munchkins out of her sight.

She exited the room as silently as she'd entered and once again found herself in the elevator watching the numbers change, this time descending. The conversation she'd had with Christina popped into her mind: Wasn't the fourteenth floor *really* the thirteenth? Come to think of it, Madeline had never been to the fourteenth floor of any Stasis Hotel.

She again swiped the key card and pressed fourteen. As the elevator slowed, she gripped the glass knife in her pocket so tightly her hand bled. A blink erased the pain.

This time the doors opened to a hallway that wasn't empty, but the family ambling towards her with luggage and bleary eyes hardly seemed to be in on the nefarious jig. She hopped out and checked a few of the numbers on the rooms just to be sure. They all began with fourteen. But before she left this place once and for all, she needed to check one last thing.

Madeline entered the stairwell and went one level down, relieved not to find a crumpled dead body on the next landing. How long until someone found him? How often does someone take the stairs to or from the thirteenth floor if they have a dedicated elevator? The key card again granted her access, but here all the rooms began with twelve. She climbed the stairs up and down a few floors, using the device to turn her fatigue into focus. Was it possible the stairs and landing between floors twelve and fourteen were slightly bigger than the others, enough to hide an entire story in between? She couldn't be sure, but *was* sure that she needed to get out of here.

Or was she?

Madeline contemplated her next move. Should she call the police? She'd killed one, possibly two people. Oh god, what had she...stop. And come to think of it, what exactly had been their crimes? She'd been taken advantage of, yes, but as far as she knew, the Eliases were unarmed and hadn't been physical, at least with her. What was she going to tell the police, that they'd violently thrown people into hell in an advanced virtual reality pachinko parlor? There weren't locks to keep people in their rooms or the building. Could she prove anything, or would she merely come off as a certifiably crazy person?

She needed to better understand what evidence and leverage she had. She reentered the twelfth floor and found her way to room 1234. If the headsets or laptop in her bag had GPS tracking, it would only give them the x and y coordinates, not z; it'd look like they were still in her original room 1334 upstairs. If they could hide in plain sight, then so could she. Madeline put her ear to the door. Again, silence.

She snuck in and was relieved to find the room clean and unoccupied. With a four o'clock check-in time, it could be twelve hours or more before someone entered.

Madeline picked up the room's phone, grateful that hotels still had such outdated devices. She needed help. That she didn't have to do everything herself was a lesson she'd learned the hard way after becoming an executive, but it was a bad habit she still had to actively resist.

She called Darwin: no answer.

Preston: no answer.

Who else's numbers did she know by heart? It was alarming how helpless she was without modern technology. Up until just now she'd thought there was something romantic about the world of analog versus digital. What a joke.

She called the landline at her parents' house: no answer. She wished she'd let the girls have phones despite their age, if only for emergencies like this.

She took out the laptop from her bag. Madeline held her breath as she opened it and waited for the Wi-Fi to connect, then smiled when it hopped on the same network it had been connected to in 1334 with full bars. 'The fastest internet in the industry.' It took her a moment to orient to using a PC after a decade on a Mac. Then she opened a browser, navigated to her email, and...realized she had two-factor authentication on everything important—anything she could use to contact those who could help. It was like she wasn't her real self without her phone, certainly as far as other technologies were concerned.

A scary thought came to Madeline: Her captors had had her iPhone and access to her biometrics. They'd also had some level of access into her mind. Could they have figured out her passwords, impersonated her, made her do or say what they pleased? Stay calm. She could deal with that later. She'd remembered one more number, and it belonged to the perfect person to help given her present concerns.

"Happy new year, Madeline," said Vipul. "It's good to hear from you. I hope you were able to unplug and rel—"

"Sorry to cut you off, Vipul. Are you at a computer?"

"As a matter of fact, I am. The engineering org never *really* gets to take time off, as you know. There's much work to do. Why do you ask?"

"I'm about to video call you from a new account. Please answer." Madeline hung up and called from the laptop.

Vipul's face appeared, flashed a look of shock, then recovered. He said, "Hi, Madeline. I hope you don't mind me saying, but you don't look so great. It's a nice hat, though. Are you sure this needs to be a video call?"

She tossed the hat on the floor and said, "I feel and smell even worse than I look. It's nice to see a familiar face, Vipul. Yes we need video because I want you to believe me, which may be difficult, and it's better to show than tell." Madeline opened the strange application ('DreamVille v1.2'), shared her screen, and donned the non-bloody headset device. Right away she began thinking—believing—she was back in the pachinko parlor elevator. Or, she realized, the device began thinking it for her. She resisted, clearing her mind.

"What on Earth are you wearing? What program is this?" asked Vipul.

"Describe a scene to me."

"A scene?"

"Describe a unique visual scene. Humor me for a moment."

"Ok...um...I spent the first ten years of my life in a small village on the bank of the Bidyadhari River at the edge of the Sundarbans in West Bengal. I'm picturing green mangroves in brown, muddy water, and a tiger prowling among them."

Madeline took the info he'd given her and let her imagination fill in the rest. The scene appeared on the computer screen, with late afternoon sun shining on the rippling water.

Vipul asked, "Is this some kind of natural language visual search engine or design program? This isn't on the roadmap."

Madeline said, "Now, change the scene in some impossible, unpredictable way."

Vipul sighed. "Ok...instead of orange with black stripes, the tiger is black with orange stripes."

"This is why you're the CTO and not on the creative side of the business." The scene updated to match Vipul's description.

"Very impressive."

"Think bigger."

"Ok...the tiger is purple with white stripes, and...wings, and I'm riding it."

"Now we're talking." Madeline focused and the scene updated accordingly, just like worldbuilding in the pachinko parlor.

"How could the program possibly know what I look like? Did you pre-train the underlying algorithm with pictures or videos of me?"

"You're seeing what I'm thinking—dreaming, actually—via the device on my head."

"...are you playing a trick on me?"

Madeline removed the headset and said, "I wish I was, because then the rest of what I'm about to tell you wouldn't be true."

"You must go to the police right away," said Vipul when Madeline finished telling him a selectively edited version of what she remembered from the past few months (had she *actually* killed someone?).

"I need more witnesses and I need to move fast," Madeline said, as much to herself as to Vipul. "Bold, decisive action. Keep the competition on their back foot and force them to respond to you. Also, this is potentially happening in dozens of countries. What about the hundreds or thousands of other victims who aren't in Tokyo? We need to help them all simultaneously."

"Listen, I know I've been wrong many times when doubting your risky ideas, but this is different. What can you possibly do? And why, of all people, did you call me..." Vipul's voice trailed off, and the look on his face said he suspected where she was going next.

"If all these simulations, or virtual realities, whatever they are, are in communication with each other, then it's definitely over TCP/IP, right? That means we can take it offline via multi-vector distributed denial-of-service attack."

"Madeline, I'm the CTO of a soon-to-be public company, not some—"

"Even script kiddies can hire botnets on the dark web for a few thousand dollars and send enough bogus traffic to temporarily bring down the services of medium-sized companies. It doesn't need to be offline long, just enough for people to wake up and remove the devices. You're the brightest engineer I've ever known, and you used to run a cybersecurity startup. Tens of millions of computers around the world run our applications. We could send a tidal wave of requests and paralyze—"

"You want to use corporate resources to commit a crime against a public company a month before going public ourselves? I'll go to battle with you any day over anything legal. Possibly even something questionably legal. But this is crazy. Absolutely crazy."

I *am* crazy, Madeline thought, but decided against saying it. "It's not against the public company. I think. This is white hat, and even I know we can cover our tracks, make it almost impossible to discern the true source of the attack. Hell, it's happened to us before. DDoS attacks account for a third of all downtime across the web. And what are they going to do, go to the police?"

"Madeline...I...you...we...would need their IP addresses. And they probably have a private network."

"I'm connected to it."

"You're connected to the...where are you?"

"A floor down. Room 1234. You're the one who always tells me not to trust hotel Wi—"

"You need to get out of there!"

"Vipul, I'm doing this, with or without your help. You can disagree and commit, or let me go at it solo. I'm still technical enough to be dangerous."

"...there are so many different geographies."

"I'll go back in and visit every floor."

"...you probably need admin privileges."

Off-screen, Madeline wiped the blood from the headset of the man she'd killed on her *Pokémon* shirt, then held it up and said, "I have those right here."

Vipul stared at her with his mouth agape for a few seconds, then put on a stern look and said, "...Ok. But I'll need to do some research first. I'm a little out of practice."

"Thank you, Vipul. Now, let's see how this thing works."

Madeline took a deep breath, then donned 'Elias's' headset and let it lay the scaffolding of her reality.

She reentered the pachinko parlor at the end of the world.

Chapter 32: Darwin

Darwin's mind booted back up to the voice of god. It perplexed him because he'd died just last week and knew no such being existed. The pain behind his closed eyes and in his head, however, made him yearn for death. He'd thought he was in bad shape before, but there was always a higher threshold of pain and suffering to attain, a new level in a terrible game.

The world swayed beneath him, caused by swells that must have been massive to rock such a big ship. It would be just his luck to end up seasick on top of everything else. Most concerning of all, his hands were tied behind his back with what felt like zip ties.

God's voice continued, which now sounded suspiciously like Balthazar. This was just as strange because his old friend also no longer existed, if he recalled correctly, although that was no guarantee. It was hard to tell how much time had passed. Fortunately he'd been knocked out—when the brain doesn't dream—and not asleep. Funny how that was preferable. The risk of sleeping after a concussion was mostly just a myth, but he now had one more reason not to do so. He opened his eyes to figure out what was going on, but the scene made him think that maybe he *was* in something resembling hell.

The remains of Sven's head still splattered the bridge. The

former captain's body had been dragged into the corner, out of the way. Preston lay on the ground next to him with his hands similarly zip tied and his eyes closed, babbling to himself. Rain splattered the bridge windows; the cyclone was upon them. And unfortunately it was the kind of storm where the rain was blood. The bullet cracks in the glass looked like dreamcatchers, now filled with skinned versions of the interdimensional beings he'd met at the men's ceremony. He winced and kept his gaze moving.

Sephira stood with her back to him, guarding the entrance to the bridge where she'd entered. Balthazar sat in his office chair on the other side of the bridge, alive but in anguish. He'd been shot in the leg and arm, and blood stained his disheveled, designer suit. Two strips of it had been torn off and used to tie crude tourniquets. His normally slicked-back hair fell in a tangled mess over his sweaty face. With his working arm he held the microphone. Behind him stood another man Darwin hadn't seen before with a pistol aimed at the tzar's head. The man wore futuristic sunglasses, which was ridiculous given the weather, though he had to admit he looked cool.

Darwin's mind focused enough to understand the pained words Balthazar spoke. "...you have fought valiantly. You have done New Libertatia proud. Bards will write songs about your bravery on this most infamous of days. Beautiful ballads. Netflix will make an award-winning docu—"

"Stop stalling," said the man behind him in some kind of Mediterranean accent.

Balthazar continued, "But I have an important announce-ment to make. And it is not one I make lightly." He paused and looked back at the man behind him with hatred. The man urged him to go on. Balthazar closed his eyes and said, "For

263

this grand experiment, this great nation, this shining city on the sea of ours to continue, for the world to have a glowing example of what a brighter tomorrow can look like, it is my final wish that you...NEVER SURRENDER! Resist until your very last breath! Kill as many—"

The man standing behind Balthazar smashed the pistol's handle into his head, causing the tzar to crumple into his chair. The man picked up the microphone and said plainly, "Anyone who surrenders immediately will live. Anyone who resists will be killed and thrown overboard, not necessarily in that order. Your tzar here just learned that the hard way."

If there was any more cheering happening below, the sounds of the storm, helicopter, and sporadic gunfire drowned it out.

The man put down the microphone, smashed his hand into the desk, and said, "This is a shit show!"

"You're awake," said Sephira, now squatting down on Darwin's left. "How's your head?"

He turned his gaze from Balthazar and got a good look at her for the first time. Like her comrade she wore black fatigues and boots with a black vest and beanie, but no sunglasses. She was further outfitted with myriad accessories, the purposes of which Darwin could only guess, including a futuristic bracelet and glove on her left hand. Her dark hair was in pigtails down to each of her shoulders. The expression on her face gave the impression she enjoyed this, like it was all some type of game. If not for the headshot she'd delivered to Sven, it would have looked like she was playing soldier and having a damn good time doing so.

Darwin's amygdala forced him to admit that she also looked...no. She was a monster.

"Sorry about that," she continued, "but presumably it's

preferable to ending up like the captain. I'm glad you didn't make me shoot you. It really was double or nothing this time. It's good to see you again, Darwin, although you look like shit if you don't mind me saying. Hell of a second date, huh?"

"You killed him."

"I've 'killed' lots of people, Darwin. I'll kill more, probably even today. To me it's no different than killing someone in a dream is to you. Or, that's how you've seen things so far. I hope you'll come around to seeing things like I do. Like we do. To me, the captain is standing right there smiling, more real than he ever was when you saw him."

Darwin just glared at her. Not this again.

"You aren't going to interrupt me? Good. It seems I have a captive audience. Then let me explain a few things that may help you. You're even smarter than I thought, Darwin. Smarter than we all thought. But you, like so many other 'smart' people, couldn't see the truth. The others wanted to permanently check you into the hotel as part of our new program, but I convinced them to give you a chance. I believed your knowledge could be an asset to us, to *them,* and it has, even if you still refuse to believe. You worked out a 'solution' to the gift we gave you only a few days after James discovered something similar. He wasn't nearly as fun as you, but equally stubborn. It became too risky to let your work proceed, so we arranged your little game of chicken.

"But *you* survived, Darwin. *They* brought you back. There must have been a reason. Don't you understand? You have worthwhile dreams left inside of you. You'll see, and you're going to get checked in after all—we're expanding into a new country. Don't worry, I'll come visit, maybe even conjugally." She winked.

Balthazar moaned. Apparently he'd come to, though he must have wished he hadn't.

Sephira said, "Your friend over there is in such agony. And he's making this much more difficult on everyone than it needs to be. But there are other ways. Let me show you." She set her rifle down and rolled up her left sleeve to reveal the fully tattooed arm he remembered. Then she unsheathed a six-inch black bowie knife from her belt, and a shiver ran down Darwin's spine.

She stared at him, or at least she tried too—her dark eyes were unfocused, darting around. Then she took the knife and carved a web-like shape into the top of her forearm. He recognized the now-familiar symbol from his research. Sephira smiled as she worked, blood dripping onto the floor. "Look, Darwin, there's no pain. Not unless you want it. Right now it tickles. And now it feels like..." she closed her eyes, "... like someone is licking me. I can make it feel like just about anything."

"I see you finally gave in and got something resembling a smartwatch," Darwin said, trying to sound braver than he felt. So, her brain had been similarly modified, but she had control over her senses, just like what he assumed had happened with Madeline. It must have been the device.

She said, "I'm flattered you remember so much of our last conversation. And yes, Darwin, things are changing fast. It's the end of the beginning. The harvest has start—"

"Hey," interrupted her partner. "Take these three down and hand them off to the new arrivals. The tzar here is still more valuable to us alive, for now, and he'll bleed out soon. Your friend there looks big enough to carry him on his back." He pointed at Darwin.

"Men. Always interrupting and thinking they know what's best," Sephira said to Darwin with a smile. She gave a mock salute to the other man and said, "Yes sir, Marcy." She helped Darwin and Preston to their feet. Outside the blood-streaked bridge windows, car-sized black insects buzzed around the smoldering, smoking ship. Presumably one was actually a helicopter, but why hadn't it landed yet given the treacherous conditions?

The other man (Marcy?) zip tied a weakly protesting Balthazar's hands in front of him, then carried him over and threaded his legs through Darwin's bound arms in a kind of awkward piggyback setup. Sephira led Darwin, Balthazar, and Preston into the elevator at gunpoint. They took it down to the deck, facing the back of the ship.

The doors opened to a scene of absolute pandemonium.

Bloody rain fell in sheets at acute angles to the deck, itself at an absurd tilt for a vessel this size. Some of the blood on the deck must have been real—there were certainly enough mangled, scattered bodies amongst the debris to account for it. Everything not secured slid or tumbled one direction then the other, some of it disappearing over the side. Different colored lightning bolts flashed overhead, illuminating the dark sky like a fireworks display, followed by booms that could have been thunder or grenades. Probably both. It looked like the wall of shipping containers blocking the helicopter pad had been intentionally knocked over so the chopper couldn't land. Clever.

"Out and to the right!" yelled Sephira over the turmoil. Darwin did his best to obey, but it was hard enough to keep his balance given the *Arianna's* motion and his physical condition, plus he now also carried Balthazar's almost-dead weight. He stumbled out into the storm behind Preston, sticking close to the tower for shelter.

They rounded the corner of the bridge tower, and up ahead Darwin saw the two sleek, black yachts moored to the *Arianna's* port side, bobbing wildly in the waves. The three-story vessels were so small next to her. Rope ladders with tiny black figures on them ran from the boats' top decks to the *Arianna*. The pirate yachts faced away, and he could just make out through the rain their names written on the back: *Morpheus* and *Hypnos*, the ancient Greek gods of dreams and sleep.

"Balthazar! You're alive!" someone yelled, running towards them with a section of pipe in his hand. Clearly he hadn't seen Sephira, who cut him down with a three-round burst when he was ten feet away. Darwin threw up.

"You have to find a way...to make a break for it," Balthazar gasped in his ear.

"And end up like that guy?" Darwin asked. "I don't want to leave you two." The many sounds of the battle and storm covered their conversation.

"That motherfucker up there was right...if I don't get medical attention soon...I'm dead. And they'll want to ensure that doesn't happen. Not yet. Also...I'm pretty sure your girlfriend back there doesn't want to shoot you. Maybe you still got it... big guy."

"What am I supposed to do if I get away?" asked Darwin. They were approaching the soccer field, which looked like it'd been similarly sabotaged so as not to provide the large helicopter anywhere to land. The chopper hovered thirty feet off the ground while someone in black rappelled down from a rope. A dozen people in black—the 'new arrivals,' presumably—worked to clear space below.

"There's a satellite phone on a separate network in the bridge...it should work when the storm passes. Find somewhere to hide...then get word out. The international community will not stand... for this shit."

"Where—"

Darwin stopped as an enormous tentacle emerged from the raging water, rising a hundred feet above him. It was so dark, absorbed so much light, that it appeared as a rip in reality's fabric, and he saw it through the negative space it created against the background. Somewhere deep down he knew it couldn't have been real, but he no longer had the mental strength to act accordingly.

Balthazar moved his head from over Darwin's right should to his left, looked out at sea, and said, "Oh my..." Was the kraken he saw real?

A titanic rogue wave broadsided the *Arianna*, causing it to pitch to the right and sending a spray of white water splashing onto the deck. With their hands tied and no way to brace themselves, Darwin and Preston lost their balance and fell hard, rolling a few feet towards starboard. Up ahead, the sudden sloping of the deck was enough to launch something person-sized up and into the rotating blades of the helicopter, which itself dipped at an extreme angle and lost altitude.

The sound of the chopper's blades hitting the deck was audible over everything else, as was the woosh of air as a black blur whipped by where Darwin had just been standing. The next sound was hard to describe, but it was followed by the crash of metal on metal as the blade remnant flew into the ship's railing and off into the ocean.

Lying face-down with Balthazar still on his back, Darwin struggled and looked behind him. The only sign of Sephira

269

was her former left arm, severed at the shoulder. The sleeve was still rolled up, revealing a colorfully tattooed forearm and the freshly carved, still-bleeding dreamcatcher web. The wrist and twitching hand still wore the device.

"This is it!" yelled Balthazar in Darwin's ear, rolling himself off his back with a gasp of pain. Balthazar picked up a shard of helicopter blade with his bound hands in front of him and held it secure while Darwin rubbed his zip tie handcuffs against it. It only took a few seconds to break free. "Go!"

The *Arianna* began to list in the other direction, towards port, the opposite reaction to the force exerted by the rogue wave. The water that had splashed onto the deck started flowing off into the sea, taking with it any light debris, including Sephira's former arm, shoulder-first.

Darwin scrambled towards the edge and slid into the railing, grabbing the hand just before it disappeared. The arm, dangling over the void as though it should have been attached to a body, was unnervingly light. Darwin scanned the turbulent, wreckage-filled waters below. It looked like one of the yachts, *Morpheus*, had been bashed into the side of the *Arianna* and sustained serious damage. Someone had managed to launch one of New Libertatia's lifeboats, but it was sinking—evidently they'd been sabotaged too. A few bodies floated in the raging water, but none that resembled Sephira.

"Go!" came Balthazar's voice through the storm.

Darwin quickly removed the device and threw the arm overboard, wondering if it would one day wash up on a beach in the South Pacific or join the Great Pacific Garbage Patch. Double or nothing, eh? Good riddance. He turned around just in time to see a blinding flash as lightning struck one of the still-standing trees in the park farther up-ship, adding to the still-burning fire.

"Preston! Stay with Balthazar!" yelled Darwin as if his dumbstruck brother-in-law had another option. He fled back in the direction they'd come, away from the new arrivals and using the chaos as cover, wishing Balthazar had given him that tour of the ship. Should he try and procure the satellite phone now amidst the confusion or hide out and get it later?

The sound of automatic gunfire raining down from the bridge made his decision for him. Best not to head back up there right now, if only to prolong what little was left of his life.

He thought about finding somewhere deep in the ship's bowels to hide but figured they'd be less likely to search for stowaways amidst the deck's madness. He wanted to be as close to the bridge as possible for the second, more dangerous part of the mission and decided to try his luck in one of the shipping containers stacked in a row just below the tower. Hopefully they were secured to the deck and wouldn't slide off into the sea.

Darwin tried to ensure no one was watching, then picked a container at random and went inside. He shut the door behind him to pitch blackness and felt his way past large wooden crates to the back. The rain outside was audible, but inside it was surprisingly dry. He realized that of course shipping containers were waterproof; they were designed to weather just this kind of weather.

He fumbled with the device in the darkness, thankful it was adjustable in size and that like the container it was also waterproof. He had an inkling of how it likely worked and could be just what he needed to control his mind until it was blown in one way or another.

Darwin laid down against the back wall, closed his eyes, and let the more-than-gentle swaying of the ship rock him to his first real sleep in weeks.

Waking up was disappointing. He'd dropped instantly into REM sleep, as one often does when extremely sleep deprived. In Darwin's dreams the *Arianna*, with Captain Sven at the helm and the pirates still on the horizon, had sprouted great angelic wings and launched herself out of the water and up above the dark clouds to safety. Sephira had even been aboard, though she'd traded her cultish obsession with dreams for one with him. He wasn't surprised to have had such pleasant dreams, even after the horrors of the recent past, because he'd had more control over them than any lucid dream he'd ever experienced before.

But now, the juxtaposition of these vivid fantasies with the impossible task and certain death that awaited him in this world was stark. At least he physically felt a bit better. It was remarkable how much even a short nap could temporarily dull the effects of sleep deprivation, especially post-procedure. His accumulated level of adenosine must have still been through the roof, and he still carried an immense sleep deficit—one kind of debt you can never fully repay. But he was now on a more level playing field with the pirates except in one area: He didn't have a gun. Where could his confiscated Glock be?

The ground was still and even; the storm had passed. He heard something outside, muffled by the insulated walls. Then the container door opened, but instead of being flooded with the bright sunlight from his dreams, all that spilled in was the gentle illumination of star and moonlight. Darwin crouched behind the crates, his heart pounding.

They threw something into the container, and it clanged as it hit the floor. His first thought was grenade, and his mind once again began its non-preparation for the end. A few seconds passed and whatever it was started hissing. The terror of being locked in the dark container with a poisonous snake briefly came to mind before being discarded as ridiculous.

A scent hit his nostrils, strange but familiar. He sniffed the air a few times to get a better whiff and found himself on a psychedelic rocket ship, blasting off into deep space. He'd been dosed with DMT again, and the new device he wore was woefully useless against these deliria.

Chapter 33: Madeline

Madeline pressed the button for '13 – Kuala Lumpur' and waited until the doors slid open. Although she'd visited nineteen other floors without issue, she still got tense every time. For complicated technical reasons Vipul had glossed over and she didn't fully understand, simply taking the elevator to a floor wasn't enough; she had to spend some unspecified amount of time there until he gave the ok. Between that, avoiding the other Eliases, and trying to seem as unsuspicious as possible, the process of acquiring everything they needed had taken much longer than she'd hoped. Hours, though she wasn't sure how many. She assumed they'd discovered one or both bodies by now and feared the distant sound of someone kicking down her hotel room door or a superadmin revoking her access.

Or worse.

She walked out onto the parlor floor, and although several of the few dozen patrons looked up at her, she knew they didn't see *her*, but some combination of their own projection of whoever they thought oversaw this place and the admin's projection of themself. After donning the dead man's headset, Madeline had found herself in the pachinko parlor elevator, right where she'd first taken hers off, except she'd been lying on the floor, where 'Elias' had been. Fortunately no one else had been there, including Madeline's avatar, which was how she now thought of the people here, and there was no blood or other signs someone had been brutally killed.

Now that she knew it wasn't real, she noticed how the parlors lacked reality's fidelity, like seeing the entire place in her peripheral vision. Like a lucid dream, except her godlike powers were no longer limited to building new worlds for the dream crawlers.

She went into the men's bathroom, where she'd recently spent more time than she had in her entire life up to this point. A man washed his hands in the sink, looking at his grizzled face and bloodshot, sunken eyes in the mirror. She noticed him tense as she entered. More than that, she *understood* what he felt. The anxiety. The fear. The hatred. It was as if she knew him so well that she could foresee his next move, because she could. Respectfully nodding to her—him—in the mirror. Turning off the faucet with his right hand. Declining to use the hand dryer because those things are fucking useless.

She said, "If you wake up in a hotel room and aren't sure how you got there, leave immediately and pull the fire alarm. Do you understand?"

The man looked at her, confused. For a second she feared he was going to attack her. He'd thought about it briefly before admonishing himself for it. But then she understood that he understood the message. He nodded and left the bathroom.

Madeline wasn't sure what she'd do if someone attacked her. She wasn't even sure what she *could* do—was physical force an option against someone thousands of miles away, or were all the overseers local? The one she'd killed had been in the same room. If violence *was* an option, could she bring herself

275

to harm one of these poor souls and cast them out, whatever that entailed?

She wondered what the overseer she'd killed had felt when she hadn't done what he'd anticipated, how jarring it would be to have your expectation so violently violated. She understood now that she'd executed something analogous to a denial-of-service attack; he'd been too busy responding to her bogus intentions to respond to her real, latent one.

Elias's handsome face stared at her from the bathroom mirror. She blinked and the eyes changed from brown to green. Who are you? *Where* are you? How badly she wished it had been this face under her boot. If only—

"Ok, I got it," came Vipul's voice somewhere far away. Damn, he was getting a lot faster. Practice makes perfect.

"Nice work. Leaving now," she said, exiting the bathroom.

"But listen, Madeline, something has changed. There's twice as much traffic on the network."

That can't be good, she thought as she walked back to the elevator. When she entered and looked at the list of buttons, she understood why.

"There's a new floor. At the top," she said when the doors closed and she no longer feared anyone would overhear. "It doesn't start with thirteen like the others. It just says 'New Libertatia.'" How bizarre. Wasn't Darwin's old college friend the president or something?

Vipul said, "I don't think you should—"

"I'm going to check it out. If that's where all the new traffic is coming from, then there could be a ton of people trapped there who need our help."

"Be careful."

"Overly careful people never do anything interesting."

Chapter 34: Together

Darwin pulled back the plunger and launched the ball into the playfield. He moved his hands to the buttons on either side of the alien invasion-themed pinball machine as the shiny silver sphere bounced around the bumpers. It fell into the dead center of the playfield, and Darwin cursed as he suspected what would happen; he'd played enough games to have a sense for when a ball was lost.

The mirrored world he'd spent an indeterminable amount of time building reflected the flashing lights of the machine as it rolled down right between the two flippers and into oblivion. Never even had a chance. The screen flashed 'GAME OVER.' Well, it was still more enjoyable than the pachinko machines on the other side of the massive, cruise ship-sized arcade. That game sucked.

A calming male voice from behind him said, "Do not despair, Darwin. You are doing great work. It is as I told you once before, in another time and place—however brief they may be and inconsequential they may seem, our actions in this world reverberate forever. The dreamscapes you create now will become part of the chosen ones' eternal home after this season's harvest."

Darwin turned around and looked into the kind face of Arlo,

the only person other than the goons he'd been able to speak to in the past...he didn't know. He also wasn't sure how or why he knew and liked this man, even if he kept spewing nonsense.

Arlo continued, smiling as he spoke. "I *know* that you do not yet believe, as you did not believe after meeting them before. And time is running short. These lives truly are ephemeral. But I have not given up hope. You may yet be converted, Darwin. You may yet join them, and us, after departing from this plane of existence. Here are some more balls, on me."

Arlo handed him a bucket of pinballs, and Darwin said, "Thanks." But he didn't feel like playing anymore right now. He had to take a piss. He walked past someone he knew as Preston, standing at the next machine over, although in his peculiar memory the man wasn't as tall or handsome as he looked now.

Darwin took the scenic route to the bathroom, stopping to gaze out the ship's windows at the endless, rolling sea of fire on which the vessel sailed. It glowed brightly against the black horizon, hot enough in parts that the blue flames looked like water. Imagine that! He shuddered at the silhouette of the large plank extending off the side of the *Epiales*, a word he knew as both the Greek god of nightmares and the name of this damned boat. Fitting.

The plank was the stick to Arlo's carrot, and two of his fellow passengers had apparently opted for the former. Their limp but not lifeless bodies were being dragged onto the platform; no one would walk under their own power to such a grisly fate. The dark outlines of cinder sharks, so large they might be megalodons, circled in the fire beneath. It was unclear if those thrown overboard burned to death before being eaten alive, and Darwin had no interest in finding out himself by rebelling against the stupid rules of this place.

Disgusted, he walked away from the windows with his head down and the distinct, well-known feeling that something didn't make sense. His baloney detection kit blared on high alert, but the clearer picture was obfuscated. It was like the indescribable semi-blindness of an ocular migraine had been applied to all his senses and thoughts. To rationality itself.

He looked up from the colorful fractal patterns in the carpet and at one of the overseers who must have just left the men's bathroom but was now standing still, staring back at him. The man resembled all the other enforcers, someone in a dark suit who Darwin had a faint, negative memory of from another life. But something was...different.

Madeline couldn't believe how many passengers were on this hell cruise. There must have been as many people as on all the Stasis Hotels' thirteenth floors combined. She paced around the large men's bathroom, one of several here, impatient for Vipul to give the ok.

"It really is New Libertatia," came Vipul's voice from the background in all directions, "which means it's connected to the others via satellite. I can still get what I need, it's just going to take a few more minutes."

"Copy," said Madeline. Networking may have been one of the less sexy layers of the stack, but boy was it critical.

Another enforcer entered the bathroom, which was Madeline's cue to leave. She exited, planning to kill the last few minutes by the elevator. Just three more floors to go after this—Jakarta, Singapore, and Manila—then they could take this damn place offline and—

Was she hallucinating, or was that a less handsome version

of Darwin walking towards her?

The device gave her no such indication. What in the worlds was he doing here? And did he know where the girls were? Forgetting the mission, she took an excited step towards him but stopped when she made contact with the floor. Something felt different. The foot she saw when she looked down was not the wing-tipped men's dress shoe worn by Elias, but her blood-stained bootie. Her dark suit flickered, intermittently replaced by women's skinny jeans and a yellow *Pokémon* shirt.

The bathroom door opened behind her, and everything went not white, not black, but blank. The color before the big bang.

Darwin's mind reeled. His heart fluttered. The person stepping towards him flashed between an overseer and...who? How bewildering to not know someone's name, to not know anything about them, but be absolutely sure you loved them.

The flickering stopped, leaving a beautiful, blond woman about his age. It wasn't quite love at first sight, because he'd seen her before, somewhere.

Someone in black exited the bathroom behind her: an overseer. The man's eyes went wide with surprise when he saw her. The goon held up a hand, and the newly materialized woman collapsed on the ground, catatonic.

Madeline heard a voice whisper, "What's going on? I've almost got it, but your connection is unstable. And it sounds like someone's banging on your hotel room door." The words meant nothing. They were just acoustic waves in the air. Patterns of noises. She was a blank canvas, an empty dream journal. She didn't know if she could move. More than that, she lacked any reason whatsoever to find out. Her hard drive had been wiped, an operating system not yet installed.

But...something began to fill the void, to illustrate the pages. At first the scenes were incomprehensible, but then she started to understand. And she knew they weren't her thoughts, either; they were being unknowingly projected into her mind from somewhere else—from some*one* else.

A rainy day. A wedding. A handsome man in a bright blue suit, smiling. Were those tears or just the rain? He spoke, said, "You look..."

Darwin cradled the head of the woman he now knew was Madeline. He remembered. He'd probably be rolled off the plank into the sea of fire for how he now acted but didn't care. This was, or at least had been, his wife. He remembered everything, and the memories raced through his mind, more real than anything around him: the wedding, the birth of their children, the arguments, the fact that she'd been lost and now—for a moment—found.

And she had recognized him too. He was sure of it. He'd seen it in her face, until she fell to the ground under this terrible spell the overseers had the power to cast. Now her blue, glassy, unseeing eyes stared not at him, not at anything at all.

But her lips moved. He leaned close and heard her say, "... *dazzling.*"

Madeline smiled and said, "What an adjective."

"What?" asked a voice she now recognized as Vipul, the chief technology officer of a company she ran, over the sound of someone kicking down a door. "The connection seems stable again. I've got it."

Her eyes focused on a perplexed Darwin, backlit by the blaze outside. The enforcer's admin device she wore had read his thoughts, bootstrapped her back into being. The love he felt for her, or *had* felt for her, was overwhelming. Had it kindled something else?

She'd have to sort that out later. She had urgent unfinished business.

Madeline said, "They're onto us. No time to visit the other floors. Shut it down."

"Here comes the flood," said Vipul. "It's going to be biblical."

"How fitting."

"Goodbye, world."

Darwin's reality slowed to a crawl. Starting with Madeline, the startled people around him blinked out of existence until he was alone in the huge arcade. Next the neon flashes and grating noises emanating from the rows and rows of machines froze, as did the rolling waves of fire outside the windows, like the speeds of light and sound had fallen to zero. His world's resolution decreased, becoming increasingly pixelated until all he saw were blocks of color. One by one they changed to black.

But he wasn't alarmed by this new darkness; something was covering his eyes. He removed the headset to find himself in a shipping container that had been converted into a surprisingly comfortable bedroom. Moonlight shined in from a window cut in one of the walls. But it made sense—he wasn't on the *Epiales*; he was on the *Arianna*, which had been taken by mind pirates. They must have put him in here after dosing him with DMT. It all came back. Sephira. Sven. Balthazar. The satellite phone! He needed to call for help.

Darwin eased open the container door to find it was one of many stacked in a ziggurat-like structure at the front of the ship. He was several layers high with a view of the immense deck up to the park, which no longer burned. Other people had already exited their rooms, and more were in the process of doing so, dazed looks on their faces. Where were the pirates? It was dark, the night still. There seemed to be few functioning light sources on the ship, but the bridge was illuminated in the distance like a rectangular moon or a UFO. It was too far away to tell if it was occupied.

He walked down to the main level, part of a growing group now in the hundreds, murmuring amongst themselves.

"Darwin!"

Preston emerged from the crowd and ran towards him. They embraced like brothers.

"What happened?" asked Darwin.

"They left," replied Preston.

"What do you mean they left?"

"Here, let me show you." Preston led him over to the side of the ship. On the black ocean water, receding in the distance, were two identical sets of lights.

With the sky clear and a rave no longer happening on the *Arianna*'s deck, the stars were the brightest Darwin had ever seen them. They spun around the sky as if affixed to the lathe of heaven. Not real—he shook his head and they stopped rotating.

He noted the constellation above the horizon where the boats were heading and said, "I wonder why they're going southeast. There's nothing in that direction for thousands of miles, and then it's only tiny uninhabited islands and atolls."

"Fuck em. Nowhere to hide out here. How could they

possibly believe they'd get away with something like this?"

"I think...they weren't too concerned with what happened after the harvest. At least in this world. Like it was the final act."

"It doesn't make any sense," said Preston.

"When has any religion had a cohesive, coherent ideology?"

"Ugh."

"Speaking of religions—have your thoughts on simulations changed now that you've effectively been inside of one?" asked Darwin.

"There are undoubtedly simulations inside of other simulations, nested many layers deep."

"Well, I prefer to be in base reality. And I have a new list of bottom five experiences, and they all happened recently."

"You remember that most of these people, including both of us, are still in the process of losing our minds, right?"

Darwin was all too aware. The water below was no longer all dark; swimming up from the deep was a radiant sea serpent, large enough to swallow the *Arianna* whole. Its watery blue glow reminded him of the blue eyes of—

Darwin stood erect and said, "I saw Madeline inside. I'm sure of it."

"Inside the simulation?"

"Yeah. It sounds crazy, but I think she may have had something to do with shutting it down."

"Nothing sounds crazy to me anymore. And it wouldn't surprise me—she's a Lockhart, after all."

"Let's find Balthazar and see what's still functioning in the medical center. I saw Doctor Goodspeed back there. I believe I know how to help not just me, but everyone."

Darwin blinked hard and the sea monster disappeared. On

the horizon, where the black water met the black sky, the lights from the two boats were indistinguishable from the stars.

Madeline removed her headset, once again in a room at the Tokyo Stasis Hotel. The computer on the desk in front of her displayed various errors. But there was no time to savor victory; the door around the deadbolt was splintering from repeated kicks.

She grabbed the makeshift knife and stood against the wall next to the handle. The door shuttered from another kick, and she quietly removed the deadbolt and waited. The next kick sent the door flying open, hopefully much faster than the kicker expected. The man stood awkwardly when his foot hit the ground, half in and half out of the room, mere feet away.

Madeline made her move, plunging the glass blade into his stomach twice, then jumping back out of his range.

She looked at the bloody knife in her hand, then into the stunned, pained face of *the* Elias Sultana. At least that was her initial impression. There was no time to confirm. He slumped against the doorframe with his hands clutching his stomach as she rushed by before he had a chance to neutralize the pain with the device.

"Madeline, wait," he called after her with what she hoped was his final strength. But she just ran to the stairs and pulled the fire alarm on the way, hoping it would spur those who'd just awoken to flee. The lights flashed and the sirens blared.

Standing on the street in the cold afternoon, her heavy breath visible in front of her, she smiled at the disheveled former pachinko parlor patrons stumbling out of the hotel into the growing crowd. It wasn't hard to distinguish them from the other guests of the five-star hotel. She recognized a dazed

Sakura and waved.

The sound of breaking glass moved her attention up. All the windows had blown out on one floor, the shattered glass raining down on the street below. Madeline shielded her eyes and counted to thirteen.

Smoke billowed from the windows into the blue winter sky.

Part 6: Waking Up

Three months later

Chapter 35: Darwin

Darwin awoke from one of the craziest dreams—nightmares?—he'd ever had, which was saying something. He must have unintentionally drifted off. Take it easy on the sauce, Dar. His mood quickly improved as understanding of his real life flooded in and drowned out the horror show. The name on the buzzing phone on his chest further expanded the smile on his face.

"Hey," he said.

"Chuckie! What did I tell you about this virus?" asked Balthazar. "I've already made enough money to build an entire fleet."

"Preston keeps reminding me. He wanted me to say thanks."

"Glad you guys are still friends after everything. I don't have enough exes to name all these ships. I'm thinking maybe I use some of yours."

Darwin chuckled. "That's fine with me."

"What was that girl's name again?"

"Which one?"

"The sexy mind pirate," said Balthazar.

"I don't know that it was her actual name." None of the names used by those associated with Circadian Capital Partners had been real in a legal sense, as far as they could tell. It was like they'd appeared from then disappeared back into the ether. *Morpheus* and *Hypnos* hadn't been seen since. "But it was Sephira."

"Ah, that's it. Fitting name for the first ship in New Libertatia's navy. Anyway, how does it feel to finally be on the cover of something?"

Darwin ran a hand through where his hair was growing back around the thin scar left by the Johnston procedure. "It feels pretty good."

"You get used to it after a while. Enjoy it while it lasts. Have you thought about taking me up on my offer? Your first medical experiment out here was a resounding success. And distributed teams will be the new normal from here on out. You'd only have to come visit occasionally. I promise all your subsequent visits will be less eventful than your first."

"I'm still thinking about it."

"Think harder. Imagine all the applications of this new dream-computer interface technology! It's going to be like science fiction. Ok, gotta go. Repairs are almost done and we're getting ready to set sail soon."

"Bye." Darwin hung up the phone. The fragmented technology left behind by the dream cult sure was impressive. How could people who were so obviously irrational build something so sophisticated? *Give them more credit, Dar.* He tried to give a lot of people a lot more credit these days. Maybe their fantastical beliefs had let them dream unconstrained by reality and innovate ahead of the field.

The stack of scientific journals on the coffee table was extra tall; neuroscience had never been so exciting. His laptop slept on top of the papers. He'd finished the first draft of *The Stardust Chronicles, Episode IX*. Lightkeeper 739 had found a companion.

Michael said it needed a lot of editing.

Movement across the living room caught his attention. The TV was still on with the volume off. The news was no doubt discussing the same events for probably the tenth time today. He unmuted it.

"...an assassination attempt on the country's prime minister. The suspect said he'd been hearing voices in his head that coerced him into doing it. In our next top story unrelated to the coronavirus, you weren't alone if you experienced internet issues today. Hackers initiated what's known as a distributed denial-of-service attack against a major internet infrastructure provider. It was the second largest attack of its kind after that against the infamous and now-defunct Stasis Hotels earlier this year..."

Darwin turned off the TV and got up. Same old scary shit. And he'd made the news after all despite his propensity for consuming it.

He let Mofongo out into the big backyard, grateful for the pleasant temperature outside and lack of wind. Your money sure went a lot further once you got outside the city, though it came with an increased risk of loneliness. Well, the amount of money he had would go a long way anywhere.

He walked by the empty home office and stepped on a few sharp LEGO pieces in the dark hallway. One of them felt like it pierced the skin. He smiled.

Darwin went upstairs, his loyal dog following close behind, past Christina and Evelyn's rooms, and to bed.

Chapter 36: Madeline

Wednesday, April 1st, 2020 — 8 hours of sleep

A train barreling through a scorching desert. The black tracks and golden dunes stretched into the distance as far as I could see. I rode on top of one of the cars. I was with someone but can't remember who. It's much harder to recall my dreams now, like it used to be. The details start slipping through my fingers as soon as I wake, as if I'm holding a handful of sand. The same is true of much of the past year, but then again, much of that was a dream, too. And some of it was a nightmare, which is harder to forget, like the people I may or may not have killed; no bodies were recovered from the Tokyo Stasis or any of the other Suspended Animation Collection *hotels.*

INTERPOL insists there never was an Elias Sultana, that he was just a construct.

Madeline closed her dream journal. She'd read through it several times in the past few months. Parts of it seemed forged, written by someone else. What relationship did she have to the woman who'd filled these pages, dreamed these dreams? The disassociation was disorienting. At least it was no longer publicly accessible on the dark web; the Dream Punx website went down with Vipul's DDoS attack and never came back up.

She paused M83's *Hurry Up, We're Dreaming* playing from her phone on the nightstand next to the lavender-scented oil diffuser and bottle of galantamine. It was getting late, and legally she *was* the same person she'd always been, which meant she had a public company to run tomorrow. Fortunately her road warrior days of unnecessary business travel were behind her, something she'd sworn even before the pandemic flared up. What a wakeup call this had been. Her company made video conferencing software, for god's sake. Time to eat her own dog food and spend more time with her own dog and family.

Speaking of family, she heard footsteps and the jangling of a collar coming down the hall.

"You fall asleep on the couch again?" she asked Darwin when he entered the bedroom.

"Sure did," he replied. "Balthazar called. I'm seriously thinking about taking him up on his offer. I think the Johnston procedure has potential to help with other kinds of brain damage."

"I will fully support and be proud of you no matter what."

He smiled and said, "Thanks. It's my *dream* job, after all."

"Good one."

"Behind raising the girls, that is. But with both of us working from home and maybe a little outside help, it could be manageable. What time is therapy tomorrow?"

"Noon."

"Perfect. Preston still thinks we should do a couples' cere-mony, by the way. He really likes the new facilitator."

"I can't believe he already went back to men's group. It can't be good for his brain after all this." The idea of completely giving up the reins and again encountering the dream crawlers, even if they only existed in the darkest corners of her mind, was a nonstarter.

"Yeah, Arlo turning out to be some kind of high-ranking cult leader really turned me off the whole thing. And I think we'll be just fine without it."

"Me too," she said with a smile.

Darwin and Mofongo climbed into bed. Madeline turned off the light, donned her eye mask, and said, "See you tomorrow."

Darwin chuckled. "Sweet dreams."

Madeline progressed through the stages of sleep and woke up in a dream.

If you enjoyed *Circadian Algorithms*, please share it with others and rate it on Amazon and Goodreads. Thanks!

Acknowledgments

Firstly, thank *you* for purchasing and reading this book. Writing is a grueling and personal endeavor, and it means the world(s) to me to be able to share it with others. Until some of the technology in *Circadian Algorithms* gets built, there is no deeper connection than between writer and reader. I also fear that reading anything more than 280 characters or a headline is fast going out of fashion as our attention spans go to zero, and I appreciate your appreciation for such an ancient, raw, and longform artform.

Thanks to everyone who read and reviewed my first book, *Mind Painter*. Your feedback was instrumental in improving my craft and inspiring me to crank out a second book during the darkest days of the Covid-19 pandemic. I will write the follow-up novel someday.

Thanks to those who read and provided input on various drafts of *Circadian Algorithms*: Alex, Jesse, Sam, Jake, Emily, Marianne, Tony, Simon, Lisa, Liza, and Scott.

Thanks to Rafael for the cover (again).

Thanks to the Fluid Interfaces Group at the MIT Media Lab and Dr. Matthew Walker at UC Berkeley for their amazing and inspirational work on dreams and sleep. Go check it out! My initial catalyst for writing about dreams was not knowing if I'd have time to write another book with an increasingly demanding career in product management and a growing family; incorporating dreams let me briefly explore many disparate crazy ideas in one novel. But the more I researched (and experimented on myself), the more enthralled I became. If you can't tell after reading *Circadian Algorithms*, I find these subjects fascinating and believe they're woefully neglected and underexplored. I recommend keeping a dream journal for a few weeks and maybe dabbling in lucid dreaming, the sources for some of the weirdest ideas in the book.

Lastly, it's difficult to truly understand your influences in today's information environment. I've consumed thousands of books, articles, papers, and podcasts over the years, and it's often impossible to discern exactly where and when an idea or viewpoint formed. So, thanks to all the wonderful, wild, passionate people out there with esoteric interests who allow me to dive down deep rabbit holes, from the simulation hypothesis and non-existence of free will to finding god during psychedelic trips and starting new countries.

About the Author

Tom B. Night is an American-Australian technologist and author whose novels include *Circadian Algorithms* and *Mind Painter.* He grew up in the Pacific Northwest then spent 15 years at tech companies in the Bay Area. He now splits time between Seattle, San Francisco, and various dreamed-up worlds. Get in touch or stay up to date at tombnight.com.

NOV 2 2

CPSIA information can be obtained
at www.ICGtesting.com
Printed in the USA
LVHW082340211022
731251LV00002B/129

9 798404 135985